MW00680211

FIREBIRD

OTHER BOOKS BY
GLEN HUSER

The Snuggly
(Groundwood Books, 2018)

The Golden Touch
(Tradewind Books, 2015)

The Elevator Ghost
(Groundwood Books, 2014)

The Runaway (Tradewind Books, 2012)

Time for Flowers, Time for Snow
(Tradewind Books, 2013)

Skinnybones and the Wrinkle Queen
(Groundwood Books, 2006)

Stitches (Groundwood Books, 2003)

Jeremy's Christmas Wish
(Hodgepog Books, 2000)

Touch of the Clown
(Groundwood Books, 1999)

Grace Lake
(NeWest Press, 1990)

FIREBIRD

GLEN HUSER

RONSDALE PRESS

FIREBIRD
Copyright © 2020 Glen Huser

RONSDALE PRESS
3350 West 21st Avenue, Vancouver, B.C. Canada V6S 1G7
www.ronsdalepress.com

Typesetting: Julie Cochrane, in Minion 12 pt on 16
Cover Design: Julie Cochrane
Cover Art: Karen McFarlane
Paper: Ancient Forest Friendly 55 lb. Antique Cream (FSC)—
    100% post-consumer waste, totally chlorine-free and acid-free.

Ronsdale Press wishes to thank the following for their support of its
publishing program: the Canada Council for the Arts, the Government of
Canada, the British Columbia Arts Council, and the Province of British
Columbia through the British Columbia Book Publishing Tax Credit program.

Library and Archives Canada Cataloguing in Publication

Title: Firebird / Glen Huser.
Names: Huser, Glen, 1943– author.
Identifiers: Canadiana (print) 20190072288 | Canadiana (ebook)
    2019007230X | ISBN 9781553805878 (softcover) | ISBN 9781553805885
    (HTML) | ISBN 9781553805892 (PDF)
Classification: LCC PS8565.U823 F57 2020 | DDC jC813/.54—dc23

At Ronsdale Press we are committed to protecting the environment. To this
end we are working with Canopy and printers to phase out our use of paper
produced from ancient forests. This book is one step towards that goal.

Printed in Canada by Marquis Book Printing, Quebec

in memory of my father, Harry Huser,
an immigrant boy, artist,
and musician

ACKNOWLEDGEMENTS

I wish to thank the Department of Ukrainian Studies, the University of Alberta, for tracking down poems and prayers and translating them for me, and for suggested readings on internments and police treatment of Ukrainians during World War I. A special thank you also to Michelle (Ukrainec) Tracy who read *Firebird* as a work in progress, checking for accuracy and for suggesting some of the Ukrainian expressions Alex and his family would have used. Also a huge thank you to my sister Karen McFarlane for her careful edit and for helping me recall the Norwegian language patterns of our father's mother and stepfather (immigrants to Canada). Thanks to Karen, as well, for creating a wonderful cover image. I am grateful to my mother, Bea Huser, for checking the authenticity of details from early twentieth-century rural life in Alberta. Thank you also to Ronsdale's Veronica and Ronald Hatch and Meagan Dyer for their close reading of the manuscript and suggestions for revision. Dianne Linden and Aaron Rabinowitz: I truly appreciate your taking time to read *Firebird* and to provide feedback.

I am very grateful for the generous grants provided by the Alberta Foundation for the Arts and the Canada Council for the Arts when I embarked on this project.

Alberta Foundation for the Arts

Canada Council for the Arts   Conseil des arts du Canada

FIREBIRD

Chapter 1

"SEE HIS WINGS?" Marco said, standing back, holding the chalk pencil he had used to complete the outline on Uncle Andrew's cupboard door. "Spread. Ready for flight."

Alex nodded. But he couldn't say anything. Sometimes his brother's skill overwhelmed him, left him mute. The detail of the fanned wing feathers had this effect, each so perfect. Alex could feel the air searching between the feather tips, could sense the urging to lift, to soar.

"Now we add the fire." Marco smiled at him as he squeezed some warm yellow from a tube onto the pie plate he used as a palette and then twinned it with a daub of orange. "It's amazing how much oil paint looks like bird droppings," he added with mock seriousness.

Alex couldn't help laughing.

Marco winked at him. "The fire burns two times the brightness against the grey-blue sky of the cupboard door," he explained, beginning to paint in one of the feathers with the fiery gold, modulating it so the tip was yellow deepening to a reddish orange as it approached the hinge of feather against the wing bone.

Marco had finished the cupboard door back in September before leaving to find work with the threshing crews.

Since then, winter had come with heavy falls of snow in November and the first week of December. Darkness had descended earlier every day, with Alex topping up the kerosene in the kitchen lamp so there was light for preparing supper and for doing his homework.

The night of the fire, Alex had been so tired he kept nodding off over his reading assignment. Uncle Andrew's foot had been bothering him again so Alex tended to all the barn chores himself. By eight o'clock he was more than ready for bed.

"*Nadobranich.*" Alex yawned. He knew how to say "good night" in English but Uncle Andrew liked to hear words from the old country.

"*Spochevi dobre.*" Across from him at the table, Uncle Andrew, looking up from the Ukrainian newspaper he subscribed to, smiled and raised his glass as if he were presenting a toast at a wedding instead of saying "sleep well" to his nephew.

Alex climbed the ladder to his bed in the loft, a dark corner. It was chilly and he wished Marco were home. The bed was always warmer with the two of them. He undid his boots and kicked them off, but deciding it was just too cold to undress, burrowed under the quilts.

It must have been hours later when he woke to the smell of smoke. The soft patch of light he expected to see below from the kitchen corner had become something stronger, a wild, dancing glow. Choking, Alex stumbled down the ladder and raced to the kitchen. He struggled to pull Uncle Andrew from his chair at the table where a quart jar of moonshine, almost empty, reflected the flames. Marco's bird on the cupboard door was the last thing he saw before a beam crashed down across his hand, his fingers laced in his uncle's shirt as he tried to get him up from his chair.

Everything was lost in a firework of sparks, and Alex howled with fear and pain as a piece of fabric—from a bed? from curtains?—flew against his face, attaching itself with an intimacy that sent him screaming through the door to the snowdrifts where he plunged his face and his burning hands into the soothing cold.

Alex wept, his tears blurring the flames of the burning farmhouse. Uncle Andrew, he knew, must have passed out, lost to the deep sleep of moonshine. Maybe he never woke up. Alex prayed he never woke.

The whole building was collapsing now, falling in on itself except for the staunchest parts of the thick, mudded walls. As it burned like a gigantic brush fire, Alex watched the sparks flying into the black sky. It was hard to tell where the sparks left off and the stars began.

It seemed they all danced—the stars and the sparks—to the music of bells, thin, tinny bells like in the English song about jingle bells they'd been singing at school. Although it pained him to move, he shifted his position in the snowdrift so that the road to the farm came into view. It was a dark, willow-rimmed tunnel in the night, but something was coming. The sound of the bells arranged themselves in clusters around the movement.

Maybe he was not to die after all. There were horses, great heavy-footed beasts, their breath swirling in clouds against the cold, and they were right beside him. If it were possible to move his burned fingers, he could have reached out and touched the hair on the leg of the closest one. Instead he let his fingers curl in his lap like the claws of a dead crow.

Someone was getting down from the sleigh, someone muffled against the cold with wraps, eyes glinting between the borders of scarf and cap.

"I think it's that Galician boy," a male voice boomed. "You know, the one that came with his brother a couple of years ago to live with Kaminsky."

"Alexander." Another voice. Someone getting down on the other side of the sleigh. It had a familiar sound to it. Gordon. Gordon Wallace.

"Oh my God!" the voice said. "Dad, he's all burned!"

The man was kneeling by him now, reaching out, touching his shoulders. "Listen, son, were you here by yourself?"

Alex looked in the direction of the fire again. There was not much left of the farmhouse. Just the glow of the flames, lower now with less to feed on. He looked back into the man's eyes and shook his head. Even the slight movement sent a fresh wave of pain along the burned side of his face.

He realized he was weeping. He could feel the moisture trickling down the skin on the other cheek. There was a kind of low, animal moaning, like he'd heard once from Uncle Andrew's dog who'd got caught in a weasel trap. The moaning was coming from his own mouth, his own throat. It turned into a scream as the big man picked him up and eased him into the back of the sleigh. "There. We'll just get this around you." It was something heavy and woolly with a smell that made Alex think of the *kozhukh*, the sheepskin coat Uncle Andrew wore.

"Your brother," the man said, "was your brother in there too?"

Alex shook his head.

"Just your uncle?"

He nodded.

"Gordie, you stay with him. I'm going to give the barn a quick check."

In the back of Alex's mind was the wish that he could stop crying, stop the moaning. If his hands didn't hurt so much, he would have made one into a fist and held it against his mouth to stop the sound.

Gordon Wallace was leaning over the front seat of the sleigh. "I'm sorry, Alex," he whispered. It sounded like he was about to cry too.

In a few minutes the big man was back and climbed into the sleigh.

"Gee-up," he said, and the sleigh started to move. Sleigh bells tinkled against the last crackling sound of the fire.

"What are we going to do, Dad?" he heard Gordon Wallace say. It was a question in Alex's mind too, but the answer was lost as he felt himself spiralling into blackness.

When he came to, the big man was moving him out of the sleigh into something else. It seemed like a small house with a stove inside, a strange sort of carriage-like sled. A woman put a cold, wet cloth against his face, covered him with a blanket, and placed a pillow behind him. In her dark fur coat, she made Alex think of a bear.

"I'm Mrs. Wallace," she said, "Gordie's mother. We're going to get you over to Mrs. Eddy's as fast as we can."

She opened a lid on the barrel-like stove and put in some wood. There was a flurry of sparks before she closed it again.

"Let me wrap your hands in these wet towels."

When she was finished, she put on mitts and gathered the horses' reins that came through a small opening.

The woman made a chucking sound and called out, "Get along now, Pepper. Star."

They were moving, the runners of the sled sawing against the snow. In the darkness of the caboose, the heat from the stove settled around Alex, and he could smell the fire mixing with the old fur smell of the coat, the raw wool of the blanket close to his face, the familiar scent of cut wood.

"Do you speak any English?" Mrs. Wallace adjusted the blanket. "Our Gordie says you don't speak much but he thinks you're understanding a fair bit."

Alex felt a noise coming from his throat.

"There, you don't worry about talking. In fact, it would be good if you can sleep. It's about a two-hour trip to the Eddys. We're so sorry to hear about what happened," she added.

He did close his eyes. He tried not to think about the pain of his burned face and hands. He tried to concentrate on what Gordon's mother was saying as they moved along through the night, tried to sort out the words.

"Mrs. Eddy's a nurse, and about once a month or so, Dr. Vendrick stops in. With Christmas so close, I don't know if he'll be coming by, but we can hope, and Mrs. Eddy will have a pretty good idea of how best to tend your burns. Lord, a burn can hurt."

He fell asleep to Mrs. Wallace's talking, her words settling in with the movement and steady sounds of the sleigh and the horses. Their stopping was what woke him, and he cried out with the sudden renewal of an awareness of his burns. From outside the sleigh there was a frenzied barking of dogs.

"There, there, now," Mrs. Wallace said. "We're here and

I'm sure all the Eddys are awake with the racket of those hounds."

"Who's there?" someone shouted from across a yard. "Jiminy! Rascal! Quit that infernal yapping!"

"It's Edna Wallace." She was out of the sleigh. "Is that you, Florence?"

"Naw, it's me, Liz, but Ma's getting up. You got someone sick? Jiminy, Rascal, go lie down!" The dogs quieted. This was a voice you didn't fool with.

"A boy. Burned bad."

"Edna?" Another voice, gravelly with sleep.

"Sorry to be bothering you this hour of the morning, but Dan and I thought it'd be best to get him right over."

"Burns, you say."

"Face and hands. He was staying over at that Galician farm on the next quarter to us. House burned to the ground and the boy's uncle with it."

"One less Hun." The first voice, the dog-threatening voice.

"Best get him in. We can put him in Robin's room. Mrs. Allen is in the spare. I'm thinking there's twins on the way and they're overdue, and her no bigger than a schoolgirl."

They were all beside the sleigh now. A woman in a man's coat held a lantern up and scowled at him. "Do we have to put him in Robin's room?"

"Don't be foolish, Liz." The older woman, the gravelly-voiced woman, holding a patchwork quilt like a shawl, was large, as big as two people. "When a bed is needed, we use it. Can you walk, boy?"

Alex tried his legs. As he half stood, half crouched to get out of the caboose, he felt he was going to fall and he reached out a hand to catch hold of the door frame. The pain of the contact with the wood made him cry out.

"Liz, give me the lantern and you carry him."

He heard her swear under her breath as she helped him out of the sleigh, finally sweeping him up with an arm behind his back and another supporting his legs. With her face so close, he could see that she was a probably about the same age as Marco. She had a rough, boyish look to her. A curl of hair escaped from a wool cap.

As she strode across the yard, images caught in the haphazard light of the lantern preceded them. A large two-storey house with a front gable, scrubby trees, shabby farm buildings. They were on the front step and through the door. The dogs were sniffing at his feet but went scattering when she growled, "Down!"

A little girl in a nightgown watched them from where she stood, illuminated by a lamp on the kitchen table.

"Who is it?" She had a small, piping voice.

"An alien," his bearer snorted, beginning to climb the stairs.

He could feel the little girl's eyes on him as they ascended, and then he could hear the soft sound of her slippered feet on the stairs, following.

"Is he going in Robin's room?" The small voice came from the end of the upstairs hall.

"Don't ask."

In the dark of the bedroom, he was lowered onto a small bed. Springs creaked beneath him, and the young woman was gone. Mrs. Wallace and the big woman, Mrs. Eddy, were beside him now. Mrs. Wallace held the lantern while Mrs. Eddy looked at his burns.

"Poor lad," she muttered. "We'll keep wet cloths on them now and tomorrow I'll make up some poultices. I think I've got some of that salve the doctor left for Elias Gardener when he knocked that pot of oil off the stove. What's your name, young fellow?"

He tried to say it, but his voice was still caught up in the pain and smoke, and it came out with strange sounds from the dryness of his throat.

"It's Alexander. He's at school with our Gordie," Mrs. Wallace said.

"Alexander." The big woman sighed. "We'd best get you out of these clothes and into bed." She turned to the little girl who had crept into the room. "Myrtle, you scoot along back to bed now."

"It's almost time to get up," she laughed.

"Go along now." They were removing his socks, undoing buttons. Alex realized he had run from the fire in his stocking feet. He was glad he'd fallen asleep with his clothes on earlier that evening. Before the fire.

"Liz, get me a basin of warm water," Mrs. Eddy called down the stairs.

Somehow they eased his shirt off without bothering his hands and they used scissors to cut away his undervest. Mrs.

Eddy washed him gently and slipped a nightshirt over his head.

"One of Robin's," she said. "Good thing it's a big size."

She made him drink a cup of water and take some white pills before getting him under the covers, and, when he was lying still, his hands outside of the top blanket, she wrapped them in cool wet cloths and put another over the burned side of his face.

"I'll just stay with him until he falls asleep," said Mrs. Wallace. "Then I think I'll catch forty winks myself before I head back home. An hour or two on your sofa will do me nicely."

He was coming to realize that Mrs. Wallace liked to talk, and he found her voice soothing. Soft and steady like the horses' hoofs on the snow.

"Do you have a mother some place in the world, Alexander? Would she be at home in Galicia, thinking about you this very minute? And a father? But then why would you be here without them and so young and all? I'm thinking you must be an orphan boy. Gordie says you have a brother. The two of you orphans, I suppose, but we'll be finding that brother of yours and the two of you will be a family, even more of a family because there's just the both of you. If he's out working, he'll surely come back this way for Christmas."

It had been a small apartment they had in Hamburg, not far from the docks. Sometimes he had walked down with Papa— *Tato*—to look at the great ships.

"*Yak mama stane zdorova*—as soon as your mother is

well—we'll be getting on one of these," he'd say, pointing across the dock. "A ship as big as a small town, taking hundreds of people across the ocean. Or, who knows, maybe even one of the smaller ones. Share the trip with cows and horses if it'll get us there."

"Will Uncle Andrew be waiting for us? Will he be on the other dock?"

"Heavens, no! He lives far on the other side of Canada. But we'll get on a train and go chugging across the land for many days, and then he'll be there to meet us. We must say prayers that your mother will be well soon, strong for the journey."

In the apartment there had been a daybed and that's where she would be when they returned from their stroll. Reading, if she wasn't too tired. She had been a governess before she married, teaching the landowner's children, reading them stories. Stories of humpbacked horses and flying ships and the magic firebird. Stories she had shared with him for all the bedtimes that brought him up to his eleventh year.

Sometimes Marco would be asleep on the floor at her feet. He had a pallet that he'd made from packing material he'd collected from where he worked loading and unloading boats and he liked to stretch out on that when he came home from a shift. Marco the prince, Mama called him.

"An emperor's son. Just look at that golden hair."

"And what does that make me?" Tato would scold, holding back a laugh.

Afternoon sun that found its way from a high window in

the apartment would make a pattern across the two of them, Marco and Mama. Sometimes Alex would see her reaching to touch the edge of that sunlight, as if she might draw strength from it into herself.

Now sunlight poured through another small window— where was he?—making a pattern of light on the quilt of the bed he was in. His own hands were cocoons of cloth. Across from him, there was a bureau with a mirror over it. He could see part of his face in the mirror, a face with a patch over half of it. Under the patch there was some kind of paste. The smell of strong tea. And something else, like Mama put in with her linens when they lived in Lviv, and then in their packing cases as they travelled. Lavender?

If he turned his head a bit, he could see a bookshelf. It held a few tattered books, a baseball mitt, a harmonica, a pencil box and a photograph of a soldier. The soldier looked as if he were ready to burst into laughter.

"That's our Robin." The voice came from the other side of the bed. It was the little girl, he remembered now. She was sitting on a braided rug playing with some toy soldiers. "He's away at the war."

"Are you . . ." His voice was working again. "Are you Myr-tle?"

"You can call me Myrt."

"Myrt."

"I wish he'd be home. Then we'd go skating."

"Soldier men?" Alex moved a bit closer to the edge of the bed so he could get a full view of the toys she had spread out on the floor. "Robin's?"

"He said I could play with them."

Suddenly the door was filled with the other one, the one who had carried him upstairs. She was still dressed like a man, with an outdoor coat on and her hair covered with a cap. The way she looked at him made him shiver and, if his hands hadn't been two bundles, he would have pulled the quilt up.

"What're you doing here, Myrtle?" The question was aimed at the little girl, but the young woman didn't stop looking at him.

"Playing."

"Well, play somewhere else."

"Phooey." She began packing the toy soldiers into a box. "I'm going to ask Mama," she said defiantly before she left the room.

The woman—Liz?—allowed her gaze to travel around the room, checking the bureau top, the bookshelf, a closet.

"You touch any of this," she said, "and you'll wish you'd gone up in smoke last night. You see that cap there on a peg, his baseball mitt, his books—you touch any of it and you're going to be sorry, and I mean really sorry, that you didn't stay back in Hun country where you belong."

She was drawing breath, Alex thought, to tell him what

other things he might be sorry for when a scream broke into her warning. It made him jump and he felt a jolt of pain along his face.

He heard Myrt's feet pounding up the stairs.

There was another scream followed by a wrenching moan.

"It's Mrs. Allen," Myrt shouted. "I think she must be dying."

Chapter 2

◇

SHE WASN'T DYING, Alex found out a couple of hours later. Screams had continued intermittently from a room somewhere on the ground floor. Screams and long, wrenching moans that made him want to cover his ears. There was a bustle of activity, feet moving purposefully from room to room, the sound of people talking. He could recognize Myrt chattering, and Liz's brusque, clipped words that sounded like someone chucking stones at a barn wall. A slower, gravelly voice must belong to the big woman he'd seen last night with a patchwork quilt wrapped around her. And then there was the voice that had soothed him into sleep on the ride to the Eddys. Gordon's mother with her strange accent.

One of the dogs howled every time Mrs. Allen moaned, and Liz hollered at it to hush up or she'd give it something to yelp about. It sounded like she threw something at it a minute or two later.

It was Mrs. Wallace who brought him up some breakfast on a tray. In the light of day, he could see she had carroty red hair just beginning to go grey. Without the heavy fur coat, her body had shrunk to normal proportions. When she smiled, he noticed she was missing a front tooth.

"What a commotion!" She shook her head.

"Someone is dying?" He was glad his voice wasn't playing tricks on him anymore. The words he was thinking actually came out as words.

"Oh, Lord no." Having set the breakfast tray down on the dresser top, Mrs. Wallace gently lifted a corner of the bandage on his face, looked at his burn, then smoothed it back into place. "There will be a new babe before nightfall, I should think. Mrs. Eddy thinks there may be two. Twins. Poor wee Mrs. Allen so small herself. It'll not be easy." She raised a glass of milk to his lips. "But how are you this morning, laddie?"

Alex took a couple of swallows of milk as he thought of what to say. The pain across the left side of his face and along his hands was constant company, even when he was lying still. And when he moved, it jabbed at him in new ways. He couldn't help thinking about Uncle Andrew, and his longing to see Marco gnawed at him.

"Hurting," Alex said finally.

"Of course you are." Mrs. Wallace's voice was soft and comforting as she spooned some porridge to his mouth. "I don't think there's anything more painful than a burn. I remember when Gordie was a wee babe and I was hurrying about the kitchen, fixing a bottle for him and sterilizing sealer jars for canning beans, and a loop of my apron tie caught on the handle of the pan with the jars and it all spilled against my leg. Well . . ." She clucked her tongue against her teeth a couple of times and shook her head.

Alex held the warm oatmeal with its bit of cream and brown sugar in his mouth for a minute before swallowing. Then he ate more quickly so Mrs. Wallace would be able to set the bowl back on the tray.

"I would like . . ." Alex tried to reach up and wipe the bit of cream that dribbled from his mouth as he spoke.

"Yes?" Mrs. Wallace tidied the bed around him.

"Marco. To be here."

"Marco?"

"My brother," Alex said.

"And where is Marco?" Mrs. Wallace had eased herself into the one chair in the room, a wooden chair with a broken spindle in its back.

"He is at a farm." Alex tried to remember the letters that had come from Marco in the past months. There had been four since Alex had started school late in September, after he'd helped Uncle Andrew with the harvesting. Marco had mentioned going into town to pick up provisions for the farmer, to get mail and post letters, once to go to a dance.

"Vegreville," Alex remembered the name of the town. "He lives at a farm and works."

"You could write to him," Mrs. Wallace said but then she looked at his bandaged hands. "Or someone could write for you. But not today. And I'd best be on my way home or they'll be wondering what happened to me. I planned to be on the road earlier but with Mrs. Eddy busy . . ." She sighed as she got up and collected the breakfast tray.

Once he could hear her footsteps on the stairs, Alex managed to get free of his covers and get out of bed, although he nearly fainted when his feet first found the floor and he stood up. More than anything else in the world right now, he knew he needed to find a chamber pot. But he didn't want to use it with the bedroom door open. Slowly he made his way across the room and used an elbow to close it. Then he knelt down and peered beneath the bed. Sure enough, there was the china pot with a handle. To get it out he had to lie on the floor and use a foot.

Although the room was cold, he could feel sweat beading along his forehead. Before he was finished, the door was suddenly flung open and he nearly knocked the pot over in his hurry to cover himself.

"What're you doing out of bed?" Myrt stood wide-eyed in the open door. And then she giggled and backed out.

Alex used his bandaged hands to push the utensil back as quickly as he could. Climbing back onto the bed, he realized his covers couldn't have been in more of a mess.

Myrt knocked before she came in this time.

"Ma told me to make myself scarce," she said. "You want me to make your bed? I know how."

"Yes." Alex knew his face was still red from embarrassment, and he looked away from her, as if he'd seen something interesting at the window. "Please," he added. "Should I be getting onto the floor?"

"Naw." She yanked at the top quilt and the whole tangled mess slipped off.

Alex was glad the borrowed nightshirt covered him as well as it did. But it didn't cover his feet and they were freezing, so he hoped she'd hurry getting the covers sorted and back over him.

From downstairs the moans of Mrs. Allen were increasing in intensity and the dog in the yard kept up a regular echo, disregarding whatever Liz chucked at it.

"Ma says moaning helps new babies figure out where to go or else they might never find the right bed," Myrt informed him as she draped a sheet over him and tucked in the corners. "Every baby knows its mama's cry and then the baby cries and if it matches up they know they should be together. She says she don't ever remember them not matching up. I guess it's kind of like a miracle."

Alex closed his eyes. He felt very tired and, with each blanket Myrt added to the bed, he could feel himself drifting closer to sleep. With the bandage covering one ear and his other pressed into a pillow, he was able to evade most of the noise from downstairs.

Faintly, he could still hear Myrt, who seldom took a break from talking.

"All done. Snug as a bug." It was almost a song. "Don't tell Ma I came in without knocking and caught you using the thunder mug . . ."

Even when she was sick, Mama would sing to him. He had his favourites. There was one about a brother:

My brother is coming and coming,
Past the gates he's walking, walking,
Bright crescent moon, beautiful star,
Why is my fate so unhappy?

Sometimes her singing would be interrupted when she couldn't catch her breath.

"When she is strong again," Tato would tell him, "then we will be on the ship. So it is my job to see she rests and has good food." When he'd left his farm to marry Mama, he'd worked as a baker in Lviv, and in Hamburg he worked part time in a bakery three streets over from their apartment. "The pay is as thin as a French pancake." He would shake his head sadly and then smile as he unloaded the wicker basket he carried with him the days he worked. "But Herr Grunberg sends me home with this hamper of milk and butter and day-old bread. It is Mama's job to eat, and your job to study and learn English."

Mama still had some of the books she had used for teaching English and French when she was a governess. She could speak Polish too, but all of her attention was focused on them learning English as they waited to go to Canada. Alex would read aloud to her from a book of English stories and, if she wasn't too tired, they would practise simple exchanges of English conversation.

"How is the weather today?" she'd ask him, glancing toward the window.

"It . . . snows."

"Is snowing," she'd correct him.

"And how is your health?"

"It is well . . ."

She raised her eyebrows.

"I am well. I am very well, thank you," he would add.

But he had been the first to become really ill and the reason their apartment had a quarantine sign posted outside. Not that a quarantine sign could keep Marco from slipping in and out when no one was watching, even if he had to go out the window and across a roof. Someone had to bring in some money and food. They had all agreed that the money set aside for the voyage to Canada was not to be touched.

By the time Alex was out of danger, both Mama and Papa had come down with the sickness. The same doctor who had ordered the quarantine took Marco's money for medicine and told him he'd have to keep the sign posted.

But the medicine hadn't helped.

Both he and Marco had tried desperately to nurse them,

but Mama slipped away first and three days later Tato closed his eyes for the last time. He had grasped Marco's hand just before he died. "Sorry . . ." His voice had been barely a whisper. "Perhaps we should not . . ."

"Don't be sorry, Tato." Marco had continued holding his hand. "You were brave to bring us this far. We will still go. It will be good."

Alex had kept to a corner where he hoped Papa wouldn't hear him crying.

In the coming days, he knew that Marco was the brave one, arranging for the burials, refusing to be bullied by the doctor and the cemetery workers.

"I am dipping into the money," Marco had said, as if it were still possible to speak to their parents. "I'm not going to leave you here in this strange city without a proper resting place." He bought sturdy wood for a grave marker as well, surrounding their names and dates of birth and death with a border copied from a book of poems Mama had cherished.

In the midst of granite headstones, marble statuary and weathered wooden crosses of the German cemetery, the brightly-painted marker with its Greek crucifix, Cyrillic lettering and gold paint looked exotic, Alex thought. You could spot it from the very edge of the graveyard.

They had gone to look at it one last time the day before they sailed. Afternoon sun had caught the gold paint, so it seemed, almost, that they were looking at treasure. Marco had sighed and put an arm around Alex's shoulders.

"There's just the two of us, Lexie," he'd said, slipping in the nickname like a gentle squeeze. "But we have Mama's and Tato's dream to hold us together. And I am hoping, enough money . . . Right, little brother? We will be a force in this new land, the two of us."

But where was Marco? In his last letter he'd written he expected to be home by December. He had never been away for so long.

Alex wondered how long he had been sleeping. The bedroom had grown dark. Could it actually be evening? In winter, of course, it might only be late afternoon. His stomach rumbled. He was famished.

The house, Alex realized, was oddly still. No moaning or screaming. No dogs howling. Not even the sound of footsteps and talking.

By bending his knees and using his elbows, he was able to get the bedcovers down without using his hands. The floor hadn't warmed up any since he'd climbed out of bed hours earlier, but there was a braided rug beneath the window and it gave some comfort to his bare feet as he stood and peered out. It didn't seem to be quite as dark outside as it was inside. Liz was going into the barn, he could see, with pails, trailed by the dogs. In another part of the yard, a bundled-up Myrt was balancing an armful of firewood, heading toward the house. He could hear the door close as she came in and the sound of the wood being dropped into a woodbox.

A couple of minutes later there was the sound of her feet

bounding up the stairs. Cautiously, she peeked into the bedroom.

"Mrs. Allen's babies came," she whispered excitedly. "Twin baby boys. Ma says she's going to name them George and Edward for the last two kings."

There was someone coming up the stairs now. Steps creaked under the weight of the person. Mrs. Eddy gasped for breath as she reached the door.

"Myrtle, light that lamp, will you, honey." She squinted as she looked at him, still standing on the rug, but turned now with his back to the window. "Boy, you best crawl back under those covers, at least until we hunt up some socks and slippers and a pair of pants for you. I want to wash the ones you had on. There should be a couple of Robin's old shirts . . ."

"I know where they are." Myrt had found some matches on the dresser top and lit the lamp. She knelt down and opened one of the drawers.

Mrs. Eddy came into the room and sat down. Alex feared for the remaining unbroken spindles on the chair back.

"Myrtle says you've been sleeping most of the day. You've been up here checking on him every ten minutes, haven't you, honey? I swear you have the makings of a nurse, just like your mother."

"I want to be a circus rider," Myrt giggled. "I want to stand up on a spotted horse and ride around in a big circle."

"Our Robin took her to the circus in Edmonton, and she hasn't had a sound notion in her head since, I sometimes think. Now, boy, you get back into bed and I'll check on those bandages."

Alex cried out as she began to lift the bandage away from his face. In places, the gauze had adhered to the wound.

"Myrtle, you run downstairs and bring me up a pitcher of warm water from the reservoir. We'll just dampen the edges a bit and it should come away fine."

In a few minutes Myrt was back.

"I only spilled a little." She grinned as she handed her mother the pitcher.

Mrs. Eddy soaked the bandages on his hands too, in places, as she unwound them. Myrt stood by with a second basin for collecting the soiled cloth. With her huge hands, Mrs. Eddy bathed the parts of skin at the edge of the burns with a gentleness that made him think of Marco sponging his fevered face when they were in Hamburg.

"I think we'll leave them unbandaged for a bit. Air can be good against a burn. And then, after supper, when you're ready for bed, we'll bandage you up again for the night. Now I'd best be checking on Mrs. Allen and those babies. Liz said she'd scare up something to eat but Lord knows what it'll be."

Downstairs, in the brighter light of the kitchen's kerosene lamp, Alex took a closer look at his hands. It was mainly the backs that had burned, the skin blistered and red, even burned away in places. The bone of a knuckle on his left hand showed. Sitting down at the table with the others, he found he could use the underside of a couple of fingers and a thumb to hold a piece of bread. It was possible to dip the bread in the yolks of the eggs Mrs. Eddy slid onto his plate from a platterful Liz had fried up. Alex found it hard to believe that bread and eggs could taste so good.

When Mrs. Eddy asked him if he'd like the last couple remaining on the platter after everyone had dished up, he nodded, and had some more of the mashed potatoes that had been reheated in a big frying pan.

Liz glowered at him through the meal.

"No letter from Robin today?" Mrs. Eddy sat back with her cup of tea. "I was hoping when I saw the mail caboose pull in."

"Just *Country Guide*," Liz muttered. "And don't you be cutting pictures out of it, Myrtle, until we're through reading it."

Myrt ignored her sister. She had eaten bits out of a heel of bread to make a horse shape that she was deftly manoeuvring around her plate and along an avenue of salt and pepper shakers, a butter dish, a pitcher of cream and a sugar bowl.

"It's been a long time since we've heard from him." Mrs. Eddy sighed. "And he's good about writing."

"Huns and their boats on the high seas." Liz looked at Alex as if he were commanding them himself. "It's a wonder any mail gets through."

Babies began crying in a back bedroom and Mrs. Eddy set her tea aside. "This has been a long day, I have to say," she said, adjusting her apron, "and it isn't over yet. Myrtle, you do up the dishes now and don't dawdle around until the water gets cold."

"Phooey." She bit her horse's head off.

"You can keep her company, Alex. It's real warm there by the stove if you sit by the woodbox."

As Myrt scraped the dishes, sending any leftover bits into a dish for the dogs, and filled a wash pan with dippers of water from the stove's reservoir, she chattered nonstop.

"You know what?" She chased a dishrag over one of the plates before setting it in the pan of rinse water, watching it float for a second before it sank. "My birthday and Christmas and New Year's are almost all at the same time."

"What age will you be?" Alex asked. The woodbox was a perfect place to sit. The stove kept his legs warm and he could hold his hands near the window where a bit of soothing outside cold seeped through a crack.

Dropping the dishrag, she held up all the fingers and thumb of one hand and two fingers of the other. "Seven. On December 27th. I can count to a hundred, and seven is my favourite number. Next year I'll go to school, and then Ma says I can learn to count to a million. I can read a lot of words and write my name. Can you read and write, Alex?"

"Of course. In two languages. Mostly Ukrainian, but also much English."

Alex thought about school. Today there would have been no one in the seat of the desk he shared with a ten-year-old boy, Charlie, who was reading in the same level of reader. Miss Anderson would have everyone practising songs for the Christmas concert. The one about the jingling bells. *Away in a Manger. Hark the Herald Angels Sing.*

Who would do his part in the play, he wondered. The part of Joseph. If he'd been at school today, he could have listened to Beryl, a grade eight girl with beautiful blonde ringlets, who was going to practise reciting *Annie's and Willie's Prayers* for the whole class. She sat across the aisle from Alex and had told him she'd been learning a verse a night for the last month.

"For presents . . ." Myrtle was holding up a handful of forks and was looking at them as if they were a congregation of people. "I want skates and a Snakes and Ladders board. I had a good one but I left it outside and it got rained on and it all fell apart. And maybe a horse and a bicycle. When you've got all your present days in the middle of the winter, you need to think about summer when there's none. But Ma says not to hold my breath on a bicycle, and I can practise with Robin's old one, but it needs a new chain. A new chain we can afford, Ma says. What are you wishing for, Alex?"

"For me?" Alex stretched his legs out. The knee breeches he had on had belonged to Robin, but the slippers had been Liz's until she outgrew them. She hadn't looked happy about seeing them on his feet. "What I am wishing for is Marco to come home. That would be the best Christmas present."

"Marco?" Myrt began drying the cutlery, wrapping it up

in a dishtowel as if she were getting the forks and spoons
ready for bed.

"He is my brother," Alex said. "For Christmas I want to be
with my brother."

Chapter 3

꙰

CHRISTMAS WAS TEN days away. At Uncle Andrew's it would have been longer yet, Ukrainian Christmas coming on January 7th, but Alex tried not to think about that. As Myrt made decorations for the tree, cutting up an old catalogue to make paper chains, he couldn't help remembering Marco helping him to paint cards for Miss Anderson and the children at school last year. Marco had been home early, with some money for his fall work, and he'd bought a thick writing pad of white, unlined paper. Last year there had been twenty-eight children in the one-room schoolhouse at Bayles' Corner and Marco had made cards for all of them. At least he'd drawn all of them, looking at Christmas designs in the Eaton's catalogue. Alex had helped to paint in the bells and stars and teddy bears and the fancy scrolled lettering that announced "Merry Christmas" inside the folded pieces of paper.

"These are wonderful," Miss Anderson had said. "Your brother is a professional." It was a word he'd remembered to tell Marco when he returned home just before the holidays.

"Professional?" Marco had looked puzzled. "Like a professor?"

Uncle Andrew had raised his eyebrows and wiggled his index finger around his ear. He'd begun celebrating early in the afternoon with his own concoction of sweetened chokecherry juice and homebrew.

"An expert," Alex said. He'd asked Miss Anderson what the word meant.

"Maybe I will dance with her." Marco was getting ready to go to a dance that evening in the schoolhouse. With his fall earnings, he'd been able to buy a dark blue suit, a shirt and tie, and oxford shoes.

Alex had thought about going to the dance too. After all, he'd turned thirteen and some of his classmates his age were going. But he didn't have new clothes. He'd been growing the past year and his best trousers, the ones he wore to school, had pant legs that ended well above his ankles and had already raised giggles at school. His coat was tight too, although he did have one of Papa's shirts with a design along its collar and cuffs that Mama had embroidered, and it was plenty big.

This fall, with his first pay, Marco had sent to Eaton's for a new outfit for Alex. Unfortunately he'd changed out of it to do chores on the afternoon before the fire, and they'd burned up. He'd be wearing some of Robin's old clothes for Christmas at the Eddys, and Mrs. Eddy had given him a vest that belonged to her husband who had died in a logging accident five years earlier. It was black broadcloth with a watch pocket. Marco had Papa's watch, but maybe Alex would be able to get one for himself now that he was fourteen.

When his hands healed, he wondered, would he be able to get some kind of job? Maybe he could work a few months here and a few months there as a farm labourer as Marco had done, or maybe he could help out at the store at Bayles' Corner, or do the janitor work at the school. Or maybe Marco would farm Uncle Andrew's quarter and Alex would work alongside him.

For Christmas Day at the Eddys, he was wearing the black vest. Liz had gone out into the backwoods to find a Christmas tree and he had helped Myrt decorate it the day before. Along with the cut-outs and paper chains, they'd strung silvery garlands. With parts of his hands still bandaged, he'd been able to do little more than hold a garland in place or steady a branch to which Myrt was attaching a bauble or clipping on a small candle in a brass holder.

"It's been two years since Robin was home for Christmas," Liz noted morosely as they sat around the decorated tree on Christmas morning. "Seems like a hundred." It was the first time Alex had seen her in a skirt and she seemed awkward and embarrassed by it and kept her feet in their riding boots in full view.

"That boy loved Christmas," Mrs. Eddy sighed. "I swear he never slept more than a wink on Christmas Eve. When he was a tiny tot, he'd be up every five minutes checking for the sound of reindeer on the roof. It used to drive Albert crazy. Do you remember that, Liz? Your dad would have to threaten to give him a good hiding and even that wouldn't keep him from bubbling up like a fudge pot on a too-hot fire."

"Can we open our presents?" Myrt did a little dance back and forth in front of her mother. She had already emptied her stocking of its candy and an orange and a little rag doll with a mop of red yarn hair.

"Not before your cousins get here and Mr. Bayles and the Greeleys." Mrs. Eddy sighed again, and settled back into her armchair. "Thank heavens we haven't got a sick person in the house today. I thought Mrs. O'Hara might be with us but she sent word that the baby's more likely to be coming just after the New Year."

Liz raised her eyebrows and looked at Alex, sitting cross-legged on the rug.

"Well." Mrs. Eddy wrapped an afghan closer around her shoulders. "Alexander isn't exactly sick. Just a bit wounded."

Liz rolled her eyes.

"Everybody needs a place for Christmas," Mrs. Eddy went on, "and we're pleased to have you here with us."

"I want to open a present," Myrt whined.

"Let her open one," Liz suggested. "Or there won't be any peace."

"All right. One." Mrs. Eddy smiled. "There's one for you there too, Alex. Why don't you go ahead and open it."

"I know where it is!" Myrt grabbed a package from the small pile at the base of the tree and raced over to him. "It's from me!"

"No." Alex suddenly felt awful. He hadn't been able to get anything for anyone and he'd hoped that no one would have felt they'd need to come up with something for him. "I am . . ." He struggled to find the right word. "Out."

"Pshaw," Mrs. Eddy grunted. "No one's out of things on Christmas Day."

Alex held the small package wrapped in green tissue paper and tied with a thin red ribbon in his hands. It was so light, it placed no burden against his burns.

"Oh boy!" Myrt shrieked. "I'm opening this one." She held a large package wrapped in store paper with a small Christmas ornament attached to the top along with a card.

"What does the card say?" asked her mother.

Myrt looked at it and screwed up her face. "I can read some but not Christmas cards in letter writing."

"Let's see." Myrt relinquished the card to Liz.

"This is in your brother's handwriting." Liz's voice took on a softer edge. "For the fearless bareback rider, it says. Choose your pony and ride your course."

"A horse," Myrt squealed.

"Yeah, that's likely."

Mrs. Eddy leaned over and whispered to Alex. "That boy picked out gifts for two Christmases when he was on his embarkation leave, if you can believe it. 'Just in case the war's not over,' he said."

Liz scratched a match to life and lit a cigarette.

"I'd appreciate it if you refrained from smoking in front of the Greeleys," Mrs. Eddy said. She looked over at Alex. "Don't ever take up that habit if you can avoid it. Nor chewing. I can't abide a man expectorating into a tin pail throughout a social occasion. I hope you don't take up chewing too, Liz, although I'm not counselling you. All I'd have to do is counsel you not to do it, and you'd be doing it the next day."

Myrt had unwrapped the package and removed a carousel music box from the carton. "Oh look." She held it in both hands like something newborn and fragile. "A merry-go-round with horses!"

"Wind up that little key." Liz exhaled a small cloud of smoke and picked a bit of tobacco from her front teeth.

Myrt wound the key slowly a few more times and then gently released it.

"Set it down now," her mother said.

When she put it on the dining room table, the carousel began to move slowly in a circle, and tinkly music played a tune that made Alex want to tap his toes.

"Oh my," Mrs. Eddy sighed yet again. "That's a tune my father played on his fiddle at my wedding party. 'Silver and Gold.'"

"Look!" Myrt had discovered a small drawer in the base of the music box and pulled it open. She frowned to find it empty.

"It's for jewellery and other little treasures," her mother explained. "You'll have something to put in it when you open the rest of your presents later."

When the music box wound down and the music stopped with a last few, tentative chimes, Myrt twirled around, momentarily intrigued by the flare of the skirt on her Sunday dress.

"Open your present, Alex." She began jumping up and down.

Alex slipped the ribbon off and pulled the tissue paper apart with the thumb and first finger of his left hand which had been burned the least. Inside were two handkerchiefs with the initial "A" embroidered in one corner.

"This is fine," he said, fingering the material gently.

Myrt leaned against him and ran her fingers over the letter on the top handkerchief. "A for Alex. I sewed it all myself. Well, Mama did thread the needle and helped me a bit. A for Alex. No one can use them but you."

Mrs. Eddy heaved herself out of her armchair and picked up the wrapping paper and ribbon, smoothing out the paper and folding it, winding the ribbon into a loop.

"I'm going to check on that turkey," she said. "Liz, maybe you can help me with the spuds. Myrt, why don't you and Alex play Chinese checkers, but you watch her, Alex. She's devious when it comes to moving those marbles around."

They played checkers until Myrt became bored. Then she got out Robin's old collection of toy soldiers and organized a game with them.

"Alex, yours'll be the bluecoats and when I close my eyes, you hide them and then my redcoats will come looking for them. When they find one it becomes our prisoner and then it'll be your turn."

"We see who gets most prisoners?" Alex looked at the parlour clock on the sideboard by the table. "Five minutes for you, then five minutes for me?"

"Okay. I'm hiding my eyes."

Myrt faced into a corner as Alex found spots for his blue-coated soldiers, inside a candy dish on the sideboard, tucked into a sash tacked to the wall, holding a tray with a scene of London's Tower Bridge and the Houses of Parliament, between copies of the Bible and a big dictionary on the book-stand by Mrs. Eddy's armchair.

"Ready?" Myrt was doing a little dance from foot to foot.

"Almost. Two more."

Alex lifted a doily on the arm of the sofa and put one there and then slipped the last behind a china ornament of a horse on the windowsill.

Myrt was managing to find them with amazing speed, and Alex realized she'd actually been able to watch what he was doing from a mirror just to one side of where she'd been hiding her eyes.

She'd found four when the dogs began creating a ruckus

in the front yard. Myrt dashed to the window and Alex followed her. A team of horses pulling a caboose halted by the front gate.

"It's the Greeleys," Myrt said before running into the kitchen. "Ma, the Greeleys are here."

Alex watched as a bent, white-haired old man climbed out of the caboose and then helped a woman in a long, fur-trimmed coat step out. She had white hair too, he could see, although her head was mostly covered by a large hat that looked like it had been made from an animal whose fur was tight and curly.

As the couple began making their way up the walk, and Liz was leading the team to the barn, an open sleigh pulled by another team came around the bend by the scrubby trees at the edge of the yard. The dogs were practically doing acrobatics and Alex could hear Liz hollering at them to quiet down or she'd set them out for wolf bait.

Myrt bounded into the living room again. "It's Gracie and Eve and Auntie Peg. Now we can open presents." She did a twirl and then a reverse twirl, chanting, "Presents, presents, we can open presents!"

Her mother poked her head into the living room. "Settle down, Myrt." She untied her apron and tucked it back into the kitchen. "And remember your manners."

In a minute everyone was at the door. Alex found a chair in the farthest corner of the living room. He wished it would be possible for him to simply disappear for the next few hours. He'd gotten used to being around the affable Mrs. Eddy and Myrt, who treated him like a brother, and even Liz with her constant scowling and complaining.

Now, however, there was a host of others who'd want to know all about him and look at him sideways, not really staring at the burns but taking in, nonetheless, how he looked. And wondering how much English he spoke and how much he understood. And talking about his future as if he weren't in the room. It had happened before, when Mrs. Allen's husband and mother had come to fetch her and the twins.

"There's not an orphanage hereabouts," Mr. Allen had said, nodding towards him. "Probably in Edmonton, but how do you go about getting him up there?"

"There's Galician priests that might know where to place him." Mrs. Allen had handed one of the twins to her mother as she got the other wrapped. "Probably in Vegreville or Lamont. Someone should ask one of them."

"They're Greek," said Mrs. Allen's mother. "Greek priests with those funny crosses."

Myrt ran circles around everyone now as Mrs. Eddy brought her guests into the living room.

"Alice, Howard, this here's Alex. He's staying with us for a bit while his burns are mending. Used to live with his uncle, but you heard about that fire on the other side of Bayles' Corner three weeks back."

The Greeleys were a matched set—old and very wrinkled, both with a heavy head of white hair. With her lace collar and cameo brooch, Mrs. Greeley made Alex think of the Polish grandmother who had employed his mother as governess for her two grandchildren. She had visited them a couple of times when they still lived in Lviv. Mr. Greeley pulled a pipe out of his pocket and began chewing on the stem.

"Alex, this is Mr. and Mrs. Greeley. Our oldest and best neighbours." Mrs. Eddy squeezed the old lady's hand.

Alex stood and ducked his head in a bit of a bow. People in Canada didn't bow. It was a habit. Even most of the children he'd known in Lviv didn't bow—it was something his mother had taught him. The gesture brought a wisp of a smile to Mrs. Greeley's lips.

The other arrivals had rid themselves of their wraps and now trooped into the room. As introductions were made, Alex noticed that Mrs. Winfield, Auntie Peg, was, in size, definitely related to Mrs. Eddy. Her daughters, Gracie and Eve, a few years older than Myrt but younger than Liz, hung back shyly for a minute until Myrt pulled them away to put the gifts they'd brought beneath the tree.

As everyone found places to sit, Myrt's cousins with Myrt on the big braided rug between the sofa and the dining room table, Alex could see the little girl's exasperation as she waited for a chance to break into the adult chit-chat. Her mother had stopped her from playing the carousel music box after she had wound it up and let it run down twice. Finally, when Mrs. Greeley and Auntie Peg had exhausted the topic of baking shortages caused by the war, Myrt exploded.

"Can we open presents now. Puh-lease!"

By this time, Liz had stomped back in to join the group, picking some bits of straw off her skirt.

"I wonder what's keeping Mr. Bayles?" There was an edge of worry in Liz's voice. "He's generally the first one here."

"Something last minute must have come up at the store." Mrs. Eddy nodded at Myrt and her cousins. "Jack won't mind if we go ahead and open gifts, I'm sure. You girls hand things around."

There was even another gift for Alex. It was wrapped in the same brown store paper with its imprint of holly that had been used for Myrt's music box. A gift tag attached with a Christmas sticker of a smiling Santa face stated, "For Alexander with all best wishes for 1916, Florence Eddy." Inside was a little leather box.

Using his thumbs to release the catch, Alex flipped the cover. Inside there was a comb and hairbrush, a razor, and a tiny pair of scissors. Tato had had a kit like this and, when Marco claimed his watch, he'd given the kit to Alex. It too, of course, had burned. He realized Mrs. Eddy had been watching him as he'd opened it.

"Thank you." Alex wasn't sure she heard him over the hubbub of everyone opening gifts, but she must have known what he was saying. She nodded to him and smiled before returning to a gift in her own lap, a cardboard box filled with small jars of preserves. Now Mrs. Eddy was reaching over and patting her sister's hand and exclaiming something about no one making jams and jellies like Peg Winfield.

When the small storm of papers and ribbon had been cleared away and everyone had examined each other's presents, Mrs. Eddy declared that they couldn't wait a minute longer for Jack Bayles. If they did, the turkey would be way overdone. In a few minutes the dining room table had been pulled apart and leaves added. Myrt and her cousins set the table with china and cutlery from the sideboard as the women began bringing in small dishes of pickles and cranberry jelly, and then larger bowls of potatoes and carrots and creamed corn. Finally the platter of carved turkey and a bowl of sage dressing.

A couple of years ago Alex wouldn't have been able to guess what some of these dishes were—they were all so different from their own Christmas fare. But last year Miss Anderson had arranged for a full Christmas dinner at the school for all the children, and she'd had them write up a menu, then pen thank-you letters to the ladies of the Bayles' Corner Red Cross group who had provided the meal.

Mrs. Winfield, who sat next to him at the table, helped him dish up and then cut his meat. For a few minutes, as everyone dug in, even the grown-ups stopped talking and there was just the sound of the cutlery against china along with satisfied sighs and people murmuring "*mmm*." Then Mrs. Eddy urging everyone to have another helping.

"Mince pie," Myrt announced as plates were cleared. "None for me. I hate mince pie."

"Oh, you do not," Mrs. Eddy chided. "You just like Mrs. Greeley's lemon pie better. Now who'd like lemon, and who'd like mince?"

"Both for me," Mr. Greeley chuckled. "You can never have too much pie."

The count was lost with the dogs barking again. Liz scraped back her chair and checked out the window.

"There's Mr. Bayles now. I'm glad we kept a plate ready for him in the warming oven. He must be starved." She slipped on a jacket and hurried outside.

But Mr. Bayles didn't come in right away. Alex guessed he must have decided to help Liz tend to the horses.

"What's keeping them?" Mrs. Eddy fussed over the place she'd set at the end of the table.

And then, as loud as one of the dogs howling, there was a human cry from the front step that made everyone hold their breath. A high, keening cry.

Liz.

"No," she was screaming. "Not Robin. Not Robin."

Mrs. Eddy went white in the face. She knocked over a chair as she rushed through the kitchen door.

"It's Robin." It sounded to Alex like Liz was pounding a fist against the door casing. "They've killed him. Those bloody Huns have killed him."

Chapter 4

꙰

MYRT AND HER COUSINS and Aunt Peg followed Mrs. Eddy into the kitchen and Liz's cries were quickly echoed by the sobs of others and Mrs. Eddy repeating Robin's name over and over again in a kind of chant. Alex watched as Mrs. Greeley's mouth opened in a small *Ooo* of horror and a thin, veined hand fluttered beneath the cameo brooch as if it were somehow helping her heart continue to beat.

"How can there be such news on a Christmas Day?" Mr. Greeley shook his head sadly and captured his wife's other hand with his own.

They were both looking at Alex.

What were they thinking? That he had somehow been responsible for Robin's death?

Alex excused himself and headed up to his room. Even there, he felt like an invader, the young soldier in the photograph grinning at him. There was Robin's baseball mitt shaped to his hand, a bicycle clip that must have circled his ankle as he'd ridden along country roads, a mouth organ that would have felt his breath and released tunes that had hovered in the air of a summer afternoon. Somehow Robin lived in all these things that surrounded Alex in his room, but they were like the ripples from a stone tossed into a pond, still visible as the stone itself sinks and is lost.

Alex heard his own breath catch, felt tears spring to his eyes. How had Robin died, he wondered. A bullet wound? The victim of a shell blast or mustard gas? Or from some disease nurtured in the mud and filth of the trenches.

Alex knew about these things, not just from the flag-waving and labels pinned on a map of the world at school, and people singing cheery songs like "Pack up Your Troubles." Uncle Andrew had kept up with the war news, borrowing newspapers from a neighbour.

He would have Marco or Alex read aloud from them. With a drink in hand he would declaim the inhumanity and stupidity of men, shouting in Ukrainian, the language they all used at home. "I would not go to such a war—young men the pawns of the tsar, an emperor, a king. All that blood for what?" He'd accent the *what* by swirling the home-brewed vodka in his glass. "No, better to fight for our own freedoms."

"Don't shout too loudly," Marco would laugh. "Papa always said you were a socialist, but socialists are not popular now, so speak in a whisper."

"What do I care for whispers!" Uncle Andrew would bang the table. "I am proud to be a voice for my fellow workers."

"Who are your fellow workers? Farmers like yourself with your own land?" Marco teased him. "You may be a voice in a jail cell if you keep ranting. It's a good thing you do your shouting in Ukrainian and none of the recruiting officers and those singing the praises of the British Empire can understand you."

"Maybe I'll use English," Uncle Andrew muttered. "They need enlightenment."

Alex wasn't sure how long he sat in his room—Robin's room. The house seemed oddly quiet, as if everyone downstairs was talking in whispers, and if they were crying, crying softly. At one point he heard Liz shouting outside, but he couldn't make out what she was saying, and when he got up and looked out the window, he saw her on her horse, holding the reins in one hand and a rifle in another.

As she looked up at the window, she raised the rifle and Alex ducked down below the sill. He heard her fire twice, but just the sound of the reports, no sound of the impact of the bullets hitting anything. She must have been shooting straight up into the air. The dogs whined and a downstairs door opened and someone—Mrs. Eddy, or maybe Mrs.

Winfield—called out, "Liz, come on back! Liz!" But this was followed by the sound of the horse galloping away over the packed snow.

When he peeked over the windowsill, he saw Liz disappearing along the field road over the crest of a hill. Heading back to the one chair in the room, Alex carefully removed one of the books from Robin's bookshelf. It was old and tattered, one that he or others must have nearly worn out. The title was *Wonders of the World* and, with its thick pages and cracked spine, it lay open easily in his lap and it was not hard to turn the pages with his bandaged hands. At least it helped the time pass.

There were pictures of the pyramids and the great sphinx of Egypt. The ruins of a temple on a hilltop in Greece. The Colosseum in Rome. Alex wondered if Robin, as he pored over these same pages, had dreamt of crossing the seas and travelling to these places. Maybe he had stood in his army uniform before the Tower Bridge in London and the Eiffel Tower in Paris. Weren't those cities that Miss Anderson had pointed out as she discussed the war with the older students at school and examined a map of the world?

Alex found he could read a fair bit of the text accompanying the engravings, but it was becoming too dark to read when there was finally a knock on his door. Alex guessed the little man poking his head into the room was Mr. Bayles, who had brought the news about Robin.

"Alex?" He had a kindly face. Bushy eyebrows and a thick mustache. He was dressed for outdoors and held a winter cap in his hands. "How'd you like to come with me, boy?"

"Come? Where?" Alex used the flats of his hands to close the book.

"To my place. To the store." Mr. Bayles shuffled from foot to foot and gazed at the floor. "It might be best for you not to be anywhere near Liz Eddy for a while. She's like a wounded bear right now. Florence Eddy figures your burns are mending fine."

"Yes," Alex agreed. "It will be the best."

To get to the porch where the old coat and cap that Mrs. Eddy had given him were hanging, he had to go past the people still in the living room. A red-eyed Myrt was on the rug, playing Snakes and Ladders with her cousins. Mr. Greeley wandered slowly up and down, puffing on his pipe, leaving a trail of tobacco smoke. Mrs. Greeley and Mrs. Winfield came suddenly into the room, easing Mrs. Eddy's bedroom door shut behind them, whispering and shaking their heads.

"Me and the boy'll be on our way now," Mr. Bayles said. "I'm sorry again that I was the bearer of such bad tidings."

Myrt leaped up. "Are you going away, Alex? I don't want you to go." She ran over and threw her arms around him and began crying.

"Best." Alex struggled to find words. "Best I go."

Mrs. Winfield gently pulled Myrt away.

"Wait," Myrt shouted. "Your presents." She ran to the sideboard and collected the handkerchiefs and the toilet kit. "You just about forgot them."

"I am stupid." Alex smiled at her.

It took a few seconds but Myrt finally smiled back at him. "Stupid," she said, and giggled.

Mr. Bayles helped Alex do up his wraps and Alex followed him to the barnyard to get his team and sleigh. As he looked back, Myrt stood in the kitchen doorway, waving, before someone urged her back inside and shut the door.

"Not much of a Christmas for you, eh, boy?" Mr. Bayles said once his team had reached the main road. The sun was low on the horizon now, molten gold caught in the branches of trees along the edges of fields.

"Our Christmas is some days to come." Alex realized his voice hardly carried past the muffling folds of the scarf Mr. Bayles had tied around the lower part of his face, knotting it carefully so it didn't press too hard against the burn. "I think my brother will be home."

Of course, there was no home to come to. How would Marco find him?

"There's a letter for you." Mr. Bayles flicked the reins. "Steady on there, Princess. She's a little skittish, not like her mate, Duke."

"A letter?"

"Yup. I meant to bring it out to the Eddys and then that wire come up from Vermilion for Florence and everything else plumb went out of my mind. It's waiting for you there back at the post office. Return address to Marco Kaminsky, Vegreville."

"Oh good," Alex whispered into his scarf. "A letter."

"That'd be your brother?" Mr. Bayles, Alex remembered from the few times he'd been into the store at the corner, liked to talk. Maybe it was all part of being a storekeeper and postmaster.

"Likely ain't heard about the fire. Odd, ain't it, the fact that someone who's gone is really still alive to people don't have the news. Like your uncle, who is still alive to Marco. And Robin, still alive to his family on Christmas day, them likely wondering how he was doing, what he'd be having for Christmas dinner. Still alive until I brung the news. Thought about holding off for a day so everyone could have their Christmas, but knew I couldn't sit through dinner knowing . . ."

"Liz is feeling very bad, isn't she?" Alex snuggled into the blanket Mr. Bayles had thrown over him. With darkness, it was getting colder.

"Yup. Like I said before—a wounded bear. Nobody better go near her for a while. She's always been a bit of a terror, but I know she thought the sun rose and set on Robin. She stuck to him like a shadow. She'd go hunting and fishing with him, and she was darn good too. Sometimes she'd catch more fish than he would, or pitch a better game of baseball—they were both good pitchers. When he joined up, I swear she was ready to cut her hair and pretend she was a boy just to be right there with him." Mr. Bayles shook his head sadly.

"She would like to kill me, I think." Alex hadn't even been aware that he'd said this aloud, but Mr. Bayles reached over and patted his arm.

"You mustn't put too much stock in Liz's threats. She's just mad at the whole world right now, and you just happened to be the red flag in front of her."

Mr. Bayles kept talking, but it wasn't long before Alex found it difficult to keep his eyes open. The still coldness of the night, the muted clopping of Duke's and Princess's hooves on the snow-packed road settled in with the sound of the postmaster's voice. Before he fell asleep, Alex looked at the sky now spangled with stars. A poor man's jewels, Mama had called them. Tonight the jewels were strewn across the heavens.

He slept until the team turned into the yard behind the store at Bayles' Corner.

"Now you be patient just a minute or two longer, Princess, while I get Alex inside and get a fire goin'. Then you'll be gettin' your oats." Mr. Bayles wrapped the reins around a hitching post.

"You awake there, sonny boy? You was off in dreamland the last five miles." He helped Alex down from the sleigh and unlocked the back door to the store.

Alex followed him up the stairs.

"We'll get some light on the subject and then we'll stoke up that fire. It's colder than an igloo." Mr. Bayles bustled around, lighting a kerosene table lamp, opening the stove door and poking at coals in a potbellied heater in the corner, then adding wood from a box beside it.

The times he'd been in the store, Alex had never thought about what was above the main floor. The sitting room was small and cozy with an armchair and a couch along one wall, a gramophone, calendars and magazine pictures on the walls. Cozy, but definitely cold. Alex couldn't stop shivering.

"It'll warm up in a jiffy. In the meantime you keep this blanket wrapped around you. I'm just going to put the horses in the stable and give them some feed."

"The letter?" Alex said, his teeth chattering.

"I'll collect it from downstairs on my way back. Have to stoke the fire in the store too so things don't freeze."

Alex could see there was a small kitchen just off the sitting room on one side and a bedroom on the other. Three little rooms above the store and post office. A little like the apartment they had in Hamburg.

It seemed to take forever for the postmaster to take care of the chores, but when he came back upstairs he had the letter.

"Yup. Marco Kaminsky," he said, holding the envelope up close to the lamp. "You want me to open it?" He already had his pocket knife out. "You just take your time reading it, and I'll get the kettle on to make us a nice hot cup of tea. And a bite to eat. Worked up an appetite myself, I have to say."

The room had begun to warm, and Alex freed himself from the quilt to grasp the pages Mr. Bayles had removed from the envelope. It was a long letter, Alex realized with satisfaction, three pages filled with Marco's handwriting and some sketches too.

My Dear Alex,

How long is it since I have written? Each week this last month I have been expecting wages and thinking not to write because I will be home faster than a letter—but Granger always surprises me with one more job to do. First it was fixing the pig barn and the henhouse. More than fixing. Like building them new. I am too much the good builder in wood. Closing in a stairway in the house. Now he has me making a cabinet for dishes and painting it. This was after I made a little picture of summer flowers on the kitchen door. The flowers were for Stella, his wife, and I will put more on the cabinet when it is done. Stella is Ukrainian too and we must be careful not to talk it when Granger can hear.

I will be happy to leave Granger who is not a nice man even if he has a big house and lots of land and money. He gets mad easy and breaks things and calls names and even sometimes hits Stella. I would like to hit him back for her but Stella says it will only make everything more bad. She is so young she should be a daughter not a wife. Did I tell you he has a hook not a hand on his right arm? He was in a war in Africa and his hand got hit by a shell and had to be cut off. Maybe that is one circumstance why he is so mean.

So far I have only a little bit of wages and for that reason I should not fight him. He is owing me about one hundred and fifty dollars.

In free time I have been going to Vegreville quite a

bit. Five miles, a long walk, but worth it to get away from Granger. I have been making a picture for Father Manihszyn for the church. Also I have been reading English books from his library to make my talking and writing improved even though the priest says it is good to keep reading and writing Ukrainian for our language to be alive in this new land. I think Mama would be pleased with how good I use English. She would be happy to see this letter, would you think?

How is Uncle Andrew? Give him love from me and say again I am sorry I was not there this fall to help. I know you were much help, Alex, almost a man now! When I am home, we can build onto the barn. That is what he has been wanting to do, I know. He will like it when I make the kolach like Papa always did for Christmas. I wish I had watched with more care when Mama made her pyrohy. The ones I made last year were not good. Most of them went in the slop pail. Maybe this year will be better. I am so longing to be home when I think about Christmas.

Here is a picture of me feeding the pigs and Granger ready to bang me with his hook if I am not more fast. We should be in the comics like the Katzenjammers don't you think? Also some pictures I copied from magazines in the library and these we could use for cards when I am home.

I will be seeing you in a week or maybe ten days. If I can catch a ride to Vermilion with someone and not take the train then it will save money.

Love from your brother Marco

Alex smiled at the cartoon of Marco feeding the pigs. He was halfway falling into the trough, a big sow had a startled look on her face, and a fat, bearded man was yelling at Marco and threatening him with his hook. On the back of the page, there were intricate pen sketches of a Santa Claus part way into a chimney, an angel blowing a horn, and a little boy with a top hat and a long trailing scarf singing Christmas songs.

The letter was dated Dec. 2.

"There now." Mr. Bayles pulled over a small table close to the couch. "Did that put your mind at ease? Things'll be just fine when your brother comes home. Might not be able to rebuild the house right away but in time . . ." He poured tea into two mugs and urged Alex to help himself to thick slices of buttered bread and cheddar cheese from a tin plate.

"The barn's in good shape, Dan Wallace told me, and he's taken the stock over to his place to look after until things are settled. For the time bein' you might even just build a lean-to against the barn and use that for living quarters, and then in the summer . . ."

Alex found a way to hold the mug and blow on the tea to cool it enough to drink. He could feel tears welling and hoped that, with the cup close to his face and the business of drinking the brew, Mr. Bayles wouldn't notice him crying. But then a great choking sob escaped as he tried to swallow.

"There now, boy." Mr. Bayles reached over and patted him. "Surely there wasn't no bad news in your letter?"

Alex handed the pages over for him to read.

"Something's just delayed him," Mr. Bayles said as he finished. "Likely couldn't get a ride straight away . . ."

"He would be home." Alex tried to keep his voice from breaking. "I think he would be home."

"Now, now . . . you mustn't be thinkin' the worst. Like I say, he was probably just delayed. Maybe had another job or two to finish before he could come. I bet he's even wrote to you, but mail moves kinda slow around Christmastime with everyone sending cards and parcels. Wouldn't surprise me if there's somethin' in the post after Boxing Day." Mr. Bayles fished a large white handkerchief out of his back pocket. "You blow your nose now and wrap yourself around some of that bread and cheese and then we'll have some of the fruitcake Mrs. Greeley sent along. I do like a piece of fruitcake—the best thing about Christmas in my mind."

He was able to eat and the tea warmed him. Before he cut into the fruitcake, Mr. Bayles searched through a stack of gramophone records until he found the one he wanted.

"John McCormick," he said, sighing over a bite of the cake, "there's a voice to make the angels weep."

It filled the small room with a Christmas song about a silent, holy night, a voice that slipped along lamplight into the shadows. Later, when Alex lay beneath the covers in the bed Mr. Bayles made up for him on the couch, the song lingered in Alex's mind. He lay awake for a long time watching the light from the stove grate shimmering along the ceiling, as if in its erratic pattern there were some answer to what was keeping Marco from coming home. And then he must have fallen asleep but he woke himself up, gasping, and the flickering light was like the fire from the burning farmhouse.

"Oh, Marco," Alex whispered, "*De ty*? Where are you?"

Chapter 5

WITH EACH MAIL delivery over the next week, Alex's despair grew. There was no letter from Marco. The days were long, with Alex staying upstairs while Mr. Bayles tended to customers downstairs. His schoolteacher, Miss Anderson, visited him one of the days, bringing him a few books.

"Why look!" She smiled at him as she eased out of her winter wraps. "You have no bandages. From what Mrs. Wallace told me, I expected to find you wrapped up like a mummy from ancient Egypt."

"They heal." Alex held up his hands in front of him. "But the fingers are hard to move. My face is a scrab."

"Scab," Miss Anderson corrected. "But that's good. It means the healing process is working as it should." She had him turn his face so she could examine the edge of the burn. "Healing nicely. Now Mr. Bayles said it would be fine for me to make some cocoa for the two of us and I have gingerbread cookies. You have a look at these books while I get things ready."

When she was seated across from him, holding a mug of hot chocolate in one hand, she reached over with her other and briefly let it rest on his arm. "I was so sorry to hear about your uncle, Alex. What a tragedy. And Mr. Bayles says you haven't heard from your brother."

"Something has happened to him, I think." Alex ran the tip of a finger, one that hadn't been burned, along the cover of the top book. He liked the feel of the binding, almost like cloth, as if it were clothing for a person within.

"I hope not. But we need to think of what's best for you while you're waiting for him. I understand that Mr. Potchak is a cousin to your uncle and I was wondering if you would like me to talk to him and see if you could stay with his family. With the children coming to school here, you could come along with them. I know there are a lot of people living in the farmhouse but . . ."

"I will go to find Marco," Alex said. He had been thinking about it a great deal, how he would get from Bayles' Corner to the railway that brought him and Marco to Alberta three years ago. There was the rail line from Vermilion to Vegreville. But he would need money for a ticket.

"Oh, Alex," Miss Anderson sighed. "How do you know where to start?"

"Vegreville. He writes from Vegreville."

"I know. Mr. Bayles told me, but maybe he's picked up work elsewhere on the way home. He could be in any of a hundred different places. Also, you need to know, Alex, that you're required by law to be going to school." Miss Anderson nibbled contemplatively on one of the gingerbread cookies. "If you really don't want to go and live with the Potchaks, I'm sure Mr. Bayles wouldn't mind keeping you on here and then you'd be really close to the school. He likes a bit of company, I think, and when your hands are better you could help . . ."

Alex didn't say anything. In his heart he knew that he had to go and search for Marco. They were meant to be together; it's what Mama and Tato would have wanted. He thought of how Marco had looked when an official checking their papers before they boarded the boat to come to Canada had said, "You can't be emigrating with a child when you're not the parent."

There had been a wild look in Marco's eyes, a ferocity. "I am his guardian," he said. "We are a family." In the end, though, he had to slip some money to the official.

"Nothing needs to be decided right away," Miss Anderson said as she got ready to leave. "You rest and I think you'll enjoy these readers I've brought. You're doing so well, I think I'll have you read along with the grade fives now."

Alex went back to school on the Tuesday after New Year's. When the children crowded around him to look at his burns,

Miss Anderson clapped her hands and told everyone to take their seats, even though she hadn't rung the bell yet.

"Alex, as you know, has had an unfortunate accident," she said, "and I'm asking you to show your best manners and not stare or ask embarrassing questions."

"I saw the fire," he heard Gordon Wallace whisper to the boy sitting next to him. "Me and Dad rescued him."

Miss Anderson levelled a gaze at him. "We'll stand now for the flag salute . . ."

Still standing, they sang "God Save the King" and then sat for the Bible reading. Returning the leather-bound volume to the small collection of books ranked between bookends on her desk, Miss Anderson smiled at them. "And now, I want to wish all of you a happy new year. 1916. Maybe everyone could say what they hope this new year will bring."

During the lunch break, Orest, the oldest Potchak boy, cornered Alex in the cloak room. "My dad says your uncle was crazy." He spoke in Ukrainian. "He said all the Kaminskys were cuckoos, even in the old country, thinking they were better than everyone else, and your Uncle Andrew always saying bad things about the Church. He says the fire was God's breath breathing on a heathen."

"*He's* crazy," Alex muttered. "My mother and father . . ."

"What happened to them for all their fancy ways?"

Miss Anderson poked her head into the cloakroom. "Do I hear you boys speaking Ukrainian? Remember, it's a rule at school to stick to English. You want to improve, don't you?"

"Yes, Miss Anderson." Orest smirked. "*Suka*," he said, under his breath, the Ukrainian word for bitch.

When the bell rang, Alex returned to his desk, disheartened. There was no bonding between the Potchaks and the Kaminskys, he knew. Uncle Andrew believed it had something to do with their parents having a rift in the old country over a cow that went missing so long ago that no one could quite remember for sure what the circumstances were.

Then, when Alex's father, Stephan, had married a governess from the Polish landowner's estate where he'd been working as a labourer, they had had a wedding to which only a few relatives had been invited, but none of the Potchaks. Add to that Uncle Andrew's tendency, at the drop of a hat and generally with a drink in hand, to deliver speeches on social justice for the working man.

"It embarrasses them that there is someone in the family who thinks beyond the pig-sty fence," he would announce loudly, sometimes within their hearing. "Who considers his fellow workers and not simply the bellies of his family."

Marco used to laugh at them all, and he liked to wink at Olga, the Potchak's oldest girl, when their paths crossed, and make her blush. Olga, Alex believed, had a crush on Marco, and that was another burr in Orest's underwear.

When classes were over, Alex waited until the Potchaks were gone, all five of them trudging off on their two-mile hike home, before preparing to head out himself.

"I'm glad you came today," Miss Anderson said, giving

him a hand with his coat buttons. "You'll find each day will be easier after this first one."

At the store, Alex put the kettle on so it would be hot for supper. He wished he could peel potatoes and carrots and do some of the other chores. It was possible for him to handle cutlery and dishes and he set the kitchen table.

Mr. Bayles beamed at him when he closed the store and came upstairs. "So, not so bad, eh? Back to school?"

Alex shrugged his shoulders. "Yes, not so bad."

"That Miss Anderson, she's very pretty, and I hear she's a good teacher too. Now the one we had before, Mr. Griswold, looked like he'd been weaned on a pickle and he had a temper..."

Vegreville, Alex thought. *I wonder if I could walk that far.* The weather had been mild today, but winter storms, he knew could come out of nowhere. If a storm came, what would he do?

"How far to Vegreville?" Alex asked when Mr. Bayles quit talking long enough to dip a spoon into a dish of stew he'd reheated for supper.

"*Mmm*. Vegreville," Mr. Bayles raised his bushy eyebrows. "That's a fair ways. I reckon it's about thirteen miles to Vermilion and then it must be close to forty, fifty miles from Vermilion to Vegreville. Fifty miles by train, I'd say. Roads, it'd depend which ones you took."

"Too long to walk."

"Oh my." Mr. Bayles poured tea from his teacup into his

saucer and then, as it cooled, took a slurp from the saucer. "Way too far to walk. Now, horseback, maybe. You're not thinking of trying to hoof it that far, son?"

"No," Alex sighed. "I know it is too far but I must go. I must get money and then I can take the train."

"Best way to go this time of year and that's a fact. Did you have money, Alex? In the house?"

"Not much. Just a few coins." He'd kept them in a china sugar bowl with a lid that had belonged to Mama. Most of the household furnishings they'd crated to bring to Canada, Marco'd sold in Hamburg just before they made the crossing.

"Keep something you'd like," Marco had said. "A keepsake." Alex had picked out a small sugar bowl and cream pitcher and wrapped them carefully in a tea cloth with a border Mama had embroidered. When he and Marco had settled in with Uncle Andrew, Alex had placed the china on the cloth draped over a packing crate by the bed in the loft that he shared with his brother. Behind the bowl and the pitcher, he'd propped Mama and Tato's wedding photo. All gone now of course.

But the stock hadn't been lost. Uncle Andrew's cow, the plough horse, a few chickens, and the pigs. One of the pigs Uncle Andrew had given to him as a birthday gift a year ago. How much money would he get from its sale, he wondered.

"Popo, my pig. He is big now and I could sell him for train ticket money." Alex added sugar to his own tea.

"There's a thought." Mr. Bayles got his pipe from a pipe

stand on the window sill. "But don't you think it'd be better to wait until your burns are well healed? While that's happening, there's a good chance your brother will get in touch with you or even show up here."

Alex dipped one of the gingerbread cookies Miss Anderson had left them in his tea and caught the corner of it in his mouth before it dissolved. "I can't wait," he said. "I have to find out. I will walk . . ."

"Now, let's just think this out a bit." Mr. Bayles struck a match and held it against the tobacco in his pipe and began sucking on the stem. "I'm not sure you'd be allowed to sell off any of your uncle's stock. You know, the Mountie was here checking on the fire since there was a death involved. He must have made some kind of arrangement with Dan Wallace to look after things until it can be decided . . ."

"But Popo is mine."

"I'm sure he is. But there is all this legal rigmarole." Mr. Bayles exhaled a bit of smoke, smiled with satisfaction, and then, with pipe in hand, regarded it with the kind of affection Uncle Andrew bestowed on his snuff box. "How be if I give you twenty dollars? That'll more than pay your way to Vegreville and back. You can owe me, pay me back when you sell your porker."

The last of the gingerbread cookie caught in Alex's throat. He felt like he could hug Mr. Bayles, wrap his arms around the old man, very carefully of course. His hands were still too sore to grasp anything tightly. But then he decided he must be more of a man, not a boy. A man who could make a trip all on his own.

"Thank you," Alex said. "I will give you money back. It's a promise. Thank you, thank you." It was proving hard to keep back tears.

"You should be able to catch a ride into Vermilion with Jim Hainstock when he brings the mail on Thursday. If Miss Anderson knows you'll just be gone a few days, she probably won't mind you missing a bit of school. But you'll need a plan of what to do once you get to Vegreville."

As Alex curled up under the covers on the couch that night, he knew it would be a while before he would be able to go to sleep. Ideas raced in his mind, all the things he and Mr. Bayles had talked over as the old man did up the few dishes and then put on a gramophone record of piano music that sounded like spring sunshine.

When he closed his eyes, Marco's smiling face was there looking at him. It seemed like Marco could always smile, even when he was climbing through that window in the Hamburg apartment, or crawling into their bunk stalls on that boat that brought them over, a cattle boat with white-wash over the manure-crusted walls in steerage.

"You are like Ivan the Fool in the stories," Mama had declared once when she was trying to be serious and Marco kept teasing her.

On that September morning when Marco had left to go and find work, he'd smiled sleepily over coffee and reached over and rumpled Alex's curly hair. A morning warmed with sun coming through the kitchen window, the air soft with the smells of early autumn and sausage frying and the sound of Uncle Andrew's snores.

"No long faces, Lexie," he'd said. "Remember what Mama always said. 'Wear a smile and confound the tsar.'"

Alex had watched from the doorway as Marco headed out on foot, turning back to wave before disappearing behind the poplar trees along the main road.

Chapter 6

❧

JIM HAINSTOCK, Mr. Bayles had warned Alex, had a laugh like a donkey braying. He was a big man too, wearing a bulky overcoat that only buttoned on the top couple of buttons, exposing a girth of ravelled sweater.

"Never say no to a bit of company," he'd boomed. "Cuts the trip, that's what I say. We should be in time to make the afternoon train."

Along with the twenty dollars, Mr. Bayles had given him a lard pail filled with sandwiches, some pieces of hard candy, and a couple of oranges.

"You might get hungry along the way, and you can save some for a bite to eat when you're on the train." Mr. Bayles patted him on the back and helped him up into the sleigh.

"Now, if your brother's not there, you be sure to come right back."

As the sleigh went by the school yard, Alex noticed Orest Potchak staring at him. The air was filled with the shouts of schoolchildren playing a game of fox and geese at recess and Alex could almost feel his own booted feet flying over the tracery of paths outlining the sliced pie circle in the snow. The knowledge that he was one of the fastest runners was a satisfaction that warmed him almost as much as the extra sweater Mr. Bayles had insisted he wear that morning.

Jim Hainstock, Alex realized as they drove along the roads toward Vermilion, knew everything there was to know about the families living on the farms they passed. A building that looked like a couple of granaries stuck together, he informed Alex, sheltered the Belvederes who hadn't had two nickels to rub together since they laid claim to their homestead ten years earlier.

"More kids and dogs than you can shake a stick at." He shook his fist at three hounds that were hurling themselves against the sleigh runners. "How they manage to feed them all is beyond me."

A bit farther along they passed a log farmhouse with a sod roof. A man carrying pails to the log barn behind waved at them.

"Bert Benson."

Alex watched Hainstock manoeuvre a plug of chewing to-bacco from a pouch in his pocket.

"A bachelor but he's got a way with the ladies, that one. More'n one young'un in and around Bayles has got carroty-coloured hair that you'd have no trouble matching up with Bert Benson's mop. Maude Fairview, when her boy Delbert sprouted curls the colour of a ripe pumpkin, she took off and went to stay with her mother over in Kitscoty before her husband got home. Ned was working in Edmonton, at the brick works I think, and no one knew better than Maude what kind of temper Ned had. She'd had some black eyes to show over the years . . ."

The afternoon sun was warm and Alex shed the blanket Mr. Bayles had wrapped around him. Where mailboxes along the way showed mail to be delivered or picked up, Hainstock seemed happy to have Alex scoot down and tend to it, adding the letters and postcards to a mailbag behind the seat. His hands must be getting better, he realized; there was very little pain as he grasped the edges of the sleigh to get out and back in.

They made their way around a lake where frost hung jewel-like on the branches of the scrubby willows bordering it and cattails poked their brown heads from the tops of snow drifts. Magpies threw their own raucous chatter against Jim Hainstock's stories.

"Now you'll find some Ruthenians living on this next section." Hainstock spat a stream of tobacco juice which didn't totally miss the side of the sleigh, adding its residue to an interior brownish crusting which must have been built up, Alex reckoned, over a long time. "Maybe you know them. The Franchuks."

Alex shook his head.

"Course you ain't been here that long, have you?"

"Three years," Alex said.

"Franchuk, I think he came over with his wife and a couple of kids and his brother and his family. They settled here even before your uncle came to Bayles' Corner. I never seen anyone work like them Ruthenians. But they done well. Got one of the best spreads in the country. A big herd of cattle. Grass don't grow under Orest Franchuk's feet. And the missus, she's been popping out babies every couple years. I lost count." Hainstock laughed and shook his head.

By the time they could see the buildings of Vermilion in the distance, Alex thought Jim Hainstock's jaw must have been aching with the workout he'd given it. Maybe the chewing tobacco kept everything oiled.

Once they were actually in town, Hainstock said, "I need to drop the mail off at the post office, but I'll go into the station with you and see that you get your ticket." Hainstock heaved himself down and Alex followed him into the train station where the big man plunged into a conversation with the station agent that seemed to be picking up from some earlier start.

"This boy here'll be needing a ticket for Vegreville," he told the agent once the story had spun to a lull. "That burn on his face is something, eh? Likely heard about that fire at Bayles'

Corner a few weeks back. Well this boy come through it, but not the uncle, and now he's looking to find his brother been working on a farm outside Vegreville."

As Hainstock passed the ticket and his change to him, Alex felt the gaze of someone behind them. When he looked around, he saw a red-faced man in a suit and overcoat.

"Train'll be along in about half an hour." The agent pointed to benches where a few people were already waiting.

When he'd bought his ticket to Edmonton, the man nodded to Jim Hainstock.

"The boy Ukrainian?" He said "Ukrainian" as if it were leaving a bad taste in his mouth. "Lotsa Ukrainian workers roamin' around doing farm work these days. Don't seem right, I say. Our boys going off to do their duty, and these Austro-Huns staying behind and reaping the profits."

Hainstock nodded his head in agreement. "Truer words," he said. "Mind you, we wouldn't want them in the forces. We don't need to be giving no enemy aliens rifles and bayonets. Might as well shoot yourself and get it over with." The donkey bray laugh echoed in the waiting room.

Alex managed to thank Hainstock before the postman headed out of the station, still laughing. A kind of helpless fury washed over him. Did they think he couldn't understand what they were saying? He found a bench where he wouldn't have to look at the flush-faced, scowling man.

When the train pulled in, Alex let the suited man go ahead and find his seat. Once inside the coach, he was relieved to see that he wouldn't have to sit beside him. Several seats farther down there was an empty space across from a soldier and Alex slipped into it, tucking his bag beside his boots, rather than trying to lift it onto the luggage rack.

The soldier was young, Alex noticed. Probably only two or three years older than himself. The cigarette he was smoking didn't go a long way to making him look like a mature man. There was a tracery of fuzz over his upper lip that made Alex smile inwardly.

"Going far?" Through a small cloud of smoke, the soldier smiled at him.

"Just to Vegreville." The soldier was looking at his burn-scarred hands and Alex tucked them inside his overcoat. "You?"

"Edmonton. I've been on leave, visiting the folks in Lloydminster. It's back to Edmonton and then embarkation for me. Hope someone's warning Gerry I'm on my way." He shrugged his shoulders as if he were shaking his uniform jacket into a more comfortable fit.

"Yup. Wilfred Fletcher on his way. Call me Wilf." He'd finished his cigarette and, stubbing out the butt, got out a pouch of tobacco and rolled another one. "Always like to have one or two on the ready." He held the pouch and papers out to Alex.

Alex shook his head.

"Oh yeah. I seen your hands. I can roll you one if you like."

"No, thank you." Alex realized how formal his words sounded. He smiled back at the soldier. "Alex. My name."

Dusk was falling as the train chuffed its way through the countryside, sparse trees and clumps of willow giving way to denser growth, larger groves of poplars and evergreens. The soldier managed to get Alex to tell, haltingly, his account of the fire and his reason for travelling to Vegreville.

"You're just over recent, aren't you?" he asked when Alex had finished his account. "Can tell in the way you talk. Ukrainian?"

Alex nodded.

"Good friend of mine's Ukrainian. He was born here though and talks like an Englishman. Name's Starsyshyn. Changed it to Smith and joined up. Nobody the wiser. All this stuff about allegiance to the kaiser's a load of crap if you ask me. Yup, Nicholas Starsyshyn, now Nick Smith. In the same regiment I'm in."

Finishing another cigarette, the soldier bunched up his greatcoat to make a kind of pillow, leaned back, and closed his eyes. Briefly he opened them again and winked at Alex. "Girlfriend didn't give me much rest last night. Think I'll catch a bit of shuteye."

Careful to use his good fingers, Alex pried the lid off the lard pail and fished out one of the ham sandwiches Mr. Bayles had made. He hadn't realized until now how hungry he'd become. The storekeeper had been generous with the mustard and Alex licked the bits on his lips.

He thought about the last time he'd been on a train. All those days and nights it had taken to go across Canada, from Halifax to Montreal, from Montreal to Winnipeg, and then on through Saskatchewan to Vermilion in Alberta. To Alex, it seemed that the trip would never end.

Marco had his drawing pad out throughout most of the trip. He'd done quick sketches of the interior of the coach, and some of the other immigrants. Sometimes he'd used his pencil to create games. In one, he'd drawn a small detail and it was up to Alex to guess what it was.

"The eye of the firebird," Alex might guess.

But no, he was always wrong. What he thought was the eye would become a gem in the tiara of a Polish princess. Or what he thought was the end of a garden spade became an iron tooth in the mouth of Baba Yaga, the witch. Marco would throw back his head and laugh, and his laughter brought smiles to the other weary travellers, Alex remembered.

Uncle Andrew had been waiting for them in Vermilion. He'd engulfed them in hugs. Alex could still feel the sheepskin of his coat, could still smell what he'd come to associate with the gruff middle-aged man, a hint of garlic and that ether of homebrew and the scent of unwashed wool.

But there was more than just a memory. It was here in the coach. Alex looked around and spotted a farmer in a heavy *kozhukh* eating some sausage and dill pickles spread out on a handkerchief on his lap.

The farmer got off along with Alex and a few other passengers when the train pulled into the Vegreville station. Looking back at the coach, Alex saw the soldier waving to him from the window as the train wheels made that chuffing sound of contained metal straining against movement. With a great hissing of steam, it began to roll, the glow of the coach lights gradually disappearing down the track.

In the darkness there was only a dim light from the waiting room windows and a couple of electric lights illuminating the platform as people drifted away and the station agent moved a wagon into a loading dock. Alex felt a flutter of fear. He tried to think of what Mr. Bayles had told him. To go down the street to the Queens Hotel and get a room for the night. "There's the Alberta Hotel, too, but I think Queens might have some cheaper rooms. Don't try to get out to the farm until the light of day," he had said. "Find out from the station agent or a storekeeper how to get out to the Granger farm."

At the hotel, the desk clerk looked him up and down.

"You by yourself?"

Alex nodded.

"Rooms ain't free," the clerk said.

"I have money." Alex reached inside his coat pocket and pulled out the change from his ticket.

"Fifty cents in advance."

After going up one flight of stairs, Alex found his room. It was small, hardly more than a closet, with a cot and a dresser and a wooden chair.

Stashing his bag behind the chair and checking that he had his key securely in his pocket, Alex made his way back downstairs and outside. Although it was cold, there was no wind and it felt good to be outside after the train ride. He walked along the downtown streets, peering at the displays in store windows, brushing past the noise that spilled out from the lobby of the Alberta Hotel, stopping to listen to music, oddly familiar, issuing from a church with onion-shaped spires.

The clerk nodded as he came back into the Queens Hotel lobby.

Alex summoned his courage and approached the desk.

"Granger," he said. "You know where that farm is?"

"Yeah." The clerk looked him over again and turned his attention to a man and a woman who had come in behind Alex. The woman, wearing a hat with a bunch of feathers sprouting from its side, looked disapprovingly at him. Alex was suddenly conscious that his overcoat was a couple of sizes too big, that his trousers were patched at the knee. He thought how he must look to these people, especially with an irregular burn-mark like a large continent on the geography of his face.

When he was finished with the man and the woman, the clerk shuffled some papers into a pile and closed the register book.

"Granger. Man with a hook instead of a hand?" He rubbed his fingers thoughtfully over his brush of a mustache. "A few miles north of town on the main road. Big yellow house with a verandah on two sides. You got business out there?"

Alex nodded.

The clerk raised his eyebrows. He was waiting to hear more.

"My brother. He works there."

"Ah." He ran a hand through his thinning hair. "But if I know Granger, he's not going to take kindly to an extra guest showing up on his doorstep. You and your brother, Galicians? I think I seen him with Granger picking up supplies a couple of times and then on his own once or twice. Tall? Straw-coloured hair?"

"Yes. Marco."

"How do you plan to get out there?"

"With walking," Alex said. "I can do it in one day?"

"Oh yeah, for sure. Might take a couple of hours but it's not really that far out of town. Actually, there's lots of farmers going back and forth on that road. You shouldn't have no trouble hitching a ride at least part of the way."

Back in his room, Alex didn't bother getting undressed, just took off his boots and pulled the top blankets over him. It didn't take him long to fall asleep. He could barely remember his head hitting the pillow.

But he was awake early. It was still dark, and when he looked out his bedroom window, only a few of the buildings had lights showing from their windows. In the hall outside his room, a clock struck five.

Checking his lunch pail, he decided to eat the remaining sandwich and orange for his breakfast, and then he'd set out. Just two, maybe three hours and, with any luck, he'd be with Marco.

With any luck.

Alex had to laugh inwardly at that. It had been a pretty scarce commodity in the years since the family had boarded a train in Lviv for the journey that would take them to a new world of golden grain fields, happiness and prosperity.

Chapter 7

∽

IT HAD GROWN COLDER overnight and it was still dark when Alex set off down the main street. It was not easy walking in the snow on the road, for the sleighs caused deep ruts. He was glad he had warm mitts and a scarf to tie over the bottom part of his face. A hint of sun began to define the ridges of trees cresting the fields outside of town. Somewhere, in one wooded spot near the road, an owl hooted and made him jump.

In the farmhouses he passed, smoke funnelled from kitchen chimneys and, where a kitchen faced the road, light glowed from the windows. It was a long way between farmhouses, though, and along some stretches Alex noticed gates to trails that would lead to homesteads back from the main road. There was the odd bit of traffic going into Vegreville—a team with a sleigh, a horse-drawn caboose, but no one heading out who might offer him a ride before he reached what was surely the Granger yard.

The house stood back from the road on a small hill, a large building with gables and, yes—a verandah stretching across its front and along one side. It was light enough now that he could see the creamy yellowish tint to the siding. Four windows stared blankly out at him. The kitchen, Alex decided, must be toward the back. As he approached the farmhouse, he could see a bit of light glinting from a window next to a door on the side of the verandah. He couldn't resist peeking in before rapping on the door.

A woman was busy at a cookstove, her back to him. She had her hair up in a coil of braids, hair as light and golden as Marco's. Stella. Alex had reread Marco's last letter this morning before he set out and the name was clear in his mind. Stella. Young enough to be a daughter. But where was the man with the hook? The woman turned from the stove to set a dish on a nearby table.

Alex quickly ducked back and stepped over to the door. The storm door was partly open, and on the inner door, a cream colour slightly darker than the siding, Alex noticed the painting of a garland of summer flowers. He traced the shape of a tiger lily with one of his good fingers before knocking softly with the back of his hand.

He could hear the woman walking across the kitchen. The door opened a crack and she was peering cautiously, shyly, at him, only half of her face visible. Marco had been right. She was very pretty. In the few seconds they stared at one another, he could see her look change to one of puzzlement, and then concern.

Alex pulled the scarf away from his mouth. "Is Marco here?"

"Marco?" She opened the door wider. And now something else joined the puzzlement and concern. Fear? She was looking at him at first and then past him, as if checking to see if anyone was behind him or coming up the pathway from the barnyard.

"I am Marco's brother," Alex said. "I must see him."

"Alex." She said his name gently, as if she had practised saying it before. "Come in. Shut the door."

Inside, they stood and looked at one another for a minute.

"He's gone," she said, suddenly looking away from him as if she couldn't bear to see his eyes, or maybe the burn. "He's been gone for over three weeks, close to a month."

"Gone? But where has he gone? I must see him."

"You must go too." She spoke quickly, almost in a whisper. "He and my husband had a big fight and the police took ..."

At that moment there was the sound of heavy footsteps on the verandah, and the girl's hand flew to her mouth.

"Oh God," she said.

Alex whirled around as the door opened. As Marco had

said, Granger was a large man with a hook and Alex recognized the beard his brother had so accurately sketched in the barnyard cartoon.

"A bit early for visiting," the man said, tossing the glove from his good hand onto the top of a woodbox, shuffling off his coat. "Who we got here then, Stella? Seems like the cat's got his tongue."

Stella had scurried across the room, back to the stove.

"Alex." Her voice came out as a little croak. "Marco's brother."

The man sat down and eased off his boots.

"Well, son . . ." He scratched behind an earlobe with the end of his hook. "I got no quarrel with you just because your brother is a thief. Maybe you came to bring back some of the money he stole. Police hardly found half of it when they caught up with him."

As Granger smiled, Alex could see there was a gap with missing teeth. For a minute, Alex felt like he might faint. He had to steady himself with one hand against a cabinet. It was blue, like the cabinet in Uncle Andrew's before the fire, but this one had flowers painted on it, not a firebird. It took him a couple of minutes to get his breath.

"Marco," his voice sounded as if it were coming from someone else, "does not steal."

"Well," the bearded man chuckled and shook his head, "I never met a bohunk yet wouldn't dip his fingers in your bankroll if a chance offered itself. I think it's just part of their nature."

Alex gritted his teeth. "Where is he gone?"

The big farmer stood up and, leaning over, laid his hook heavily against Alex's chest. "Aren't you forgetting your manners, sonny? I think what you meant to say was, 'Could you please tell me if you know where he's gone. Sir.'"

For a second, Alex looked away. Stella, the girl, was standing beside the stove now, looking at him, trying to tell him something through her eyes.

"Could you tell me where he's gone?" Alex whispered. "Sir."

"Well I couldn't tell you for sure but my guess is he's working on a rock pile somewhere for the Mounted Police. They don't take no more kindly to thieves than a hardworking farmer does."

"A rock pile?" The man was speaking in riddles.

"Or else in one of those camps I hear they're setting up for enemy aliens, that's the ones they don't ship back to Hun-country where they should have stayed in the first place."

"Camps?"

Granger laughed mirthlessly again and patted an ear with his good hand. "You noticing an echo in here, Stella?"

"Breakfast is on the table," she said. "We should feed the boy and let him warm up anyway."

"Kindness is Stella's second name." Granger nodded. "Looks like you got a mite too close to the cookstove sometime not too long back."

"My uncle." Alex found himself looking down at the braided rag rug on the kitchen floor. "His house burned and I got hurt."

Alex heard the girl gasp, and Granger must have noticed it too. He looked at her, his shaggy, raised eyebrows seeming to offer a question of their own.

"Your uncle?" Stella asked.

"He is dead."

"Sorry to hear it, boy. Now why don't you shuck yourself of some of them wraps and pull up a chair and have a bit of breakfast before you head off wherever you're off to, although, if you don't mind listening to a little advice, I'd give up on connecting with your brother. When he's through doing his time . . ."

Alex was about to turn and leave when Stella caught his eye and gestured urgently toward the extra place she'd set.

"The police . . ." She poured coffee into her husband's cup as he poised a fork over his plate of fried eggs, bacon and biscuits. "They'd know where Marco . . . ?"

"I suppose you been asking?" His voice sounded like a whip. "I told you to forget you ever seen that smirking light-fingered garlic-snapper."

"Edward!"

"Pardon my French!" He winked at Alex. "Eat up, boy. The walk's going to seem longer back into town."

Leaving his bag and coat by the door, Alex sat down at the place Stella had set for him, but hungry as he was, he found it hard to get any food down, and Stella looked as woebegone as he felt. Only Granger shovelled his breakfast down with a studied, unconcerned air."

"Stella," he belched. "Why don't you take the boy up to the attic and get those few things that bohunk . . . that Marco left behind."

She looked warily at her husband, Alex thought, as if she were trying to guess what he might be up to.

"He did leave a sketchbook," she said as they climbed up two sets of stairs to a tiny attic room with an iron cot neatly made up. "And he forgot a vest in the wardrobe." She turned to him when she found the garment, holding it close to herself, one hand caressing the embroidered fabric.

"He was my friend," she said, and Alex thought she might be having trouble holding back tears. "I am not permitted many friends."

"Don't be all day now," the voice boomed from two flights down. "That boy's got to get back to town and figure out what to do, and he probably wants to do it before nightfall." Stella folded the vest and put it into a paper bag with the sketchbook.

"I hope you find him and he is not where my husband thinks he is. I wish we met under better . . ." Alex felt she was struggling to find the right word. "In better times. I think of him when I see his paintings."

Granger was waiting for them at the bottom of the stairs, holding Alex's coat and bag.

"That's it, then?" He opened Alex's bag so he could stuff in the paper bag Stella had given him. But not before he opened it as well and checked to see what was inside.

Alex looked at Stella when he said thank you for the breakfast. Briefly her hand rested on his arm when he was bundled up and ready to go.

"Good luck," she said.

He thought he heard Granger chuckling at her words.

It did seem like a longer walk back into Vegreville, and the snow seemed even deeper on the road. The whole way, Alex felt empty. What could he do, except go back to Bayles' Corner and wait for a letter from Marco? If he had been put in jail, would Marco even be allowed to write letters?

Stealing Granger's money! Alex felt like screaming with the outrage of it. It must have been his wages. Granger must have tried doing him out of what he'd earned in the months he worked for him. He gritted his teeth again as he thought about the farmer. They'd met a few like him since they'd left Galicia. That doctor in Hamburg who'd looked like it would be best if the whole family simply lay down and died when they were quarantined. The man who made them pay extra to let Alex on the ship. Liz was as strong a hater as any of them, aiming her gun at his face in the window.

Why? Alex wondered. *What had they done to the world to deserve this?*

A collie dog came out from a farmyard and followed along behind him for a ways.

"All right," Alex said, "maybe you don't hate us." But when

he turned and coaxed, "Here boy, here," the dog suddenly became skittish, turned tail and ran.

He caught a ride the last part of the way with a farmer bringing cream to town. Alex was grateful that the farmer was a man of few words. In the silence, except for the rhythmic sound of the horses and the wagon runners on the snow, Alex was able to focus his thoughts on the police. Always, they'd believed, police were best to be avoided. In Lviv. In Hamburg. Would they be any better here?

Uncle Andrew, always in fear of his still being discovered, could spend a good half hour going on in detail about the kinds of punishment he felt might best be applied to any police force. Would they tell him where they'd taken Marco? Were there even any police in Vegreville, or did they just pass through from time to time? If he talked to them, would they want to put him away too somewhere?

When he got back into town, Alex slipped into the railway station. It would be a place to think what to do next, where he could stay warm for a while and collect his thoughts. Perhaps he should just do what Mr. Bayles had told him to do: take the train back to Vermilion and then try to get back to Bayles' Corner somehow. Wait for a letter from Marco.

The station agent in his wicket was looking over his glasses at him and Alex decided to get his ticket and, if he'd missed today's train, see if he might be allowed to stay in the station waiting room until the next one came through. He reached into his coat pocket for what was left of the twenty dollars.

But there was nothing there. He tried his other pocket. A handkerchief. Nothing else.

Stolen. Granger must have taken it, a final bit of revenge against the Kaminskys.

Alex felt a sob rise in his throat. No wonder Stella had been looking at her husband so strangely. She must have guessed he had something in mind when he'd asked her to take him up to the attic, away from his bag and coat.

The station agent was coming out of his office.

Alex grabbed his bag, hurried to the door, and then ran as fast as he could down the platform and away from the station.

Chapter 8

❧

ALEX DUCKED BEHIND cars on a siding and stopped to catch his breath. He wasn't even sure why he was running. Maybe it would have been best to simply tell the station agent what had happened. But then what? Maybe he would be put some place where homeless children are kept. He thought he had seen such a place in Hamburg on the street that led to the bakery where Papa had worked. Forlorn faces of boys peering out of dirty upstairs window. Once a boy in the yard being whipped and dragged into the building.

He had to think. There had to be some kind of an answer.

"Y'look lost."

Alex was startled by the man who seemed to appear out of

nowhere. He was stocky. Just a bit taller than Alex, with a heavy black mustache and a few days' growth of chin stubble. The wool cap on his head was a bit askew, revealing a matt of dark hair. He rubbed his chin with a gloved hand, fingers poking through where the glove had cracked apart.

Alex thought about picking up his bag again and running. But the man smiled.

"Thinking about riding the rails for a ways?" He spoke with an accent that Alex recognized. He must have come from some part of Galicia or Ruthenia.

"I'm trying to find my brother," Alex said in Ukrainian.

This made the man laugh softly and he patted Alex's shoulder.

"We are brothers too, I see." He responded in Ukrainian. "You expect to find him in the rail yards? Here, come with me. I know where we can get a cup of tea and warm our toes, and these cars aren't moving anywhere. I think there's a freight coming through in a couple of hours, though. We can talk about that." He flung his pack over his shoulder.

Alex followed the man out of the yards and through the streets to the back door of a house by one of the onion-spired churches.

"I know the housekeeper here," the man said and winked at Alex. "She cooks for the priests but she likes a bit of company. A bit of male companionship."

She scowled at the man, though, when she opened the door.

"Magda." The man ducked his head and removed his wool cap.

"Back again, Ivan?" She spoke in Ukrainian too. "I thought you were off to find work in Edmonton. It's not a bottomless soup pot we have here."

"I ran into some fellow travellers," he admitted, "and we had a little party down by the river."

"It's hard to leave when there's a quart of moonshine being passed around, I bet." She was peering past Ivan now, though, and looking at Alex. "Who's this then?"

"A lost boy. Checking out the rails with the rest of us." He gave Alex a gentle poke. "You must have a name, though."

"Alex."

She was a heavyset woman with greying hair, her shirtwaist and skirt pretty well hidden by a huge bibbed apron. Her hands looked as if they'd be equally at home doing field work as cooking and cleaning, but when she reached out and touched the edge of the burn on his face, there was a gentleness in the touch.

"Kaminsky," he added. "Alex Kaminsky."

"How'd this happen then?" Her sturdy hand held his chin and tipped the burned side of his face more toward the kitchen window.

She made a pot of tea and had them sit at the kitchen table while Alex told his story. Alex paused from time to time to nibble at thick slices of buttered bread the woman added to the table.

"Granger." The housekeeper refilled their tea cups. "He's the one that married that girl from over near Brush Hills. I think she was no more than fifteen. That would've been five, six years ago. She was one of them Skrupniks, poor as dirt, and they said at the time that old man Skrupnik pretty well sold her to Granger."

"Miserable bugger." Ivan combed some bread crumbs from the stubble of his beard. He sighed and gave Alex a sympathetic look. "I think he might have had your brother arrested. I heard about it from Balyk, a buddy of mine.

Police came through a few weeks back and picked up two Galician farmhands in the rail yards here, and one German—Schneider—who didn't have any papers. Three or four others planning to hitch a ride on the freights managed to get away. There was quite a scuffle with the one Galician. That might've been your brother."

"Where would they take him?" A piece of bread caught in Alex's throat.

"Probably to Edmonton." Ivan glanced at the clock on the kitchen counter. "You might want to check at the Mounted Police headquarters there, but it would be tricky. Have you got any papers yourself?"

"Papers?"

"Naturalization papers."

Alex remembered Marco and Uncle Andrew talking about getting some papers before Marco had left to find work in the fall.

"We need to be here three years," Marco had said. "We have some months to go still, but you should get yours."

Uncle Andrew had grunted. "Agh, just the government making work for itself. I've been here for ten years and don't need a British Empire certificate to say I exist."

Marco had just shook his head and laughed. "I will apply for all of us when I get back this fall."

They had no papers.

Ivan topped up his tea. "Police are checking everyone these days who's come from Austria-Hungary. No papers, or if you get accused of stealing or rowdy behaviour, or let's say you did your service years in the army back home—right away you might find yourself on the way to a concentration camp. I hear there's one in Lethbridge down in the south."

"Concentration camp?"

"I've been hearing about those," Magda sighed. "They're awful places. One of the families in our parish, the Kubenecs—Elsie's husband Steve was looking for work in Edmonton, and he was picked up and sent somewhere in the mountains. If it weren't for us helping the family, who knows what'd be happening to them. No money for nothing. Living on fried dough and lard when the priests got wind of the state they were in."

"Freight'll be along in about half an hour." Ivan finished the last of his tea with a slurp of satisfaction. "You want to come along with me, I'll help you hop a car. At least that might get you into Edmonton, barring no trouble from the yard men along the way. When you're there, maybe you can figure out a way to get someone to go in and ask about your brother and then tell you what they found out."

The housekeeper shook her head sadly. "You come over here," she said to Alex and drew him over to the cupboard. She dipped her fingers into a jar and carefully spread grease over his burn scar. "Best not to let that mess get too dry."

With their boots and coats back on, Ivan gave the house-keeper a noisy kiss.

"Ah, get off, you great smelly brute." She laughed and slapped him playfully. Turning to Alex, she said, "I'll ask the good father to say a prayer for you, Alex. For you and your brother. Now get along."

It was late in the afternoon when the freight pulled in. With Ivan beside him, Alex watched from behind a shed, listening to the bustle of activity on the station platform, and the sound of the train engine, like a great beast, idling, snorting streams of steam.

"Damn," muttered Ivan. "I don't see no cars with their doors open. But there's that hopper. Gonna be cold though. What do you think?"

Alex nodded his head.

They waited until the train started to move, then Ivan gripped his arm and they began running alongside.

"I'll boost you first," Ivan shouted against the noise of the engine and the squeal of the wheels.

He chucked their packs into the bin first. "Climb that bit of a ladder and hoist yourself over. I'll be right behind you."

Grasping the ladder made Alex yelp with the sudden pain to his hands but he moved as quickly as he could and hurled himself into the open-topped car. It was half-filled with coal, he realized as he rolled against the lumps, trying to protect his face.

In an instant, Ivan was tumbling over him.

"Damn," he said, grabbing hold of his pack. "I was afraid it might be coal. Let's hope they're not unloading it in Lamont."

Ivan helped him get settled, scooping out spots for them and placing their bags as buffers against the coal. The activity had raised a small cloud of coal dust that set Alex sneezing.

"Here, boy," Ivan said, "curl in close to me for warmth, and pull your scarf over your mouth so you don't breathe in the dust. It's a shame with all this coal we can't set some of it on fire."

As the train gained speed, the cold became bone-chilling and Alex, teeth chattering, took Ivan's advice. The man smelled of tobacco and barnyard and raw wool but it was somehow comforting.

"How is it you are riding the rails?" Alex asked.

"Y'know, I tried homesteading for a few years." Ivan searched in his pocket for some tobacco and got a cigarette going. "But I guess I wasn't cut out from that piece of cloth. Crops, when I did get them planted, failed. Never managed to get enough money ahead to buy stock and a team of horses."

Ivan's sigh became caught in the train's mournful whistle.

Likely approaching a road crossing, Alex thought. From where they nestled in the coal, they could see only the sky, growing darker by the minute, and, in places, the tops of trees.

"I was a miner back in the old country. Handled my share of this stuff." He picked up a small lump of coal. "But when I got to Canada I made a vow I'd never go down a shaft again. Never got around to getting my Canadian papers, so I've got to steer clear of the police. What I'm aiming to do is get across the border into the States. Get some work as a labourer there."

"The States?" Alex snuggled closer into Ivan's wool coat.

"It's a ways, I know. But I figure I can ride the rails to Medicine Hat and it's only a rabbit's hop away from the border.

The train pulled into a siding at Lamont while what must have been a passenger train went through. Ivan scrambled up over the coal and peeked over the edge of the hopper.

"Watch it. There's a yard man checking the cars." He ducked down again and told Alex to lie face down against his pack. After putting some lumps of coal on Alex's back, Ivan pulled his own coat over his head and somehow managed to burrow into the coal pile. But no one climbed up and looked into the bin. In about half an hour the train was moving again.

It was well into the night when the train lumbered into the Edmonton yards. Again, Ivan clambered up and peered cautiously over the rim of the car.

"All clear," he whispered. "We need to get out of the yards fast though. In the city there's always yard men around somewhere and they're meaner than trapped weasels."

As they scurried over the tracks, they passed quickly through a yard light and Ivan laughed. "Oh my God! We are black as crows!"

He was still laughing as they found an opening in the fence and Alex squeezed through. His laughter froze, though, when he looked up to see a policeman watching them. He was on the platform at the other end of the yard.

"Run!" Ivan cried, giving Alex a start with the back of his hand. "Go a different way from me," he hollered in Ukrainian as he headed across a vacant lot.

As the policeman took off after Ivan, Alex began running along the outside of the fence, putting as much distance between himself and the station as possible. There were buildings up ahead, and Alex saw what looked like an alley between warehouses. Reaching the alley, he looked back just in time to see Ivan being grabbed by the policeman.

Halfway down the alley, Alex collapsed behind a collection of garbage, what appeared to be wood scraps and a small mountain of shavings. Although he was warm from running, he could feel the coldness of the night and, taking a cue from Ivan and the coal car, he began burrowing into the shavings, pulling them over him. He used his bag again to make a support for his head. Somewhere nearby there must be a street; he could hear horses and the creak of a wagon, what might be a streetcar, and, from the rail yard, there was the sound of another train pulling in. A dog barked. A light was extinguished in a warehouse window across the way.

Before he pulled up his scarf to cover as much of his face as possible, he looked up at the night sky. It was clear and stars spun their patterns with the same beauty and impassivity as they had over his upstairs bedroom in Lviv and the flat in Hamburg and the loft in Uncle Andrew's house before it burned down.

Alex wondered if somewhere Marco might be looking up at this same sky, or would he be trapped in a jail cell? He was too tired to think about tomorrow. Finding Marco had taken on the riddled magnitude of the hero of a fairy tale on an impossible quest. But first, Alex needed to sleep in his nest of wood shavings.

Chapter 9

∽

BEFORE THE BLOCKS of wood hit him, a car honking and a train shunting back and forth in the yards had stirred Alex to a state of half-wakefulness. One of the pieces of wood hit his ear, making him yelp and he struggled up out of the heap of shavings.

"Yumpin' Yehosophat!" A man laughed.

Alex tried to shake some of the shavings off himself.

"What we got here?" The man spoke with an accent, an accent that had kind of a musical lilt to it. Not Ukrainian, Alex decided. He was wearing carpenter's overalls and he had hold of a box which must have held the shavings and scrap pieces of wood dumped over him.

Alex couldn't think of what to say. He reached down into the dump pile and retrieved his bag.

"Small for hobo." The man smiled at him. "You must be froze. Run off from train yards, yah?"

Alex nodded.

"Come in shop and get warm." He gestured to a door that had been left ajar.

Alex hesitated and the man took hold gently of his arm.

"Nobody going to eat you. If he see you—a starving bear walk away. Look for something better." He was tall, very tall, with blue eyes that seemed to be laughing all on their own. A wisp of blonde hair escaped from the tam on his head.

Alex allowed himself to be ushered inside.

There were three men, also in carpenter's overalls, busy making furniture. The nearest one to the door was using a treadle to operate a wheel, and he held a chisel against a whirling piece of wood. When he paused, his gaze took in the two of them, his eyebrows came together in a frown and he shook his head.

"You find the damnedest things out in that alley, Karl. Last week it was a half-starved dog and what've you got here now? Looks like something's been tarred and feathered."

The man laughed. "Not sure what it is. But ain't no dog or cat. You got a name, boy?"

By now the other two workers stopped what they were doing and came over.

Alex mumbled his name.

"Looks hungry," one of the men, his overalls covering a well-padded stomach, decided. "Better take him into the washroom, Karl, and see if you can get off a layer or two and I'll scare up some coffee and biscuits."

"This ain't no refuge for strays and runaways." The man working at the wheel—Alex heard someone call him Jesse—shook his head again. "Go ahead, Karl, get him washed up."

Alex followed Karl to a small room at the far side of the workshop containing a toilet and a sink.

"Here," he said. "Best not we use towels—I get some rags." He let the water run until it became hot, stoppered the sink and pushed in a cake of soap.

When he returned with the rags, Alex had his mitts off and was testing the water with the tips of his good fingers.

"*Uff da!*" Karl caught his right wrist and took a close look at the hand. Then he looked more closely at Alex's coal-smudged face. "Here, let me." He soaked a rag and began to work some of the coal dust off Alex's face, patting the cloth against the scarred patch. He kept rinsing the rags and changing the water, even running a wet cloth over Alex's clothes.

"Such burns," he muttered. "How you get them?"

As Alex told Karl about the burns and how he'd got to the yard behind the shop, the pile of shavings grew by his feet and, in a cracked mirror over the sink, he could see his face go from ashy grey to something closer to his real skin colour.

Later, around a table in a corner of the shop, Alex had to retell the story to the other three as they sipped coffees and he devoured several of the biscuits the chubby man set out on a big napkin.

"Sounds like the cops've got him all right," the man with the biscuits decided. "If he's Ruthenian and he's got no papers, I'd say they've tucked him into a jail cell somewhere. Maybe here in Edmonton."

"Naw." The scowling man who'd been operating the wheel drained his coffee cup. "They don't keep no aliens here. Lethbridge. I hear there's a big POW camp there."

"Is Lethbridge a far ways?" Alex asked.

"Lord, I'll say." The fourth worker was an older man with eyeglasses and a full beard. "Calgary's a long way off and Lethbridge is even farther."

In the midst of debating how far it was to Lethbridge, Jesse reminded the men that there was work to be done. He turned to Karl, though, and said, "If I know you, Karl, you're aiming to take this ragamuffin home same as you did that flea-bitten dog so best do it right now and, on the way, you can deliver Mrs. Sutton's washstand and that chair we mended."

"You stay with us. For a little while," Karl said after he had hitched up the company's team and loaded the furniture to be delivered. "We see. Mrs. Arneson, I tell you, Alex . . ." He didn't finish his sentence but raised his eyebrows and shook his head. "We give her some time."

"Thank you," Alex mumbled. "Thank you. I know you're not Ukrainian but I have appreciation."

Karl reached over and patted him on the shoulder. "Not

Ukrainian, true. I'm from Norvay. But what it is to be new to this country, that I know."

"How much—how many the years since you came?"

"Sixteen. Easy to remember—same as number for the year. Little older than you be now. We go to school when we get here. Learn some English. Still learning," he added. "Then was what you say—apprentice—at Lancaster's. After two years, full time. Finishing carpenter. That is when I marry Maria. Eleven years ago. Oldest boy, Einar, soon be ten."

"You have many children?" Alex asked.

"Four. And one more coming. Einar and Gunnar, then Astrid and Oleanna. If new one is a boy, we name him Norman. A girl, Edel."

"But first we must pay attention and deliver furniture to Mrs. Sutton. She lives just close by," said Karl. It was only a few more minutes and they arrived at Mrs. Sutton's house. Alex did what he could to help Karl unload the repaired furniture.

As soon as they had finished the delivery, they once again mounted the wagon and Karl urged the team towards a big iron bridge.

"That big building, is that a church?" Alex asked as they began to cross the bridge. On the crest of the river hill, the domed top of the building rose over the surrounding rooftops.

"No. Where government happens." Karl hollered at the horses as they began the incline from the other end of the long bridge. "Get a move on, Clopper. You too, Mabel. Gee-up."

They'd gone a few blocks south of the bridge when Karl called out "whoa" to the team and leaped down from the wagon box to tie the reins to a fence post. They were in front of a two-storey frame house set back on a lot. Flanked by a large, leafless poplar tree, only a bit darker greyish colour than the house itself, Alex thought the home looked uninviting, the windows staring blankly at him. But a shaggy brown dog, hurling itself at the fence as it barked and wagged its tail, offered its own welcome.

"Down, Queenie," Karl laughed. "You think I been gone two weeks, not two hours."

The dog must have decided anyone Karl was bringing home was worthy of the same adoration as she bestowed on her master. Inside the yard she ran circles around Alex, interrupting her route every couple of seconds to leap against his back and sides, almost knocking his bag out of his hands.

"Queenie, stop," Karl scolded and the dog raced ahead of them as they headed to the back porch.

Before they could open the door, though, it was flung open and a tall woman, broom in hand, shouted, "Queenie! Go lie down." She shook the broom at the dog, and in the process, nearly prodded Alex off the back steps.

Mrs. Arneson, Alex decided. She frowned as her gaze took in the two of them. Her mouth opened and Alex could hear her inhale, as if she were drawing in a reserve of air for a volley of some sort. The broom seemed to still hold the possibility of a weapon.

"*Min kjaereste*, here is Alex." Karl nodded toward him. "He will be here with us. Just a few days. You know, can be some help . . ."

"Help!" Mrs. Arneson seemed to pluck the word away from Karl, and Alex couldn't decide if it was hanging in the air as a term of scorn or a plea to the heavens to assist her. "One more mouth to feed, you mean. Did you bring another dog too? Maybe cat?"

"Now, Maria." Karl reached out and touched a strand that had come loose from her dark, upswept hair. "We find him sleeping in sawdust pile in yard back of shop."

Mrs. Arneson raised her eyes skyward and shook her head. Alex noticed a little brown-haired girl peeking shyly at him from the door. "Astrid, go inside. Or you be getting pneumonia."

Karl gently pushed Alex forward. With the little girl back inside, his wife turned and began to say something but her attention was caught by the wound on Alex's face. She reached a hand toward the burn, almost touching it with her fingertips.

"How . . . ?"

"House fire." Karl answered for him. "Burned hands too— but getting better. Coffee on? I can steal a bit of time." He winked at his wife.

In the kitchen, a blonde-haired toddler began to whimper.

Karl swooped her up into his arms and began rocking her and crooning a little song. "Ole, Ole, Oleanna . . ."

Mrs. Arneson checked a coffee pot at the back of the stove and added water from a tea kettle.

Karl nodded his head reassuringly to Alex. "Little one here is my Oleanna and hiding behind the cupboard—Astrid. Come out, *den lille*."

The warmth of the kitchen enveloped Alex. It seemed like almost every space on the walls was filled with pictures and calendars, photographs, wood-carved ornaments, plaques with odd writing. A cupboard with some fancy turned pieces in its design held a set of china canisters with a blue border pattern that Marco would have liked, Alex thought. Along with the smell of coffee, there was the aroma of cinnamon, and something starchy boiling on the stove.

Putting the baby down, Karl helped Alex get out of his boots.

"We put something on chair before you sit." He got an old towel from under the washstand.

Mrs. Arneson set out mugs on the flower-patterned oil-cloth that covered the table top, and used the bottom of her apron to wrap around the handle of the coffee pot as she poured the steaming, dark brew. As she sat down, Karl leaned over and gave her a half-hug. She scowled but when he made a sad clown face at her, her lips twitched into a tiny smile. Karl picked up the baby again and held her as he sipped his coffee. Astrid had climbed up on her mother's lap but was still hiding her eyes from Alex, her head buried in the apron bib.

"Dirty clothes you wear—they all you got?" Mrs. Arneson spoke, as Karl did, as if her words bobbed up and down, almost musically. "How much hot water and soap to get those clean?"

"In my bag," Alex said, "I have some more clothes." The Red Cross ladies at Bayles' Corner had added a few hand-me-downs to those Mrs. Eddy had given him.

After Karl had gone back to the wagon, she watched with some satisfaction as he emptied his bag. She picked up Marco's vest and admired the embroidery on it. Alex showed her the comb and brush set he'd been given for Christmas.

"Before you wear clean clothes, you need a bath. A big wash. Get tub hanging in porch."

When Alex brought it into the kitchen, she set it on the stove and, handing him a pail, told him to partly fill it with water from the cistern.

"Not too much or we never get it off stove. Some day we get hot water and bathroom," she sighed. "Wait for water to be warm. I will change baby."

It took a while and, once the water was ready, Alex tried to lift the tub but the handles cut into his burns and made him yelp with pain.

Mrs. Arneson hurried back into the kitchen. "You leave. I do it." She lifted the tub, setting it close to the stove, and added more water dipped from the stove's reservoir. From a cabinet in the porch, she found a washcloth and a bar of soap and folded a towel over the back of a kitchen chair, then gestured toward the waiting bath.

Alex looked questioningly at her. He could feel his face going red.

"*Uff da*. I will not see." She shook her head again but Alex thought he saw a little smile play across her lips. "I will be with babies in living room. You leave water in tub. I use to give dirty clothes first wash."

Alex couldn't remember anything feeling as good as the warm water of the bath. It was a round galvanized tin tub and Alex could barely fit both his bottom and his feet into it. Carefully he soaped his hands and face. There was still enough coal dust on him that the water turned dark. It was black enough that when Mrs. Arneson came back into the kitchen she told him to throw it all down the sink after all. She had him stow his dirty clothes in the porch.

He was hanging the tub back up when the two Arneson boys tumbled into the porch, home for lunch, Queenie dancing and barking around them.

"Who're you?" The oldest boy had his father's blonde hair and blue eyes. "Mommy, who's this?"

"Be polite," Mrs. Arneson yelled from the kitchen. "That is Alex. Now wash for lunch. Queenie, get outside!"

There was a washstand in the porch and the younger brown-haired boy made a dash for it. "Beat you, Einar," he said, pouring water from a pitcher into the basin.

But Einar's attention was focused on Alex's face and hands. "What happened to you?"

Mrs. Arneson was standing in the doorway now, between the kitchen and the porch. "Wash! Not necessary to know everything in the world first minute you are home."

For lunch they had large bowls of boiled rice with milk poured over it, each dish topped with a pat of butter, some brown sugar and cinnamon. Alex answered their questions as he ate. He realized that what Karl had implied was true— his wife, cranky as she could be, was softening towards him. She deflected the boys' questions when they got too personal. And once they'd headed back to school, she noticed how tired he'd become, barely able to keep his eyes open.

"Alex, you will fall asleep at table and bang your head," she said. "Go upstairs. Lie down. First bed is boys'. Just pull quilt over yourself."

There was a steep unbacked stairway leading from the living room to the upper floor. Most of the second storey was open space with a couple of beds and a crib and clothes on hangers hooked onto a clothesline across one corner. A bedroom with a large bed, a dresser and a chest of drawers was curtained off in another corner. A hole with a wooden grate allowed heat to drift up from the living room heater below.

Alex lay down on the bed closest to the stairs, pulled the patchwork quilt around him and fell asleep almost instantly.

A wet slurp across his face woke him up. Queenie was lying beside him and Einar, the blonde-haired boy, sitting beside Queenie, was giggling over the dog's affectionate means of rousing him.

"You awake? Mama said to call you for supper."

"Supper already?" Alex rubbed the sleep from his eyes.

Einar stood up. "We've been home from school for hours but Mom said we had to be quiet and stay downstairs and let you sleep. I did my arithmetic homework so we can play a game after supper. Do you like Rummy?"

"Rummy?"

"Einar," Mrs. Arneson called from the bottom of the stairs. "You up there talking Alex ears off? Better not Queenie be up there, you know what is good for you."

"She snuck up," Einar called back. "I'll get her back into the porch."

"Right now, or she be back to alley where Papa find her. And hurry up. Supper is ready."

Once everyone was at the table, Mrs. Arneson nodded to Einar who sang a short grace in what must be, Alex thought, Norwegian.

There was a large bowl of boiled potatoes, a platter of fried fish and another with thickly-sliced bread.

"So, Alex, you spend afternoon sawing logs?" Karl laughed as he dished a second helping for himself.

"Sawing?"

"Daddy means sleeping." Gunnar chased a piece of fish around his plate with his fork.

"Food is to eat, not to play with," Mrs. Arneson said, pausing in her own meal to feed the baby from a high chair pulled up to the table. It was advice lost on Oleanna, though, who managed to fling a spoonful of mashed potatoes onto the floor.

"Einar, you clean up," Karl said.

Einar sighed and went searching behind his mother's chair.

"You like to fish, Alex?" Karl asked. "Boys and me, we ice-fish last weekend. Jesse from shop, he take us."

"I caught three," Gunnar announced at the top of his voice. "More than Einar."

"Just one more." Einar contributed the potatoes he'd scooped from the floor to Queenie's dish by the stove.

"Use floor rag. Clean up good." Mrs. Arneson gave Oleanna a piece of bread to chew on.

There was a chorus of *taak for maten* as the boys finished their meal and left the table. They looked over at Alex, waiting for him to say something as well.

"*Taak for . . .*"

"*Maten,*" Gunnar said. "*Taak for maten.*"

"Means *thank you for what we eat.*" Karl laughed. "We keep some Norwegian to remember old country."

As Alex helped the boys with their after-supper chores, he noticed that his clothes were hanging from the clothesline outside. Mrs. Arneson must have washed them and hung them out as he slept.

"Thank you." Alex caught her attention as she finished changing the baby. "For cleaning the clothes."

"Three rinses," she said. "Next time you ride train, don't go in coal car."

"Yes," Alex agreed. "That would be good."

As Einar and Gunnar taught him how to play cards and Mrs. Arneson put the babies to bed, Karl got his violin down from where it hung by a ribbon from a nail in the living room wall over a table holding knickknacks. He tuned it, carefully adjusting the pegs and then began to play softly a tune that set everyone's toes tapping. Alex listened, amazed, missing opportunities to build his Rummy hand.

How was it possible for music, such a complication of music, to live in the mind and fingers of someone like Karl? Alex hadn't heard music like this since they lived in Lviv and a friend of his mother came for visits, always carrying with him a bandura. On the stringed instrument, he played jaunty tunes and wild, haunting pieces that brought tears to his mother's eyes.

"Dmytro," she would say. "You break my heart with that music." Then she'd laugh and say, "Play some more."

Later, after the boys said their prayers and crawled into bed, Alex climbed in beside them. The music hovered in his mind. Warm beneath the covers, with Gunnar snoring gently into his shoulder, it wasn't long, despite his afternoon nap, before he fell asleep.

Chapter 10

∽

ALEX WAS AWAKE for what seemed like a long time before anyone else in the house began to stir. Gunnar was a restless sleeper and Alex, after one kick, had reached down to retrieve covers, to be startled by Queenie's wet nose against his hand. When someone finally did get up, it was Karl, dressing quietly in the dark in the little curtained room, and, as he tiptoed by the sleeping children, he whispered, "Come, Queenie. Best go downstairs."

Alex dressed himself quickly and descended the stairs as quietly as he could into the dark living room below. An electric light glowed from the kitchen where Alex found Karl rebuilding the fire in the cook stove.

"Last year we get hook up to electricity," Karl said. "We need new coal furnace and Maria wants we build a bathroom and get water heater. But money, it is not growing on trees. Still, we get on. Do little bit at a time, that is what I say." When the kettle boiled, he spooned some coffee from a canister into the coffee pot, filled it with water, and set it forward on the stove.

"I been thinking," Karl said as they waited for the coffee to be ready. "I work today—special order to get out—but next Saturday is day off. I go to police station. Ask about brother. Not good you go yourself if you got no papers. We have to make a story though. Why I want information."

"A story?" Alex carefully rubbed the scab on his left hand. It was itching.

"Yah. Like brother—Marco—be neighbour who disappear or something like that. Maybe we say there be death to know about. And that be no lie."

"Maybe he will be there. In the police station."

"Well, there is jail downtown. Is possibility."

Karl got a couple of mugs and filled them with coffee. "Do you have idea what you do if he is there—in jail?"

Alex sighed. "No. How long would they be keeping him? Can I visit?"

Karl shrugged. "I will try to find out. While you wait, maybe you stay in Edmonton and go to school. Maria thinks there might be home for boys, for orphans."

"Could it be possible . . . could I stay here with you?"

As he sipped his coffee, Karl scratched Queenie behind her

ears, and she made little moaning sounds of appreciation. "That is crossing bridge before we get to river," he said softly.

"A week." Alex tried his coffee but it was still too hot and he blew on the surface. "Seven days. Could you go at night?"

"Who is at police desk when it be night? Might be somebody help us more in daytime. Say nothing to Maria. She should not have worries . . . cooking, cleaning, looking after children and baby coming."

Alex heard bedsprings creaking and then the sound of tiny feet scurrying across the living room linoleum. It was Astrid who, spying him, hurled herself into her father's arms and hid her face against his chest.

"A shy one, our Astrid," he chuckled. "Alex is no stranger now. Remember from yesterday?" Astrid peeked through her fingers and then hid her face again.

The boys were up now too, wandering sleepily into the kitchen.

"Good," said Karl. "You let Mama sleep this morning." He set Astrid on a chair. "Einar, he is our cook, making milk toast." He ran his fingers through the boy's tousled hair. "I cut bread and you show Alex how we do it."

Quickly Karl slathered butter on some of the pieces and cut cheese from a block on the cupboard counter to make sandwiches for himself before heading off to work. He was getting his coat and boots on when Maria came downstairs, carrying the baby. She looked tired but, with her hair not pinned up, she appeared younger and, Alex thought, not as hard.

"I'm making breakfast," Einar announced.

She sat the baby in the high chair and went to the door to give Karl a kiss. Alex looked away quickly, ashamed that they might think he was watching, but he had to smile when Einar and Gunnar and Astrid all rushed to the door for their own goodbye kisses while Queenie danced around them barking.

"Bye, Alex. Give Maria help with chores today," Karl said as he headed out.

Einar got his mother a cup of coffee and checked the milk warming on the stove.

"So ..." Maria Arneson looked across the table at him. "You and Karl sort out the world this morning?"

"Sort?" Alex turned his attention to Oleanna who had begun to cry. To quiet her, he handed her a cloth doll she'd been playing with the day before.

"That man." Maria shook her head and then got up and went to the cupboard to get the baby's bottle ready.

The boys went out to play, and Alex helped put the breakfast things away and dried the dishes that Maria washed in a dishpan on the stove. It seemed like every day he was able to do more things with his hands although the scabs, at times, cracked open and were especially sore when this happened.

Then he filled the tub for Oleanna's bath, and later he helped Maria heat water for washing clothes.

"It should not be bad," she said, working the baby's diapers through a ringer she'd attached to a tub. "Living for a while at boys' home."

Alex didn't say anything.

Later in the evening, as he helped Gunnar with his arithmetic homework at the kitchen table, he became aware of Maria and Karl talking in the living room. Most of it he couldn't make out—they were talking in Norwegian—but at one point, he heard Maria switch to English, "You are not meant to be looking after whole world."

The next week was a long one with Maria, it seemed, getting testier by the day. Saturday morning, she watched Karl from the corner of her eye, Alex noticed, as he made a list of things he needed to do now that it was his day off.

"Anything you need downtown? I pick up hardware for shop and I get some violin strings." He was talking to Maria but he was looking at Alex.

"Can I go with you?" Einar begged.

"Me too!" Gunnar suddenly woke up from playing with his cereal. "I want to go downtown."

"Hold on," Karl laughed. "My list is too long today. You come next time and we will all get soda. How would that be?"

"Leave Papa alone." Maria began feeding Oleanna her breakfast. "If you get chores done this morning, you go skating this afternoon."

After lunch, while he waited for Karl to come home, Alex knew he was betraying his anxiousness. Maria looked at him sharply as he carried the baby from one front window to the next and kept looking out. Since the boys had gone skating, he hoped she would think he was waiting for their return.

When he finally saw Karl coming up the walk, Alex noticed

that he seemed lost in serious thought. Alex felt himself overcome with a hollow, sinking feeling and he put Oleanna down on the living room rug with her toys.

It was a few minutes before Karl was alone with him while Maria prepared their afternoon coffee.

"Not good news," Karl said quietly. "Mountie will not check at first. Says not my business, but I tell him there is death in family Marco Kaminsky does not know about. So he do some checking. Is gone for half hour. Comes back and tells me he be charged with robbery and fighting. Like you guess, when they see he got no papers, he is sent to prisoner of war camp in Lethbridge."

"Prisoner of war? But he is not doing any war." Alex felt tears coming and brushed angrily at his eyes with his sleeve cuff.

"Enemy alien. That is what Mountie call him. No camp here so he is sent down to Lethbridge. But he can write to you. Mountie said that. You can write and tell him about your uncle. He even gives me camp address."

Alex couldn't help himself. He began crying and he was unable to make himself stop. He was thankful the sounds of his sobs were covered by the noise of the boys returning from skating. Karl moved closer to him on the living room bench and put an arm around his shoulders.

"There now," he said. "Camp is not great place to be, but he be alive and he be with other Ukrainians. All being looked after."

"I must see him."

"I do not think prisoners have visitors. But, like Mountie say, you can write."

"*Komme og spise*," Maria called from the kitchen. "Coffee is on the table." She came to the living room door and eyed both of them with the same look she levelled at Einar and Gunnar when they were misbehaving. When Alex gritted his teeth and brushed at his eyes again with his shirt sleeve, the look changed to one of question and he noticed Karl shaking his head as if to say, "Not now."

Karl gave him some sheets of writing paper so he could work on the letter to Marco that night, writing at the kitchen table as the boys played checkers. Violin case in hand, Karl had gone to play at a dance that evening and Maria, wearing earrings, a brooch made from a whale's tooth that had been crafted by her father, who'd been a sailor as a young man, and a yellow ribbon in her hair, had gone with him. She'd folded a diaper and reviewed the procedure for changing Oleanna if necessary. Alex prayed the baby would sleep through the evening.

"Good to have own babysitter, yah?" Karl said as he helped his wife with her wraps. "You boys be in bed by nine o'clock."

For a long time Alex played with his pencil, wondering how to begin. Should he write in Ukrainian or in English? Karl said something about the letters likely being opened by guards. Maybe they wouldn't let Marco receive letters in Ukrainian; maybe they'd think he was sending Marco secret war plans. Alex smiled ruefully at the thought.

He'd written no more than *Dear Brother Marco* when the

boys began squabbling over their game of checkers and Alex suggested they all play Rummy.

"We won't tell if you let us stay up later," Einar declared when the clock in the living room struck nine.

"One half hour," Alex agreed. "Then you must hop into bed without a noise. It must be a promise."

They kept their promise and Alex, tucking them in, checked on Astrid, asleep on her cot and Oleanna in her crib. He crept quietly back downstairs and took up the pencil again. It took him over an hour to finish the letter, writing in English, and he read it over three times.

He tried to imagine Marco receiving it, reading the news about Uncle Andrew and all that had happened to Alex in the weeks since his death. Would a guard be watching him? What kind of place was this prison camp? Was it stone walls and bars on windows?

Alex didn't know what to put on the envelope as a return address and, as he waited for Karl to get back, he wrote another letter, a short one to Mr. Bayles, telling him what had happened to the money and how he'd come to Edmonton. He'd left the letter unfinished, hoping he might put at the end: if a letter has come from Marco, please send it on.

It was close to midnight when Karl and Maria returned. As Maria checked on the babies, Alex asked about the return address.

"Yah, sure, put our address on. Even if you go stay someplace else, you visit us and we know where you be. I make sure you get letter soon as it comes." With one of his big carpenter's hands, he clasped Alex's shoulder and gave it a reassuring squeeze.

Maria came back downstairs, smiling. "Thanks, Alex, for looking after everything. Long time since I been out for an evening."

Her mood changed over the week that followed, though, especially on the day Karl brought his pay home and it wasn't quite enough to pay the grocer and set aside what they'd planned for when the baby arrived.

"One more mouth does make difference," he'd heard her hiss angrily at him. "He is big, growing boy. There is orphan home . . ."

"I eat not so much myself." Karl's voice was barely audible.

"Oh, fine!" Maria had given up trying to be quiet. "Starve yourself. That makes a lot of sense. And what about when he needs new clothes and bigger boots?"

Alex had wished he could simply disappear.

Following church the next Sunday, Karl took the boys sledding. There had been a new snowfall and they were anxious to use sleds Karl had made each of them as Christmas gifts. When Alex said, "I should come too?" Karl's face got red.

"Maria not feeling very good today. Maybe you give her hand with babies," he said, but there was a sad, weary edge to his voice that alarmed Alex.

He was hardly surprised when the Lutheran minister

arrived a few minutes later. Maria looked embarrassed and began fussing over coffee and cookies and then said, "I will leave you two alone for few minutes. I give Oleanna her bottle and put Astrid down for nap."

"So you're the Galician boy I've been hearing about." The minister looked over his glasses at Alex as he dunked a piece of almond cookie in his coffee. "The Arnesons are fine Christian folk but they really can't afford . . . and, well, they don't really have space, with their own family growing."

Alex tried to take a swallow of coffee but he started coughing.

"I suppose you are from the Greek Catholic church?"

Alex looked down at the pattern on the oilcloth. Roses arranging themselves in clusters that made diamond shapes with little avenues of yellow between them.

"You really should be with your own people," the minister continued. "You'll be able to talk with them better. You don't want to be a burden . . ."

"I have no people," Alex said. "I have only my brother."

"I don't mean relatives." The minister had a fat neck and his collar, Alex decided, must have been bought when he was a size smaller. A little roll of skin hung over the starched stiffness. "I mean people of your own . . ." He struggled to find a word. "Ilk."

"*Ilk?*" Alex questioned.

Maria had come downstairs, carrying Oleanna. Her eyes were red.

The minister quickly interjected, "Alex here will get his things together and I will drive him . . ."

At that moment, though, there was a commotion in the porch and Karl burst into the kitchen, the boys trailing him.

"No," he shouted, "Alex will stay here." He had a wild look in his eyes, Alex thought. "What is one boy, Maria, I ask you? Are we so poor?"

For a minute, it looked as though Maria did not know what to do. Then quietly she said, "Yes, he will stay." She turned to the minister and handed him his hat. "I am sorry for the trouble."

"Well . . ." the minister sputtered, swallowing a last bit of cookie. "I was only trying . . . He might be happier among Galicians."

"He will be fine here with us," Karl said. "Do not hurry with your coffee. Have some more."

"No, I really need to be going. Mrs. Bergstrom, she's expecting me home . . ."

Queenie followed the minister out, barking his way to the gate and his car.

"Even Queenie thinks you should stay," said Gunnar.

"Smart dog," Karl noted.

"Are we still going sledding?" Einar asked.

"Yah," said Karl, "but Alex is going with us. And Queenie too."

Maria sighed. "Get along, all of you. Do not come back with broken bones."

Chapter 11

∽

ON MONDAY, Alex went to school with Einar and Gunnar. It was a large two-storey red-brick building and, at the boys' entrance, a group gathered around him. Mitts hid the damage to his hands, but it was a mild morning and he hadn't bothered to cover the burn on his face with a scarf.

"Holy! What happened to him?" One of Gunnar's friends, with a piping voice, asked.

Einar took it on himself to relate the details but the bell rang before he was finished and they scurried into the building. Einar grabbed hold of Alex's sleeve and steered him toward the principal's office.

"Excuse me." Einar peered over the counter and addressed

a woman behind a typewriter at a desk. "This is my cousin, Alex, who's going to be living with us." It was a story Karl had rehearsed with them the night before. "His house got burned down."

The lady stood up and came over to the counter.

"And you were burned." She looked at the side of Alex's face and made a little clucking noise of concern.

Alex nodded.

"He doesn't speak much English," Einar added.

"What's your name?"

"Alexander Arneson." The words felt weighted with the lie. "It's just a little white lie," Karl had reminded them. "Otherwise the police might be called and who knows where Alex might end up. I heard they're putting women and children into some of those camps."

"Norwegian? That's your language?"

Alex didn't deny it.

"Were you going to school here?"

"In the country," Einar said, "but he has to live with us in the city now. He's partly in grade five and partly in grade six."

"I see." The lady smiled at Einar. She had rimless glasses and she wore a little clock, Alex noticed, on a ribbon pinned to her blouse.

"You run along to class now, Einar. We'll let Mr. Edgerton decide what class Alexander will go into."

"See you at recess," Einar whispered as he backed out of the office.

"Have a chair." The lady pointed to one beside the door. "I'll check to see if Mr. Edgerton can see you now." She went over and knocked at a door with a frosted window on the other side of the room.

"Yes?" Mr. Edgerton had a voice that carried through walls.

Alex watched her go in and then come out again in a minute, beckoning him over.

"This is Alexander Arneson," she said to a man behind a big oak desk. "He doesn't speak much English."

The man wore a suit, and a striped, shiny tie was knotted beneath a white collar so starched it looked like it might be made out of thin bone. A thick, sandy mustache had been combed to fine points at each extremity. He nodded at the lady and she left the room, quietly closing the door.

"Alexander Arneson. Scandinavian?"

Alex looked at him questioningly.

"Did you bring any papers, reports from your previous school?"

"No papers," Alex admitted, reluctantly. He thought of what Ivan had said about papers being crucial or you might be given over to the police.

Mr. Edgerton rose from his desk and, going over to a bookshelf behind him, selected a reader and gave it to Alex.

"See if you can read any of that."

It was not a difficult passage, a story about Robin Hood and his men. Alex stumbled on only three or four of the words. Miss Anderson had read a book about Robin Hood aloud to the class last October, a chapter each day before dismissal.

"Pretty good with the grade five reader," Mr. Edgerton noted. "Let's see how you do with grade six arithmetic." He wrote a piece of long division for Alex to calculate and, when he got that correct, told him to calculate the volume of a cylinder—which he couldn't do.

"Well, Alexander, we'll try you in Mr. Dallaine's class. Grade six. I think it's probably the right spot for you."

"Thank you," Alex said, the words coming out like a whisper.

The class was laughing over something when Mr. Edgerton brought him in but they stopped quickly upon seeing the principal and chorused, "Good morning, Mr. Edgerton."

"Good morning, boys and girls." Mr. Edgerton beckoned the teacher from the front of the room. "A new student for you, Mr. Dallaine. This is Alexander Arneson. He has limited English but reads not too badly. I know your class will do what it can to make him feel at home." He gave Alex a pat on the back before heading back into the hall.

"Welcome to grade six." Alex could tell the teacher was trying not to focus on the burns on his hands and face. He smiled at Alex and looked around the room for a spare seat. "Why don't you sit with Eric, that third desk over by the window. Eric, you'll have to quit spilling over onto that side."

He led Alex over to the double desk. A freckled, sandy-haired boy lifted the desk lid and retrieved some books and papers while Mr. Dallaine brought a slate, a scribbler and a pencil and a pen over and placed them in front of Alex.

"We're short some readers," Mr. Dallaine said. "So follow along with Eric. We were just in the middle of *The Yarn of the Nancy Bell* so we'll continue. Eric, you can be Alexander's guide today. Show him where things are, take him around."

Alex noticed that Mr. Dallaine walked with a limp. At the front of the room, he sat on the edge of his desk and continued reading the poem, twisting his face and using a queer accent. The children giggled and Alex found himself laughing with them although he couldn't make head or tails of what the poem was about.

"Mr. Dallaine." One of the girls put up her hand. "People wouldn't really eat each other, would they?"

"You might be surprised, Alicia, what people can bring themselves to do to one another." Mr. Dallaine closed his book and removed the glasses that clipped onto his nose. "But remember that W.S. Gilbert calls this a yarn—it's a tall tale. Now, let's move from the ridiculous to the sublime. The poem I'd like you to begin copying out for handwriting today is 'Invictus' by William Ernest Henley. We'll do a verse a day and then discuss the poem on Friday."

"Use my ink." Eric screwed the lid off the bottle in his inkwell. "I've got lots."

When he'd first gone to Bayles' Corner School, Alex had been able to print using the English alphabet but, over the last year, Miss Anderson had taught him to write in script. It was something he did well. But now, while his thumb was fine on his right hand, the finger he normally used to hold a pen was still sensitive from the burn and he was disappointed in the results when he used his middle finger.

Out of the night that covers me,
Black as the pit from pole to pole,
I thank what gods may be
For my unconquerable soul.

Alex looked at the results of copying the verse. In the first line the pen had stuck on the paper and left a blotch. The writing did seem to get better by the fourth line. But his hand was beginning to ache. The teacher limped over and was watching over his shoulder. Looking down, Alex could see that one of Mr. Dallaine's feet had a special boot with a thick sole. He quickly looked up.

"Pretty good, Alexander." The teacher smiled at him.

When he wiped his pen and replaced it in the desk groove, he sighed with relief.

Looking around, he noticed that many of the students were sneaking glances at him. Suddenly he felt conscious of the fact that he was a couple of years older than most of them, fitting awkwardly into the desk beside Eric, who was a bit on the small side. And his clothes were ill-fitting and patched. Maybe it wasn't just his burns they were looking at.

It seemed like a very long day and Alex had to fight not to

fall asleep while Mr. Dallaine played a gramophone record late in the afternoon after talking to the class about the music, a piece called "La Mer."

"Close your eyes and imagine being beside the sea with waves rolling up onto the shore. Imagine smelling the salt air and hearing gulls cry off in the distance." Mr. Dallaine, the wizard of voices, spoke in a tone as soft as a sea breeze, and he paused for a few seconds before placing the needle onto the record. The room was warm and, from somewhere down the hall, there was a faint chorus from a class reciting their times tables.

When Alex closed his eyes, he could feel himself drifting. Eric gave him a small, friendly poke.

Like Miss Anderson, Mr. Dallaine read aloud from a novel for the last twenty minutes of class. He took a few minutes to fill Alex in on the story about a boy named Oliver Twist who was running away from a place where he'd been bullied and abused to lose himself in the big city of London.

For Alex, the school day was not over with dismissal. Mr. Dallaine asked him to remain behind. He went over the few pages in the arithmetic text leading up to the lesson they'd had earlier and he gave him a paper with a map of the world on it and a list of places to label.

"But tell me about your family and the fire." Mr. Dallaine removed the glasses from his nose and sat back with his hands folded in his lap. He had warm brown eyes with little flecks of light in them that reminded Alex a bit of Queenie's eyes.

Haltingly, Alex told him of the sickness that had taken his parents as they waited to make the voyage over. He didn't say anything about Hamburg and he didn't mention Marco by name, just referring to him as "my brother." He hadn't even come to the part about living with Uncle Andrew and the fire when Mr. Dallaine reached over and gently touched Alex's sleeve.

"You're not from Norway, are you?" he said.

"No," Alex sighed.

"Where are you really from?" Mr. Dallaine gave him a reassuring nod. "I won't tell anyone if it involves your safety."

Alex looked at the map lying on top of the arithmetic text. He put his finger on the spot he thought must be north of the Mediterranean and west of Russia.

"From Lviv," he said.

"From Galicia?"

Alex nodded.

"And your brother? Where is he now?"

In a minute the whole story was spilled out.

Mr. Dallaine was silent for a few seconds when Alex was finished. "This war . . ." He shook his head. "It chooses some odd victims. Go home, Alexander, and don't worry about doing any homework tonight. I think you need to get a good sleep. By the way, as long as you're in this class, your name is Arneson."

"No, I will do some." Alex tucked the map inside the arithmetic text. "Do you think Marco is hurt? Is that why he does not write?"

"Give it a few more days," Mr. Dallaine said. "If you still haven't heard from him, perhaps I can do some investigating."

But there were letters for him when he got home. Maria had propped them against the sugar bowl in the middle of the kitchen table.

"Read your letters," Gunnar shouted. "I want to hear them."

"Leave Alex alone," Maria scolded. "Let him read letters himself. You go ahead, Alex. No chores that need doing this minute. Einar has filled woodbox and brought in pail of coal."

Alex took the envelopes and went into the living room. The letters were both from Marco but one had been forwarded from Bayles' Corner. He opened this one first, using the letter opener with a carved wooden handle that Karl displayed on the parlour table.

Dear Alex,

A terrible thing. I am in prisoner of war jail far away. How did this happen? It was the fault of Granger who did not give me all my pay. Just half. But I fight with him and take the rest. He chase me to Vegreville. Police are there and believe him, not me. Granger lies and says he pays me at the end of every month. Police give him most of the money back. Is that justice? They do not believe me in Vegreville. They do not believe me in Edmonton. I am there for some days and then I am sent to Lethbridge with

*other prisoners. I have no citizen papers. Those ones we
were going to get now we be here three years. At first I think
we cannot write letters and then I see some other men
writing and I know I can but must show everything before
sending. I hope you are well and I am very sad I am not
being there for Christmas and to make cards for school.*

With love,

Your Brother Marco

The letter was dated December 30, 1915. Alex quickly
sliced open the second letter and unfolded it. This one was
dated January 17, 1916.

My Dear Brother,

*What sad news! It is hard to believe Uncle Andrew is
gone. I am so sorry about your hurt face and hands and
most sorry I am not there to help. I feel like making a loud
yell but what would that help? It was good your letter
came yesterday and I have news of where to write to you
because tomorrow I will be going to a different camp. This
one is in the mountains. You will be surprised that someone
you know is going with me. His name is Ivan Sherbeniak.
He was picked up in Edmonton when he got off a freight
train—when you were both running away. He says hello
and is happy that you have a good place to stay. I am happy
too. Maybe the war will not be very much longer and soon
we can be together. On the back of this letter is a picture of*

*a firebird I have done for two hours today. Remember the
story Mama would tell us of the firebird rising again, more
brighter than ever before from ashes. You are a firebird,
Alex. Alive out of ashes. I have no paints but there is a box
of crayons here with the paper and pencils so the firebird is
in crayon colours. I will write soon from the new camp so
please write back when you have my address.*

With much love,

Marco

For a long time, Alex looked at Marco's detailed sketch of
the firebird. Somehow he had managed to make the crayon
colours blaze. The bird, its head in profile, gazed at him with
its red, jewelled eye.

"Golly." Gunnar peeked over his shoulder. "What's that?"

"A firebird." Alex held it so Gunnar could have a closer
look.

"Let me see too." Einar abandoned his homework and
hurried over. "What's a firebird?"

"A magic bird," Alex said. He thought of the stories Mama
would tell. Stories of a firebird seducing a tsar and his family
with the magnificence of one captured feather. Stories of the
bird dying in the fall, then, in the spring, rising in brilliance
from its own ashes.

"What kind of magic?"

"Magic to burn up and come back more brighter than
ever."

Karl had a look at the picture too when he got home from work.

"He is good artist."

Alex flushed with the compliment. Karl himself was an artist in his work with wood.

"Ivan is who you hide with in coal car?"

Alex nodded. "He tells me he was trying to get to the United States."

"It is good you do not get down to Lethbridge," Karl said. "Who knows where camp in the mountains is. We will know more when he writes again. Now, better get washed up for supper. Maria makes stack of pancakes like small mountain."

The next day Alex took Marco's letters with him to school. When Mr. Dallaine finished a chapter of *Oliver Twist* and announced "Class dismissed," Alex remained behind.

"How'd you make out with the homework?" The teacher gestured for Alex to take a chair next to his desk.

"I can do it," Alex said. "It is like arithmetic in Bayles' Corner. The map I will finish tonight but I must have with me a book with countries."

"Of course. A geography, an atlas. I should have given it to you yesterday." Mr. Dallaine shook his head as if forgetfulness was something that plagued him from time to time.

"I have to show you . . ." Alex retrieved the letters from where he'd been keeping them in the back of his scribbler. "Letters did come."

"You've heard from your brother?"

"Yes, he is in jail in Lethbridge but will be going to the mountains."

"The mountains?"

"It is in here. In the letter." Alex unfolded it for Mr. Dallaine to read.

"Hmm. I read something about there being trouble when some of the prisoners were put to work in the coal mines near Lethbridge. Taking jobs away from free miners, I suppose. I'm sure they'll think of some kind of work for them to do in the mountains. I'm glad you've heard from him, though, and he'll be writing to you again once he gets settled wherever they're taking them."

Mr. Dallaine studied the drawing of the firebird. "He's very good. Can you draw like this, too, Alexander?"

"No," Alex laughed. "Mama said Marco went back and got a second helping when God was giving out art . . ." What was the word Karl used? "Talent, artist talent."

"Yes, definitely talented. You miss your mother, don't you?"

"I think," Alex said, "every day. I wish every day so hard that she could have been not sick and have been coming to Canada."

"I lost my mother too." Mr. Dallaine took off his glasses and closed his eyes for a second. "I was nine when she died. I think, like you, I've missed her every day." He sighed and then pushed himself up from the desk. "Now, let's find you an atlas."

When Alex got home, Maria was perched on a stool by the sink, trying to peel potatoes with Oleanna curled up on her lap. Astrid, playing with a rag doll on the kitchen floor, gave him a shy smile.

"You take baby, Alex." Maria sounded weary. "I think she is not feeling good. Much crying today."

From the living room, it sounded like Einar and Gunnar were in the middle of a fight over toys.

"Einar," Maria yelled, "you go upstairs and lie on bed, and Gunnar you sit in Papa's chair and don't move until I say."

Oleanna whimpered as Alex took her but she settled against his chest when he walked around the room, gently rocking her.

"Oh, I almost forget," Maria said. "You get another letter today." She pointed to an envelope propped against a canister on the cupboard.

Alex didn't recognize the handwriting on the envelope. It had been addressed to him at Bayles' Corner and must have been forwarded by Mr. Bayles. With Astrid in his lap, he opened the letter, and saw it was wrapped around another envelope with the name Marco Kaminsky written on it. Alex glanced at the signature at the bottom. In a childish script, close to printing, the name read "Stella."

Dear Alex,

You will be surprised to get this letter. Inside I give you a letter for Marco which I beg you to pass on to him if it be possible. It is very important. My biggest hope is that he is *with you at Bayles' Corner and you can reach over and put the envelope into his hand.*

I am writing to you from the Vegreville Hospital where I go when my husband Edward Granger breaks my wrist. From the beating my face is hurt bad too and I tell the doctor I will not go back and live with him. They let me stay in the hospital for a few days and then I must look for someplace to live.

I must tell you Marco and I be more than friends in the time he stay with us. Edward guesses this and I think that is why he makes a fight with Marco and does not give him his money. He knows policemen in Vegreville so they believe him.

Maybe I should be beaten. But Edward I never loved. He gives my family stock and money if I marry him when I am fifteen. My family is very poor—not even enough to eat. My father says that is what I must do. I been with Edward five years. But I would sooner die than go back and live with him now. He can be very mean. I was afraid he would beat you too when you came to the farm. I hope you get home safe.

I will write to you again when I find a place to stay.

Yours truly,

Stella

"Bad news?" Maria put the potatoes on to boil.

"Bad in a way," Alex admitted. "But maybe good in a way." He passed the letter over to her to read.

"Would not surprise me there is a baby coming." Maria held up the sealed letter as if she were hoping she could see through the envelope paper to what it said inside.

Alex looked at her wide-eyed. "Marco's baby?"

"Just a guess. He is there for a long time. That girl been with Granger for many years and there was no children."

"Mama, can I get down now?" Gunnar whined from the other room. "I'll be good. I'm tired of sitting here."

"All right. And tell your brother he can come downstairs." Maria folded up the letter and gave it back to Alex.

Later, as Alex held Oleanna and gave her her bottle after supper, he couldn't help thinking about Maria's notion. Of course it was just a thought. But Granger had given her a pretty fierce beating, bad enough to break her wrist, and something must have provoked it. Or maybe he was the kind of man who would beat someone for not having supper on the table on time. Marco a father! Alex inhaled the soft smell of talcum and flannel and warm milk from the baby he held in his arms.

Although he couldn't help thinking about Marco—it seemed like almost every waking moment—Alex found comfort in the routines of home and school over the next few days. He was good at checking what was cooking on the stove for dinner when Maria was busy with the baby. At the homestead, all of them—Uncle Andrew, Marco and he—had taken turns cooking.

His hands were healed enough that he could peel potatoes

and Maria had been pleasantly surprised one morning when he made oatmeal porridge that was creamy and free of lumps. He helped the boys keep the woodbox and the coal scuttle full and the ash pans from the stoves emptied, and he gave them a hand with their arithmetic homework.

He didn't tell Mr. Dallaine about the letter from Stella—he wasn't sure why—even though he stayed after school for at least a few minutes after dismissal each afternoon to talk to the teacher and find out what he might do to catch up. Mr. Dallaine brought in an extra copy of *Oliver Twist* one day.

"This is not an easy book," he said, "but try reading the first chapters to catch up. Make a list of the words you don't understand and we'll discuss them—and bring the book to class so you can follow along when I read aloud."

By Friday the class had copied out all four verses of "Invictus" for handwriting practice and Alex looked with satisfaction at how much better each stanza looked.

During the recess breaks, Alex had at first sought out a solitary spot in an alcove at the back of the school where he could lean against the wall and keep out of the wind. Einar and Gunnar would sometimes whirl by with their friends, giddy with their few minutes of freedom. When Eric discovered him there, though, the following Monday, he hollered for Alex to join a group playing tag. By the end of the week, Alex was accepted as one of them and it was a matter of course that he would join them in whatever game they decided to play.

Eric's mother often sent candy or pastries with him to

school and Eric began sharing these with him. Some of the students in the class, he knew, kept away from him because of his lankiness and his patched clothes and broken English. But Eric didn't seem to be bothered by any of this. Had he ever known anyone like Eric who found so much to laugh about? If a wind caught one of the girl's skirts and exposed her bloomers, Eric would fall on the ground laughing. Even in class there were times when Mr. Dallaine had to scold him or send him into the hall to recover himself.

"Hey, Alex," Eric whispered to him as they worked on a geography assignment the next Friday afternoon, "come to the movies with me tomorrow. It's Charlie Chaplin. You'll die laughing. Mom says you can come for dinner afterwards."

"I'll ask," Alex whispered back. About a year ago, he'd gone to Vermilion to see a picture show with Uncle Andrew and Marco and he'd loved it. It was a film with cowboys and a train robbery. Uncle Andrew had fallen asleep but Marco whistled with appreciation when a heroine with cascading ringlets smiled demurely from the screen before being swept into the cowboy's arms.

"How much is the cost?" Alex asked.

"Just a nickel. But don't worry. I've got enough for both of us."

When he got home from school that afternoon, he asked Karl, and Karl said that of course it would be fine. He wouldn't mind seeing Charlie Chaplin himself.

"They want you should have supper after? Richards? Live in that big fancy house I drive by sometimes?" He nodded to

Maria. "We are not so poor. Alex shall have his own nickel."

Maria scowled as he brought the cocoa tin that served as a coin bank from the top shelf of the cupboard and plucked out a dime for him. "Here. For the show tomorrow. Some extra for a treat."

"Gunnar's boots need resoling," Maria reminded her husband.

"I should make him some wooden shoes," Karl laughed. "Would you like that, Gunnar?"

After he had done his chores, Alex hurried over to Eric's. It was a few blocks away, closer to the river, and the houses, as Karl had noted, were fancier than the ones on the street where Karl and Maria lived. Eric had told him the number on the house and Alex paused to look up at the windows glowing in the winter evening from three storeys.

When he rang the bell, a young woman in an apron and a little white hat answered the door and had him wait on the rug by the door while she went to get Eric.

"Hey, Alex!" Eric bounded into the hall. "Can you come then?"

"I have money too." Alex showed him the dime.

Eric walked him half the way back, as far as the school.

"See you tomorrow!" He turned and hollered and waved before disappearing around the corner.

Alex spent Saturday morning doing everything he could think of for Maria. She seemed to have forgiven him for causing Karl's extravagance with the dime in the coin bank. Just before noon, she let him take his bath in the kitchen. And later, as he dressed upstairs, putting on his Christmas shirt and vest, she surprised him by climbing up and presenting him with an unpatched pair of trousers.

"These I make over from pair Karl have when we marry. Waist a couple sizes smaller then. I do not want you to be looking like a tramp when you are visiting Richards.'"

Alex held them up. They were dark flannel, pressed with a fine crease.

"Thank you," he stammered. "Such a kindness."

But Maria seemed almost as embarrassed as he was and, saying something about the baby crying, hurried back downstairs. She must have worked on the trousers for a long time after he had gone to bed the night before to get them finished for today. They fit perfectly.

Alex met Eric at the corner by the school and they walked to the theatre on Whyte Avenue. It was packed, mainly with children for the matinee. Eric seemed to know several of them and got into a friendly tussle with one of the boys over a balcony seat. Alex noticed two girls from his class who smiled and nodded at him and then broke into a fit of giggles.

"Hey, Millicent," Eric shouted over to them, "where's your loverboy today?"

Millicent responded by sticking her tongue out at him.

"That means kiss me but don't slobber!" Eric managed to

holler before the lights dimmed and the movie serial began. During the Charlie Chaplin feature, Eric laughed so hard, Alex was afraid he might choke on the candies they had bought on their way. But Alex had to laugh too as the little tramp caused total havoc in a department store. It felt good to be in the middle of this world of happy children, cocooned in the darkness of the theatre, with nothing but the flickering, silvery images on the screen to think about.

Eric practised walking like the little tramp on the way back to his house, his feet splayed out, bumping into fences, falling into snowdrifts.

"You should be in the picture show," Alex said.

"Maybe I will," Eric decided. "Maybe that's what I'll be when I grow up—a movie actor."

"I would come to see you."

Once they had reached Eric's house and had taken off their wraps, Alex felt a fluttering in his stomach. He couldn't help thinking about dinner. Would he manage to get through it without embarrassing himself? Maria had told him there would be cloth napkins and more silverware than any one person really needed. She had helped serve at fancy meals a few times before she married.

"Just watch your friend and do what he does," she had said.

He was glad they wouldn't be eating right away. Maybe the flutters would go away.

Eric's room was on the top floor, just below the turret roof. From the rounded bank of windows, it was possible to look across the river to the buildings on the north side and see the electric lights growing brighter as the afternoon darkened. Eric had a train set that wound around his bed, and he showed Alex how to stage a spectacular crash of two engines before they were called for supper.

All of the Richards were at the table in the dining room by the time Alex and Eric had washed up. Eric had two older sisters who, he told Alex with some disgust, treated him like a baby. It looked to Alex like they were dressed in party dresses with lace and jewelry. Amanda, who was studying to be a nurse, had a close look at the burn on his face and made an announcement about it being in a terminal stage of scabbing. Eric made cross-eyes at her that brought a complaint from the other sister, Laurette.

"Now, children," Mrs. Richards chided them. She wore lace and jewels too and Alex thought she looked a little like the portrait of Queen Mary that hung beside the Union Jack in Mr. Dallaine's classroom. For that matter, Eric's dad looked a little like King George. At least he had the same kind of moustache.

Mr. Richards said a grace that sounded to Alex more like a command than a blessing.

"Eric tells us you're new to Canada," Mrs. Richards said as a maid served everyone a bowl of soup.

"Quite new," Alex admitted. The soup was a rich, creamy chowder and Alex did his best not to make a slurping sound as he ate it.

"And where would you be coming from?" Eric's father said, carefully blotting his moustache with his napkin.

"Uh . . . Norway." Alex looked down at his soup bowl.

"Norway. Did you come over directly or did you leave from Liverpool?"

Alex felt his face becoming red. "From Hamburg. My brother and me."

"Hamburg!" Mr. Richards said the name of the city in a way that made it sound like something he'd tasted that had gone bad.

"Papa, this is supper not an inquisition," Laurette reminded him.

"Hamburg!"

"Daisy, you can clear the soup now." Mrs. Richards hailed the maid who'd been waiting by the dining room doorway.

"That fire must have been a terrible experience." Amanda smiled sympathetically at him. "Does anyone know how it started?"

"From a lamp, I think," Alex said. "My uncle, he falls asleep, I believe, and is making it tip."

"I hope your uncle wasn't hurt." Mrs. Richards nodded at the maid to begin serving the roast beef.

"I told you his uncle died," Eric muttered.

"Oh my. How dreadful!"

Mr. Richards, Alex noticed, watched him closely as the rest of the meal was served and, just as the dessert was being cleared away, the man whipped his napkin off his lap and declared, "I'm thinking you're not from Norway. I never heard a Norwegian accent that sounded like that. What I want to know, young man, is where you're really from."

"William!" Mrs. Richards clutched the pearl choker at her neck.

Alex felt the last bite of lemon cake sticking in his throat.

"I stay with people from Norway," Alex said, although he wasn't sure his voice carried to the other end of the table.

"I'll state my question again." Mr. Richards was getting very red in the face. "Where are you from, boy? Who are your people?"

"I come from Lviv . . ."

"Lviv? Where in God's name . . . ?"

"Eric, you and Alex may be excused . . ." Mrs. Richards interrupted. "Why don't you show Alex your stereoscope slides?"

"C'mon, Alex. I got a whole set about the last days of Pompeii." Eric ushered Alex past his glowering father and up the stairs to his room.

"Are you really from that other place . . . that Lu-view? How come you weren't telling nobody?"

"My brother . . ." Alex tried to think of what he might say but he felt suddenly sick to his stomach, and before he could manage to get another word out, he threw up all over Eric's model train crash.

Chapter 12

∽

IT WAS DAISY, the maid, who helped Alex get cleaned up and it was Daisy's husband, Jim, who drove Alex home in the Richards' automobile.

"You all right there now, sonny? If you feel like another upchuck, holler and I'll stop and you can present your offering to a snow bank. Mr. Richards is cranky enough without his upholstery needing to be cleaned." Jim grinned at him as he manoeuvred the automobile through the snow that had begun to fall. "Daisy says you got him in an uproar about something. Probably thinks you're trying to bring down the British Empire. He was an officer in the South African War and, to hear him talk, you'd think he won it single-handedly."

"Thank you," Alex managed as the automobile pulled up and settled, its motor purring, in front of the Arnesons. The nausea had vanished but his teeth were chattering.

"Don't let the old man worry you. He gets his tail-feathers in an uproar about something or other every couple of days," Jim said as he got down and opened the car door for Alex. He gave him a friendly pat and laughed at Queenie's antics on the other side of the gate as he drove away.

Karl was with the boys in the living room when Alex came in. It looked like he was practising a new tune on his violin, a music book open in front of him.

"So, you have good time?" Karl looked up at him and his eyes quickly took on a look of concern. "You feeling all right?"

"I got sick," Alex said, dropping his coat and easing himself onto a chair.

"Too much excitement?"

"Mr. Richards . . ." Alex choked back a sob.

"What happen?" Karl leaned the violin against the coffee table, and Gunnar and Einar paused in their game of cards.

"He would not believe I am from Norway. He is mad when I say Hamburg." Alex felt a shudder work its way from his feet up to his shoulders. "Eric's toy trains . . . I got sick on. He goes in another room and I don't see him when I come home."

"Sorry you have bad time."

Maria had heard this last bit as she came down the stairs. "I am afraid something like this happens," she said. "Lying . . ."

"Alex, I think is good you go upstairs and go early to bed."
Karl picked up Alex's coat from where he had dropped it and
went to the porch to hang it up.

"Has Alex got the measles?" Gunnar asked.

"No, stupid, he doesn't have any spots." Einar poked his
brother with the fan of cards he held in his hand.

Maria felt Alex's forehead. "Gunnar thinks being sick and
having measles is same thing. All but Oleanna have measles
in fall. Karl is right. You should go up to bed. I will bring you
hot water bottle."

When Karl took the boys sledding the next day after church,
Alex stayed back, curling up on the couch with a blanket over
his legs, reading *Oliver Twist* while Maria did some mending
and Astrid gave her dolls and Queenie a tea party.

"I hope that man, that Mr. Richards, forget about you not
being Norvegian." Maria threaded some yarn into her darn-
ing needle. "Saying lies is like shaking feathers in the wind.
Who knows where they land. Oh!" She looked up, suddenly
startled. "That little one kicked me!"

Alex thought about Stella, and Maria's suspicion that she
might be pregnant. Had Stella found a place in Vegreville to
live? Would it be possible for someone like her to really get
away from a man as big and mean as Granger? Who would
support her?

"When . . . when does the baby come?"

"Three months. April." Maria got up and stretched and

felt Alex's head again. "You have not fever—so just upset stomach. Better now? Tomorrow you go to school."

He did feel better and was glad to be at school on Monday. Eric forgave him for getting sick all over his train engines. "Laurette and Amanda are calling it 'The Great Train Disaster!'" Eric laughed. "Daisy washed them off and cleaned the floor."

"I am very sorry," Alex said.

"Aw, they're good as new. Maybe I'll call that part of the track the Puke Station now."

"Your father? Is he still being angered?"

"Dad? He's always mad about something or other. He'll get over it. That was a pretty good story about you being one of the Arnesons. How come you aren't using your real . . . ?"

Mr. Dallaine had his eye on the two of them, so they turned back to the arithmetic questions he'd set the class.

When Alex returned home from school on Tuesday, there was another letter from Marco. Maria didn't even scold him for failing to hang up his coat and cap as he hurried to open it.

My Dear Brother,

Ivan and me, we arrive in the beautiful mountain town of Banff today. When it is holidays, some people are staying at the Banff Springs Hotel. Very fancy. Not Ivan and me. We stay at the Cave and Basin prisoner hotel and we have a special escort to get there—ha! ha! There are hundreds here and many guards. Some of the prisoners are not looking so good. One man tells me he was in the hoosegow for three weeks because he tells them he will not work. He says no one would ever want to go to the hoosegow. You may not get out alive. They tell me other things too but I think it is not permitted to write them in a letter. I hope you are better from the burns and that things are still good with the Arnesons. No one tells me how long I will be in the camp. Ivan says until the war is over. I hope not. I hope Granger is found out for not paying me and I will be set free.

I would draw you a picture but it is very cold in this place and my fingers are stiff. Tomorrow Ivan and me will be going out to work on rock crushing to build a road. I hope it is warmer.

I would give the world to see you.

I wait your letter.

Much love,

Marco

"He is in this place called Banff," Alex said, handing the letter over to Maria.

When Karl returned home he read and reread the letter. "Banff! Prisoners of war in a mountain park! I was in Banff once, year before Maria and me get married. Remember, dear, I go with Bjorn and Nils that summer." Karl sighed.

"Must be making prisoners do park work. I wonder they get some pay?"

The next day Alex took the letter to school with him to show Mr. Dallaine but, during the last half hour before dismissal, while Mr. Dallaine was reading about Oliver Twist being caught by Nancy and Bill Sykes after living at Mr. Brownlow's, the school secretary came to the door and asked for Alex to come down to the office. She wasn't smiling.

"Mr. Edgerton wants to see you," she said, motioning him to the chair he'd sat in before.

"Me?"

The secretary didn't say anything. She checked the time on the little watch she wore on her blouse, returned to her desk, and a couple of minutes later, when the principal opened his door, nodded for him to go in.

The principal was standing behind his desk with his back to Alex. When the secretary closed the door, he turned around.

"Alexander?"

Alex nodded.

"But it's not Alexander Arneson, is it?"

Alex looked down at the floor.

"Mr. Richards just happens to be on the school board and he was not amused to discover that we have students attending our schools under assumed names. Neither am I, I have to say. What is your real name, Alexander?"

"Kaminsky," Alex mumbled.

"Speak up."

Alex drew in a breath. "Alexander Kaminsky," he said, quite a bit louder.

"Austrian?"

Alex didn't say anything.

"You speak when you're spoken to," the principal shouted. The ends of his moustache quivered.

"From Lviv," Alex said. "That is where I come from. My brother and me."

"Somewhere in Austria-Hungary, I believe. An empire that has driven the free world to war. An empire stained with the blood of young men fighting for decency and freedom. It makes me sick to my stomach to think that you believed you could sneak in here."

Alex shook his head but didn't look up. He believed he was probably more sick to his stomach than the man shouting at him.

"You should hang your head in shame." Mr. Edgerton picked up a wooden pointer and slammed it against the top of his desk, making a loud cracking sound. "I have a good mind to give you a hiding you wouldn't forget and then call the authorities. If you're concealing your name, you're concealing it for a reason."

Alex swallowed hard. He still couldn't bring himself to look up at the principal.

"But I don't believe in caning someone who has been wounded. You can thank your burns for saving you from that. For your deceit, I am expelling you today. You will not return under an assumed name. This is a public institution, though, and if you wish to return under your correct identity, that is up to you. But, should that happen, I will invite the authorities to determine who is your legal guardian. Do you understand?"

Alex, finally, did look up. He felt like he'd already been beaten.

"I will record your name and check with the police." Mr. Edgerton made a shooing gesture with his hand. "Now get out of my sight."

Alex bolted, not even stopping in the classroom for his coat, and raced for the exit. He was breathless and shivering by the time he got to the Arnesons' back porch. The tips of his ears were icy cold.

"*Mine himmelin!*" Maria was washing the kitchen floor and she motioned him back from stepping onto it. "Why you be coming home early! Without your coat? You want you should get pneumonia?"

"I don't care." Alex dropped into a corner of the porch and let Queenie climb onto his lap. Her fur was warm and he leaned one side of his face against her side.

Maria made him get up and wash his face in warm water. When he was finished, she held a hand towel she'd warmed on the oven door against his ears. At the kitchen table, as she made a pot of tea, Alex told her about the trip to the principal's office.

"Is not good. I guess you should have been going with Reverend Bergstrom." Maria sighed. She repeated this observation to Karl when he got home.

"Yah." Karl toyed with a spoon in his cup of tea. "But that is spilt milk. We need to think what will be good for Alex now." He gave Alex a small smile. "I am glad you stay with us."

"Is Alex going to leave?" Einar leaned against his father's chair.

"We do not know." Maria put a lid on the stew simmering on the stove and looked at Karl until he couldn't help but meet her gaze. "I think we ask Reverend Bergstrom. There is ladies' tea at church tomorrow. I will talk with him."

"Maybe we should ask Alex what he wants to do," Karl said.

"I could stay here and help Maria." Alex nervously rubbed the scar on his left hand. "I could study here. By myself. In Hamburg when Mama was sick so long, I study by myself."

"It may not be so easy." Karl let Astrid climb onto his lap and gave her a hug. "That principal or Mr. Richards might do some checking. They know where you been staying."

While Maria finished getting supper ready, Karl took his violin from the wall and began playing a song that Alex recognized from hearing Mr. Bayles play it on the gramophone. It had a sweet, haunting melody that seemed to settle everyone's nerves. Even Oleanna quieted down in her high chair and chewed contentedly on the corner of a biscuit.

"That song is about Danny?" Alex got the plates and cutlery for the table.

"'Danny Boy'. That is right." Karl spent a minute tuning a couple of strings on the violin and then began to play a waltz that made Maria stop what she was doing. She turned around, stew ladle in hand, looked at her husband, and shook her head as if the music notes were swarming around her. Alex noticed him wink at her.

Alex's hands were well enough now that he could wash and dry the dishes by himself, a chore he insisted on doing so Maria could relax for a little while before getting the babies ready for bed. He was scrubbing out the stew pot when there was a knock on the door. For a minute there was absolute silence. Even Queenie seemed to catch her breath before going into a barking frenzy. Who would come to the front door? Alex felt a wave of panic wash over him. Police? Mr. Richards or Mr. Edgerton?

But it was Mr. Dallaine who was standing there with Alex's coat and cap in hand.

"It's my teacher," Alex said to Karl. He quickly tried to dry his hands against his trouser legs.

"Einar, put Queenie in back yard." Maria's voice was sharp.

"Do you mind if I come in?" Mr. Dallaine smiled. Along with Alex's coat and cap, he had a briefcase in hand.

"Oh, sure thing." Karl sounded as if he were ashamed of himself for making the teacher stand on the front stoop for even a few seconds. "Come in, Mr. . . . ?"

"Dallaine." He shook Karl's hand. "Mrs. Arneson." He nodded to Maria before catching Alex's attention. "How are you, Alex?"

Alex could feel his lips tremble but there were no words.

"I know. It's been an upsetting day." Mr. Dallaine slipped off his overshoes and let Karl take his overcoat.

"You like coffee, Mr. Dallaine?" Maria was poised to take the babies upstairs. "Hot water is in the kettle," she said to Karl. "Alex, you know where is almond cookies."

"That would be lovely." Mr. Dallaine limped over to a chair at the kitchen table Karl gestured to. "But don't go to any trouble." He nodded at the boys who were standing shyly by their father.

"Einar, I know a little bit because I conduct the chorus at school, and your brother ... ?"

"Gunnar." Karl smoothed Gunnar's cowlick. "Now you boys take homework off table. Enough for tonight."

"Yay!" the two chorused.

"He has a good ear for music, Einar," said Mr. Dallaine.

"Gunnar even more." Karl busied himself at the stove, pouring the boiling water over the coffee grounds. "He will be old enough for choir next year. And to both I will be teaching violin."

Alex took the cookie tin from the cupboard and arranged a few on a china plate decorated with a flower design that Maria liked to use for guests.

"All right, boys," Karl said. "Two cookies each. Take into living room. You can play checkers before bedtime."

"This hits the spot," Mr. Dallaine said. "I worked at school late tonight. I want to apologize for what happened to Alex today. I feel it was in some ways my fault. I know he's been attending under an assumed name." He paused and took another sip of coffee. "I felt he was justified and I continue to believe that. However . . ."

"Going back to school could be not good. Maybe police . . ."

"Exactly." Mr. Dallaine shook his head the same way he did at times when someone's behaviour seemed beyond comprehension. "For that reason, I wish to make a proposal."

Maria had come downstairs and rejoined them. She looked hopefully at the teacher.

"If Alex is in agreement, I will have him stay with me until the weekend and then we'll take the train to Calgary. I've contacted my aunt there and she is quite willing to have Alex live with her and resume his studies under her guidance—at least until his brother is released."

"Is very kind . . ." Maria straightened the cloth on the table and poured herself some coffee.

"My aunt is a kind woman," Mr. Dallaine said. "You're looking at someone she raised when my own mother died when I was a child. And she has little tolerance for injustice. Her gardener, Otto, who came from Germany when he was a boy and is now in his sixties, was taken in for questioning and has to sign in regularly with the authorities—as if he might take up his garden spade and lead an attack against the home front."

"What do you think, Alex?" Karl gave his shoulder a little squeeze.

"You would also be closer to the prisoner of war camp in the mountains. I believe it's near Banff . . ."

"Cave and Basin." Alex found his voice.

"Then it's right in Banff." Mr. Dallaine looked surprised. "Aunt Mattie thought it was out at Castle Mountain. There must be more than one."

"I will go with you." Alex nodded to Mr. Dallaine. "And I will work for your aunt. My hands are better. I am a good worker."

"Don't be worrying about that right now." Mr. Dallaine helped himself to another cookie and gave Maria an appreciative look. "But she'll expect you to work hard on your studies. Unless she's changed a great deal since I stayed with her."

As Alex gathered his things together upstairs, Einar and Gunnar came and sat on the bed.

"Do you have to go?" Gunnar asked.

"I will write you letters." Alex had secured his own letters from Marco in his bag.

"I can write you a letter too." Einar ran his hand along the handle of the packed bag. "We're doing it in school now."

"Me too. I'll write you a letter, Alex." Gunnar began bouncing on the edge of the bed.

"You don't know how."

"Do so."

"Both of you." Alex took a quick look at the babies. Astrid wasn't asleep yet and she stared at him, wide-eyed.

"Bye, little Astrid." He blew her a kiss and she smiled.

It was Maria who hugged him the hardest, though, before he headed out the door with Mr. Dallaine.

"You come back and visit," she said, and there were tears in her eyes.

"With Maria, is an order," Karl reminded him.

Chapter 13

IT WAS BEGINNING to storm as Alex and Mr. Dallaine made their way to the streetcar stop.

"I live in an apartment not far from the legislature," Mr. Dallaine said as they hurried through the snow. "The streetcar stops just a couple of blocks from it."

Fortunately, they didn't have to wait long for the trolley car.

"It's rather beautiful, isn't it?" Mr. Dallaine urged Alex to sit next to the car window, and, as it clacked across the top of the High Level Bridge, he could look out and see the snow eddying around the lights on the banks of both sides of the river.

"I really feel sorry about what happened," Mr. Dallaine said, once they'd shaken the snow off themselves and were in the apartment. "I'm afraid Mr. Edgerton isn't one of my favourite people. There's no love lost between us or he might have come and discussed this whole business with me, but then I understand Eric's dad had been in and taken a strip off him earlier in the day. Men fighting their little wars whenever they have a chance."

Alex looked in wonder at Mr. Dallaine's apartment. It seemed as rich as the rooms inside the Richards house except the furniture wasn't all curlicues and shiny cloth. When Mr. Dallaine turned on a gas radiant, the lights from the flames seemed to scatter over the warm varnished woods of the tables and sofa frames and an upright piano against one wall. There were paintings that Marco would have loved seeing, real paintings of mountains and houses and gardens.

"Sit down, Alex." Mr. Dallaine gestured toward a sofa covered in fabric the golden orange of pumpkins with a variety of different coloured cushions over it. "I'm going to rustle myself up a bite to eat."

He put the kettle on to boil in the kitchen and then reappeared at the parlour door. "Most of the paintings were done by my aunt. The mountains are ones you see around Banff. She has a cottage in the park and in the summer she goes there to paint."

Alex followed Mr. Dallaine back into the kitchen. "I'm just fixing a sandwich. Maybe you'd like one too?"

Alex nodded. He couldn't believe he was suddenly hungry again.

Mr. Dallaine chuckled. "When I was in my teen years I don't think I could ever get enough to eat. My aunt used to declare that I'd eat her out of house and home, and she has a pretty fair-sized home as you'll see when we get to Calgary. Did you travel through Calgary when you and your brother arrived in Canada?"

"No. We are coming another way." Alex watched as Mr. Dallaine cut the sandwiches into quarters and placed them on a couple of china plates that looked like they should have been used only for Sunday dinner. "Saskatoon. Lloydminster. Vermilion. My uncle meets us in Vermilion."

"Ah, yes. The Canadian Northern." He poured tea into cups that matched the plates. "Let's eat in the other room, by the fire. It's definitely a night for it."

Alex was glad Mr. Dallaine gave him a large, cloth napkin. Even with it, he was concerned that he might be dropping crumbs on the sofa or the rug. The sandwich had a kind of cheese and sausage meat that made Alex think of food he'd eaten in Hamburg.

"You'll be all right here tomorrow? You have your books and school supplies so you can do some work and I'll leave a key for you in case you want to go out for a bit, although, if it's really storming, you may not want to. Excuse me if I take off my shoe and put my foot up. It often bothers me when I've been on my feet a lot during the day."

Alex tried to look at other things in the room as the teacher took off his built-up boot and then the other boot and eased the crippled foot onto a footstool.

"Ah, that feels better."

Alex sneaked a quick glance at the odd-shaped stockinged foot on the stool.

"It's a club foot," Mr. Dallaine said without embarrassment. "I was born with it."

"You make piano music?" Alex nodded toward the upright.

"I do." Mr. Dallaine let Alex collect the dishes and take them into the kitchen. "At one time I thought I wanted to be a concert pianist. But I realized at some point that I was never going to be quite good enough, and that's when I decided to become a teacher. Not just a teacher of music but of ideas . . . and stories and poetry. My aunt said it was just as possible to become a virtuoso teacher as a virtuoso pianist."

"Virtu . . . ?"

"First class. Genius." Mr. Dallaine leaned back in his chair and briefly closed his eyes. "How's that for blowing your own horn?"

"You play the horn too?"

"Oh dear, Alex. It's an expression. It'll take a genius to teach you the English language."

The living room sofa collapsed to make a bed, and even though he was more than comfortable with the blankets and an extra pillow Mr. Dallaine gave him, Alex had trouble falling asleep. A light from a street lamp shone through a breach in the curtains of the living room window, making a strip across the floor, catching some of the geometric patterns on the rug.

It seemed that Mr. Dallaine was having trouble falling asleep too. From the crack beneath his bedroom door, Alex could see that the bedroom light stayed on. He was probably reading. Alex thought about turning one of the living room lights back on and reading some in the *Oliver Twist* book, but he wasn't sure where the switch for the light was or where Mr. Dallaine had put his bag.

Finally he did drift off and didn't wake up until Mr. Dallaine was getting his wraps from the hall closet, ready to set out for school.

"Hi, sleepyhead," he said, checking his briefcase. "I'm off now. There's porridge on the stove for breakfast and a sandwich and milk in the icebox for lunch. Fruit in the bowl on the kitchen table. Help yourself—and I'll be home to make supper."

Alex watched from the window as the teacher left the building and struggled through the drifts of snow to the end of the block, and then he crawled under the covers and went to sleep again. It was almost noon, he could see by the mantel clock, when he woke up again.

His books were on the kitchen table along with a note from Mr. Dallaine about which pages to work on in arithmetic, and a chapter to read in a history of North American exploration. He did the arithmetic questions quickly but he had trouble concentrating on the history book. Instead he read another chapter in *Oliver Twist* and spent some time wandering around the apartment, looking at each of the paintings and the photographs displayed on shelves and the top of the piano.

Foremost on the piano, in a silver frame, there was a photo of a middle-aged woman wearing a gigantic hat thick with feathers. From beneath the brim, her eyes stared out at the world with a kind of disarming clarity and there was just the hint of a smile at the edges of her mouth, as if she was privately amused about something. A smile like Mama's, Alex thought.

"Is that your aunt?" Alex asked Mr. Dallaine when he got home.

"Yes," he said fondly. "A few years back. Mathilde Lafontaine. Aunt Mattie. I think she had that photo taken around the time I graduated from university, when I was in Toronto."

"And this is when you are younger?" Alex pointed to a photo beside it of a dark-haired little boy in a sailor suit, sitting in an armchair, one leg crossed over the other, perhaps to hide a misshapen foot.

"None other," Mr. Dallaine laughed. "I hated getting my picture taken—still do. But Aunt Mattie wouldn't put up with my shyness and we had a cousin who was a photographer, so I think I have a portrait for every birthday of my life until I moved out on my own. How about you, Alex? Did your family take pictures?"

"We had some." Alex thought of Mama's and Tato's

wedding picture. There had been, too, a few snapshots a friend of Marco's had taken in Lviv, and one a street photographer in Hamburg had taken of the four of them when they first arrived in the city, while Mama was still well enough for them to go out for walks. "They are burned."

"You lost so much in that fire, didn't you?"

"Yes. Much."

"Now, you must think of what's not lost." Mr. Dallaine eased himself into the armchair as he had last night and put his foot up on the footstool. "You have your brother and, even though no one would wish to be where he is, in some ways he's safe. At least he's not in the trenches. It's ironic— your brother is safe behind barbed wire; I am safe behind my club foot."

"Safe with your foot?"

"No one makes a soldier of a man with a deformed foot."

That evening, Mr. Dallaine played the piano for an hour before it grew too late. Alex felt he could listen forever, music such as he'd never heard before, beautiful and somehow sad. Music that a person might want to gather and keep in the way that Mama gathered flowers from her small garden in Lviv and pressed them in her Bible.

"Mendelssohn. They're called *Songs Without Words*," Mr. Dallaine said. "But I am rusty—I need to practise more."

"Can I write to Marco?" Alex asked as Mr. Dallaine took out a set of papers to mark. "And tell where to write back. In Calgary?"

"Of course. What a good idea. I can mail it tomorrow on my way to school." He let down the desk cover, converting the piece of furniture into a writing table, and took out paper, pen, and a blotter. "There, you're all settled, and I prefer marking papers from my armchair."

In his letter, Alex didn't write much about what happened at school. He had the feeling that he should spare as many unpleasant details as possible from Marco.

My teacher is taking me to Calgary where I shall be living with the aunt of Mr. Dallaine. Maybe I can go to Banff and see you. Are you let to see visitors? I hope the answer is yes. Mr. Dallaine is saying Banff is not a far way from Calgary. On Saturday he will ride with me on the train to Calgary. I hope I will like Aunt Mattie. She has a nice look in the photo on the piano. Some day I wish you will meet Mr. Dallaine who is being so kind. He would like to meet you too. I forget to tell you the aunt paints pictures. So you will like to meet her too I think.

They had to get up early on Saturday to catch the train. It was still dark for their chilly walk to the station, streetlamps casting a glow on the snow piled away from the street and sidewalks.

"I'm glad we don't have to go far in this," Mr. Dallaine muttered through the scarf covering the bottom part of his face.

Alex pulled the flaps of his cap tighter over his ears. After only a few minutes the station loomed above them on a rise over Jasper Avenue. It was a huge chalky building with double rows of windows and a flat roof swept by a wind that sent sprays of snow over them as they approached the entrance.

Inside, they hurried away from the door to a warm corner to set the bags down and loosen their scarves. Alex hadn't been in anything this big since the shipping terminals in Hamburg and Halifax and the train stations in Montreal and Winnipeg.

The lofty-ceilinged waiting room, rather than echoing noise, seemed to create a church-like muting of sound so that a baby crying barely registered. The noise of some men talking together and laughing at a coffee bar was as soft as the smoke that curled from their cigarettes. There were people waiting on benches and others queued before wickets at the ticket counter. Alex stayed by the bags as Mr. Dallaine joined a line.

"They're already boarding," he said, returning with their tickets.

A conductor ushered them up into a passenger coach. They were lucky to find empty seats where they could face one another. Alex felt the train's awkward heaving into action, the chuffing and lurches, vibrating through his bones before it found its pace. It felt good to be moving. With his face pressed to the window, he was surprised to find they were heading over the same bridge they had ridden on earlier in the streetcar, and halfway across the bridge, a streetcar travelled alongside the train. He could see the passengers inside the trolley looking back at him—all of them riding in the sky.

Barely across, the train stopped at another station on the South Side where more passengers got on. Once past the city limits, they chugged through the prairie countryside. With the sun now up, fields gleamed with ice and snow, pinned here and there by small groves of leafless poplars. In the bitter cold, smoke ribboned from the chimneys of farmhouses. At the stations where the train whistled its way in, then paused, making a sound like a great beast straining in confinement, passengers got off and on and people hurried about their tasks on each platform, plumes of frozen breath smudging their faces.

"Few sounds are more mournful than a train whistle, don't you think?" Mr. Dallaine opened a basket he had packed with food for the trip and offered Alex a muffin.

"Also fog horns," Alex said. "In Hamburg when Papa dies, fog is everywhere and boats on the sea are making *whooo-whooo*." Some people had turned to look at him when he imitated the foghorn and Alex blushed. "A noise like it is sad for him," he added.

"Tell me what it was like before you left Galicia. Why did your family decide to leave?"

Alex drew a big breath. Where could he start? "Lviv is a nice city with streetcars and big buildings and many parks.

We go many times to be in the parks and Mama and Tato, that is Papa—go sometimes to a building like the government building in Edmonton where there is singing and music. But we live in a small place. Papa works where bread is made. And cakes and pies. We have not much money. Uncle Andrew writes come to Canada where land is there for free or almost free. You can make a farm, be your own, how do you say it . . ."

"Master?"

"Master. It belongs to you, not somebody else. Marco, he is working doing different things and Mama still teaching some lessons so there is money we can save. Two years we save to take the train, to take the ship. Uncle Andrew is sending us money too. Then it is enough and we go."

Mr. Dallaine closed his eyes for a minute. "It is almost impossible to imagine. Such an undertaking, such a journey." He brushed the muffin crumbs from his coat and then stood up to take their bags down from the overhead rack. "Let's read for a while." He fished out a book he was halfway through along with Alex's copy of *Oliver Twist*. "It makes the time pass. Did you read on those long train journeys you had to get to Alberta?"

"Yes. Reading sometimes newspapers when other people is finished. I am practising to read in English but we have some Ukrainian writing too. And Marco has pencils and drawing paper so he makes drawings."

They read off and on until it began to grow dark and then

they both fell asleep even though the conductor came by and lit lamps in the coach.

Alex woke first. From the window, he could see a distant parade of lights along the skyline.

"Calgary." Mr. Dallaine was awake now too. He covered a yawn and stretched.

"When I telephoned Aunt Mattie, she said she'd send Otto with the car to meet us. I'm glad. I'd hate the idea of waiting for a streetcar in this weather."

In the crowd at the Calgary station, a red-faced man with a bushy white mustache hailed them from across the waiting room.

"Over here, Mr. Dallaine!"

"Otto!"

Alex followed behind his teacher, trying not to bump any-one with his bag.

"Otto, this is Alex, and Alex, Mr. Schaeffer. I was telling Alex how thoughtful it was for you to get the car out in this kind of weather."

"No trouble, Mr. Dallaine." Otto led the way out of the station. An icy blast of air hit them. "Miss Mattie will be happy to see you. She's been in the kitchen most of the day helping Alma. You have not been home since Christmas."

"I know," said Mr. Dallaine, as they got in the car and he wrapped a rug around Alex and himself in the back seat. "But that's only a little over a month ago."

"For your aunt, that is too long." Otto laughed. "She still

can't believe you chose to take a job in Edmonton rather than Calgary."

"Testing my wings," Mr. Dallaine sighed. "Sometimes we need to fly free for a while."

They made their way through downtown streets clogged with snow and traffic to a riverside drive where large houses sat in yards of drifted snow back from the road. Otto pulled off onto a semicircular driveway and parked in front of a house where lights glimmered in most of the front windows.

"We're here!" Mr. Dallaine called once they were inside. "Anyone home?"

A door at the end of the hall opened and a woman hurried toward them, peeling off an apron as she came.

"Martin!" She enveloped Mr. Dallaine in a hug. "The train must've been terribly late. And this must be Alex." She released her nephew and hugged Alex. The lace edging on her blouse tickled his nose. He inhaled a bouquet of powder and a flowery perfume. "Welcome, Alex. Martin's told me all you've been through."

She stood back from him, but still grasping his arms. "You're a good-looking lad for all you've been scorched around the edges."

Alex was looking at Aunt Mattie too. She was older than the woman in the piano picture or maybe the photographer had used his art to get rid of some of the wrinkles. But then Mr. Dallaine had said it had been taken a few years earlier. Her hair, wound into a bun on the top of her head, was mostly grey with just a hint of the reddish-brown it must once have been. Here and there a strand escaped the confines of the bun, and the one drifting down her forehead onto her nose she tried impatiently to secure in place once she released Alex.

"You must be famished. Dinner will be on the table in two shakes but you'll have time to freshen up, and Martin, you can show Alex his room. I thought he could have your old room and you could take the guest bedroom for this visit."

Alex followed Mr. Dallaine up a curving staircase to the second floor.

"This was mine for a good part of my life," he said, opening the door to a small bedroom with a bookshelf on one wall and a desk beneath the window. "It gets the morning sun, and it's right next to a study that you can use as a school-room. There's a globe in there and a small library, and a window seat that's perfect for reading. Even the small piano I used to practice on."

The bathroom was down the hall and Alex carefully washed his hands and face and tried to tame his curls with water on his comb. He worked carefully at the last bits of scabbing on his face. Most of the crust had peeled off, leaving puckered skin the colour of borscht. He was glad the burns on his hands were pretty well healed over too.

In the dining room, the table was set for five. Mr. Dallaine looked questioningly at his aunt.

"It's a celebration. I asked Alma and Otto to join us."

The two emerged from the kitchen bearing platters of food. Alex looked wide-eyed at the feast. Roast beef and some kind of puffy biscuits over which Alma drizzled a rich gravy. Mashed potatoes, creamed peas, cabbage salad and pickled beets.

"Otto's been finding out about the mountain camp." Aunt Mattie urged Alex to take a third piece of roast. "He knows a couple of people who've been interned."

"They were in tents at Castle Mountain." Otto paused from slicing his meat. "Almost freezing before they decided to move the camp to Banff at the Cave and Basin. Half-starved, working without boots. Quite a few ran off the first chance they got."

"What happens?" Alex swallowed a forkful of the biscuit and gravy Mr. Dallaine called Yorkshire pudding. "When they run away. What happens?"

"Some've been shot by the guards. Some picked up by search parties. Some disappear into the mountains." Otto shook his head sadly.

"My nephew, Bernhard," Alma noted indignantly, "he is behind barbed wire simply because he was forced into the army for a couple of years when he was a young man, not even nineteen, in the old country. The last thing he wants to be again is a soldier for Austria."

"I think it's dreadful." Aunt Mattie waved her fork in the air as if it were a weapon. "Calling these poor people 'enemy aliens.' Most of them did everything they could to get away from places of oppression and injustice and poverty. That's why they came to Canada. Talk about taking advantage . . ."

"I think it would be wise for Alex to have a different last name while he's staying here," Mr. Dallaine suggested later, when Alma served the dessert, which turned out to be apple strudel topped with a thick cap of whipped cream. "And it might be wise not to use the name you used in Edmonton. Maybe pretend you are Norwegian again—just don't talk much if anyone is checking you out. Did you know Norwegian men changed their name with each generation before they came to Canada? What's your father's name, Alex?"

"My father is Stephan."

"Well, there it is. I christen you Alexander Stephanson."

Chapter 14

∽

MR. DALLAINE HAD taken Monday off from teaching, pleading a doctor's appointment. Sunday, they accompanied Aunt Mattie to church and spent the afternoon with newspapers and books. Mr. Dallaine went over Alex's schoolwork with his aunt.

"Especially, he needs to practise composition." Mr. Dallaine was writing down topics that they would want him to write about, not just history and current events, but personal thoughts too. Alex tried to pretend that he was not listening, but it was finally too much and he escaped to his room.

In the evening, Mr. Dallaine played the piano for a couple of hours in the parlour. One of the pieces, sweet and somehow sad with a part that sounded, Alex thought, like a sudden summer rainstorm, brought tears to Aunt Mattie's eyes.

"*Liebestraum*," she sighed. "By Franz Liszt, my husband Emile's favourite."

Alex had coffee with Mr. Dallaine before he left to go back to Edmonton on Monday. Aunt Mattie fussed over her nephew in the dining room, renewing an old argument about why he should be teaching in Calgary rather than Edmonton as Alma brought in scones and blueberry jam.

"You could be here and have Alma cook for you and then you might not look like such a scarecrow." She shook her head and eyed a buttered scone as if it were part of some conspiracy to keep her nephew away.

"I like Edmonton. I like being on my own." Mr. Dallaine sighed. "I leave you Alex to look after."

"I love having Alex," Mrs. Lafontaine said, reaching over and gently patting Alex's hand. "But why can't I have both of you?"

"I'll come back down in a couple of weeks to see how things are going."

"At least, with you here, Alex, I think he'll be making more frequent visits," Aunt Mattie declared at the schoolroom window as they watched the car drive off. She moved around the room, spinning the globe, taking a book off one of the shelves, opening it and then replacing it, straightening a stack of writing paper on the desk.

"I was a teacher before I married Emile Lafontaine," she said. "I was actually Emile's teacher. It was quite a scandal when I married him. There are probably still people in Toronto talking about that!"

"He is dead?" Alex ran a finger along the smooth oak edge of the desk.

"He died in the last year of the last century. I did so want him to see this new one, although with the world the way it is now, perhaps it's better he didn't."

"My mother was a teacher too." Alex plucked a straight pen out of a clay container by the writing paper and felt the nib tip with the end of a finger.

"Was she?"

"She teached before my birth for the Malyki family who owned a big house and much land outside of Lviv."

"A governess?"

"Yes. Teaching little children of the Malyki family. They are rich Polish people. My father worked there in the fields. That is where they meet."

"You know, Alex, I think we will be good company for each other. You can work on your lessons and I have canvasses to paint. I'm working on one now. Come and see." She turned an easel facing into a corner around. On it was a partly finished oil painting of a lake at the foot of a large mountain, with a range of peaks in the background.

"Oh, that is beautiful. The paintings at Mr. Dallaine's— they are also beautiful."

"I studied in France," Aunt Mattie mused. "A year in France. It was a gift from Emile for our tenth anniversary. What a wonderful year! He came to spend time with me twice, although he was very busy with his company. The weeks we had in Paris! Such memories feed us and keep us alive, don't they, Alex?"

She was an early riser, Alex discovered, and was often in the study, busy working on a canvas when he came in to tackle his schoolwork. As she painted, she had him read aloud from *Oliver Twist*.

"One of the best ways for you to develop a feel for the language," she informed him, "is to read from the masters. Listen to the rhythms and the cadence; savour the vocabulary. Now read that paragraph again and pay attention to where Dickens has inserted commas. Every comma offers you an opportunity to pause and survey the road ahead."

Much of what Aunt Mattie had to say was a mystery to Alex but he grew to love being with her. Sometimes, as she watched him struggling with a piece of prose or frowning over the outcome of an arithmetic problem, she would break into laughter, startling him from his work.

"Don't be so serious, dear boy." She'd shake her head and laugh. "Part of being human is being able to relax and laugh, remember with delight things in the past, engage the present with vigour, and anticipate the future. I saw that poem 'Invictus' that Martin had you copy out in your scribbler. It's all very fine for William Ernest Henley to go on about horrors and darkness and the menace of the years, but he should mention that one of the things that keeps our souls unconquerable is a good laugh now and then."

Alex didn't have the heart to ask her what she was talking about. When it came to science and arithmetic, even Aunt Mattie was hard-pressed to find anything to smile about, but she was a good teacher and Alex could feel that he was catching up quickly.

Like her nephew, she loved music and took him to a recital one evening in early February. Alex wore a shirt that had belonged to Mr. Dallaine when he was a boy, a white bow tie that Aunt Mattie found somewhere, his black Christmas vest and the dark flannel trousers Maria had made for him. Alma had curled Aunt Mattie's hair and she wore feathers that stuck up from a jewelled band that circled her head. There were more jewels at her neck. She had a dark velvet cape that she slung carelessly over the back of a chair in the concert hall.

Alex felt as if he were sitting beside a queen.

They were both enthralled by the Schubert music.

"He was poor all his life," Aunt Mattie told Alex over hot chocolate after the concert. "But the people who knew him said he had a wonderful spirit and a sweetness of nature that was unforgettable. And such a drive to create! He died so young—only thirty-one—and yet, when you think what he accomplished . . ."

In Alex's mind, the recital music continued to run and cascade. He nodded his head.

"That last piece we heard is sometimes called *The Trout*. It always makes me think of a fish on its journey along a mountain stream, swirls and eddies and leaps. My husband, Emile, loved to fish, and two years before he died he had a cottage built in Banff. We called it The Aerie—our own little mountain nest. He would fish and I'd tag along with my sketchbook. Sometimes, if it wasn't too difficult to hike, Martin would come along too. He would have been twelve or thirteen. So, Alex, you can imagine the trio—Emile out in a stream with his wading boots on, rod in hand, Martin and me somewhere on the bank, me trying to capture the scene in charcoal or watercolours, Martin lost in one of the books he packed along wherever he went."

"It was a good time?" Alex looked at Aunt Mattie's face, the half-smile on her lips as she relived the past, complete with a child and a husband.

"Yes, Alex, my dear." She reached over and put her fingers gently over his left hand. "It was a good time." She traced the pattern of the burn. "I think I'll have Dr. Abraham come over and look at your burns this coming week, just to make sure everything has healed all right. He's a family friend."

"Nature's done its work nicely," the doctor told Alex and Aunt Mattie after he'd checked Alex over thoroughly the following Wednesday. "Something people have been dealing with in country cottages for centuries—burns. And some of the old wives' remedies work as well as anything. Lavender and honey and even boiled potato peelings."

The doctor, a thin olive-skinned man with a shock of black, wavy hair, had taken Aunt Mattie up on her offer of a glass of sherry, and she had joined him and even poured Alex a thimbleful.

"You have not become part of the great movement by the ladies of the province for total temperance?" Dr. Abraham smiled as he held the cut crystal sherry glass up so it caught the window light.

"You know me, Aaron," Aunt Mattie laughed, "I'm not likely to join any kind of stampede. Stay out of the way of the buffaloes, I've always said."

"Wise woman." The doctor turned his attention to Alex. "Mattie tells me you have a brother in the internment camp at Banff."

"Yes," Alex said. "He is moved there from Lethbridge. To do work, I think."

The doctor sighed. "I've had two cases of TB from the Castle Mountain camp sent here to the hospital. They're pretty badly off before the camp doctor releases them for treatment. But if your brother is strong and healthy . . ."

"Marco is when I last see him. Strong and healthy."

"It's ridiculous, scandalous." Aunt Mattie drained her glass. "Rounding up farmers and miners and men desperately searching for work. Corralling them behind barbed wire like cattle. When I was in Banff in August, there were even excursions by some of the tourists to go to Castle Mountain and look at them as if they were animals in a zoo. The commandant's wife would serve them tea from her tent as part of the outing, if you can believe it."

When the doctor had finished his sherry and left, Alex stayed in the drawing room with Aunt Mattie. He had with him a book of Robert Browning's poetry she had given him to read—for "the sound of the ways in which English words can work together." Alex was thinking more, though, of the words that had passed between Aunt Mattie and the doctor. Did the prisoners have barbed wire around them at the Cave and Basin too? Were tourists stopping by to stare at Marco and Ivan and the others?

Aunt Mattie, who was reading the newspaper, snorting every few minutes at something that struck her as absurd, put the paper down when she saw that Alex was lost in worry.

"What's troubling you, Alex?"

"The days," Alex said. "All the days I have sent Marco a letter and no letter has come from him."

"We really have no idea how the mail works in a prisoner-of-war camp," Aunt Mattie tried to reassure him. "Perhaps they send letters out only once a week."

"He would write at the first chance."

"Give it a few more days. I'm sure a letter must be on its way at this very minute."

But at the end of two weeks, when Mr. Dallaine came down on the weekend, there was still no word from Marco.

"I think bad is happening," Alex confided to the teacher. "Maybe Marco is very sick . . ."

Mr. Dallaine sighed. "It is perplexing. We might try writing the commandant or telephoning the camp, but the attention it might focus on your brother may not necessarily be a good thing and I'm not sure they'd even entertain responding to civilian enquiries about prisoners."

It was Aunt Mattie who came up with a plan, announcing it over the roasted chicken on Saturday night.

"If there is no letter by Monday, Alex and I will take the train to Banff."

"Do you think you should?" Alex could see that Mr. Dallaine was trying to think ahead, imagining what would happen when they got to Banff. "You should send Otto down a day early to take down shutters, thaw the place out. It's pretty cold."

"What do you think, Alex?" Aunt Mattie looked at him from across the table, candlelight reflecting off her glasses. "Would you feel better if we went to Banff?"

"Oh, yes," Alex said.

Alone with Alex in the classroom, Mr. Dallaine had a look at Alex's work in composition and listened to him recite a few lines from Shakespeare:

Full many a glorious morning have I seen
Flatter the mountain tops with sovereign eye,
Kissing with golden face the meadows green,
Gilding pale streams with heavenly alchemy . . .

"Excellent." He clapped his hands. "And you've written to the Arnesons. Einar told me when we had choir practice this week. That was thoughtful."

"I have written to Mr. Bayles as well. If any letters come from Marco, I have asked him to send them on. I would like to write to Mrs. Eddy and Myrtle, her little girl, just to let them know what is happening now in my life, but I think I better not."

"Because of the older girl?"

"Yes, Liz. I think she would like to shoot me."

"Well, I'm not sure that's the case." Mr. Dallaine tested the keys on the little piano. "But it's probably wise to keep your whereabouts secret. This piano is very out of tune."

When Otto brought the car around and it was time for Mr. Dallaine to go, Alex rode with him to the station.

"I know it bothers you to be accepting so much from Aunt Mattie," Mr. Dallaine said as they pulled into the parking lot, "but you need to realize, Alex, that you are giving, as well, to my aunt."

"Giving?"

"She's been lonesome these last few years. And she's always been one to take up a cause. I guess I inherited that from her. I think you've become a good companion and you've become the focal point for a cause she has come to care about passionately."

Alex thought about what Mr. Dallaine had said as Otto drove home. It was as if Aunt Mattie were part of the wind that had blown himself and Marco across half the world,

part of that force that hadn't yet dropped them as it had their
parents and Uncle Andrew. It made him feel as if he could
look out and see the great lighted stretch of Calgary below
him and the railway tracks taking Mr. Dallaine to Edmonton
and that other track heading west to Banff.

Yes.

To Banff.

Chapter 15

BY THE TIME ALEX and Aunt Mattie headed to Banff, the weather had grown milder. From the coach window of the train, Alex watched as the snowcapped mountains drew closer. Once they were actually in the Rockies, his breath was almost taken away by the towering peaks. In places, even the clouds seemed to be pierced, and mist unravelled along the upper slopes. From the storms of the past weeks, a deep snow covered the Bow River Valley and branches of evergreens were still laden with snow.

"I'm glad I brought my sketchpad along," Aunt Mattie said as the locomotive rumbled through the mountainscape. "It's quite amazing, isn't it, Alex?"

"Amazing." More and more he was picking up Aunt Mattie's words, weighing them, trying them out.

Otto met them at the station in Banff with a hired sleigh and team.

"Oh good." Aunt Mattie sorted out luggage and food hampers on the platform. "You knew I'd end up bringing the kitchen sink, didn't you, Otto?"

The kitchen sink? Alex decided not to ask about it. As he breathed in the fresh mountain air, he was struck by the fact that somewhere close by, within a mile or two, Marco would be drawing breath from this same mass of air. In his mind, he felt he could reach out and touch him. Finally. Alex wanted to shout but he didn't. He helped Otto load the back of the sleigh.

The Aerie was twice the size of Uncle Andrew's farmhouse. It looked like mountain stone had been used as a base for the log walls. The roof, with its wide overhang, was covered with a perfect cap of snow. Inside, Otto had a fire going in the fireplace as well as the kitchen stove, and the rooms were snug and warm.

After Alex had settled into one of the small bedrooms, Aunt Mattie insisted they have tea and something to eat before venturing out.

"We need to think this out carefully," she told Alex as they nibbled on biscuits and egg salad Alma had sent along. "If the prisoners are being kept at the Cave and Basin, there's going to be sentries all around it and we don't want to be noticed if we have to keep going back. I think today we will simply be sightseers out for a stroll, happening to stumble on the site. Get a feel of how it is set up."

"They don't work on Sundays," Otto noted. "I was able to find that out from the man who rented us the sleigh."

It was late in the afternoon when they set out from the cottage, walking first to Banff Avenue and then crossing the river.

"Keep to our right here, Alex," Aunt Mattie said once they were over the bridge, "that'll keep us on the Cave Road; that other one goes to the Banff Springs Hotel."

They were by a recreational area, with park benches poking out of the snowdrifts, when Alex looked back and saw them coming—what looked like a parade of prisoners, marching in pairs, guards in uniform at the head and back of the line.

As they came closer, one of the guards in front nodded at Aunt Mattie. Alex's heart seemed to have lodged up in his throat. For a minute he could barely breathe. Could Marco be among them? But as they trooped by, he could see there was no one of Marco's height and build. No Marco. But there was something familiar about one of the prisoners at the end of the line, though, just in front of the rear guard.

Ivan.

He looked wide-eyed at Alex and half-stopped until the guard behind hollered at him to keep moving. As he continued on, he looked back briefly. Aunt Mattie and Alex watched them disappear down the road toward the springs.

"That was Ivan." Alex clutched the sleeve of Aunt Mattie's coat.

"The one who looked at you?"

"Yes. Ivan, who took me in the train car with coal to Edmonton. Do you think he comes every day this way?"

"Most likely." Aunt Mattie had caught some of his own excitement. "He must know if your brother is all right."

They continued along the Cave Road, both of them lost in thought, stopping when two other work parties returned from park sites. Alex searched the faces as they passed. But Marco was not among them.

The Cave and Basin pavilion was fronted by huge stone walls surrounding two pillared towers with broad octagonal roofs. Tower tops that looked exotic, almost like the roofs he'd seen in pictures of Japanese pagodas.

"This is where the swimming pool is," Aunt Mattie said. "Obviously there are no prisoners here. Let's go around to the side."

As they rounded the corner of the pavilion, they saw two guards positioned in front of what looked like a station house.

Aunt Mattie began trekking toward them and Alex followed in her wake.

"Is this the way to the Springs Hotel?" she asked the nearest sentry.

"No, Ma'am." The guard smiled at her. He was a young man with apple cheeks who looked like he was trying to grow a moustache. "You're on the wrong road altogether. This here's the Cave and Basin—for the hotel you need to veer left after the bridge. But the hotel's closed up in the winter."

"Are you guarding the Cave and Basin?" Aunt Mattie feigned amazement.

"Not the swimming pool in the Cave and Basin, Ma'am. But there's about three hundred prisoners of war in back of us and that's what we're guarding."

"Oh my!" Aunt Mattie clutched at her bosom, as if she expected to be momentarily assaulted. "Aren't they behind walls?"

"Don't you fret, Ma'am," the guard assured her. "The prisoners' barracks are surrounded with barbed wire and secure gates—it just looks open here where we are, so the attractiveness of the pavilion ain't spoiled. Any enemy alien that's looking to escape will find himself staring down the barrel of a gun."

"Well, you do put my heart at ease." Aunt Mattie heaved a sigh. "And thank you for your directions to the hotel. We've heard it's a beautiful edifice and we wanted to view it. I have no idea how we could have become so lost."

As they headed back, Aunt Mattie said, "Do you think Ivan might try to talk to you, or get a message to you?"

"Maybe he would," Alex decided. "But how, with the guards?"

"I'm not sure. But it might be worthwhile for you to be here when the work party returns tomorrow."

That night, Alex found it hard to sleep. He even thought about getting up and dressing, then going down to the Cave and Basin. Perhaps hiding in the trees he could see in the distance beyond where the prisoners' barracks must be. But what would he accomplish? He'd be able to see the barracks. He would be closer to where Marco actually was. But that would be all.

When he did fall asleep, he slept through until close to noon. Aunt Mattie had gone out but she was back for the lunch of roast beef sandwiches Otto set out on the dining room table. Tea was steeping in a pot with a Chinese design.

"I went and visited Mrs. Billingsgate." Aunt Mattie poured the tea. "She lives here year round and, if anyone knows anything about what's going on in the town, it's Anthea Billingsgate. She said there's work parties all over the place. Working on the roads. Fixing up the grounds here and there. Building a bridge over the Spray River. In her words, you can't turn around without bumping into an enemy alien. She says her husband keeps a gun by their bed at night he's so sure something dreadful is going to happen."

"Marco, he is maybe working somewhere in Banff?"

"It's possible." Aunt Mattie passed the sandwiches to Alex. "Why don't we just walk around the town? Maybe stroll to the Banff Springs Hotel. We'll keep an eye on the clock, and I think you should go over to the Cave and Basin around the same time as yesterday, where we saw the work party heading back. Just in case Ivan has figured out some way to communicate with you. I'll let you go by yourself, though. I don't think the guards paid much attention to you but they'd take notice if they saw me again."

During their walk, they didn't see any prisoners working within the town site itself, and Aunt Mattie headed back to the cottage to help Otto fix supper while Alex walked to the recreation park where the work detail had passed by. When he saw them coming, he put his jacket collar up, pulled his cap down well over his eyes, and pretended to walk in the same direction they were moving.

As they caught up to him, a guard called out, "Work party coming through," and Alex stepped to the side of the road. He could see that Ivan was in the same position he'd been in the day before, and, once Ivan spotted him, he stumbled and fell.

"Get up, you clumsy fool," a guard yelled at him. As Ivan struggled up again, the guard prodded him with his rifle. "Stupid bohunk, you should be able to keep one foot in front of the other."

Ivan didn't look back this time, but Alex knew the stumble hadn't been accidental. When the work party was out of sight, he walked cautiously over to the place where Ivan had collapsed. Alex could see, from under a clump of snow, the edge of a piece of paper. He quickly grabbed it, brushed off the snow, tucked it into his pocket, and hurried to a corner by the bridge where a street lamp had come on.

The note had been scribbled in pencil, and it was written in Ukrainian.

Dear Alex,

What a surprise to see you by the Cave Road yesterday when we were coming back from working. I know you must be worried to death about Marco. We are all worried. Shortly after we got here from Lethbridge, Marco got into a fight with a guard. The guard was making Marco go to work when he was sick with the flu and called him a name. Marco got mad, swung at the guard, and the guard hit him with his gun. In the end, Marco got sent to the hoosegow for three weeks. He was let out two days ago but I barely know him. He has lost so much weight and he is coughing bad. Right now he is in the hospital. If he does not get out of here, I think he will die. Our best hope, I believe, is to run off when we are going to work into the trees which are very thick along the way. Prisoners have done it before and a few have got away. First he must become better enough to go with me on the gang, though. I will try and visit him in the hospital tonight.

Your good friend

He hadn't signed the note, Alex suspected, in case it did fall into the hands of a guard. After reading it, Alex hurried back to the cottage.

Aunt Mattie was helping Otto cut up vegetables and Alex could smell meat being braised in a big pot on the stove.

"He is in the hospital!" He got out of his boots and coat as quickly as he could and hurried over to the kitchen table to show Aunt Mattie the letter. "Ivan made a little fall to the ground when the workers were coming back and this I find beneath some snow."

"Has Marco been hurt?" Aunt Mattie put aside the cabbage and the chopping board to examine the letter. "I think you'll have to interpret this for me, Alex."

"Oh! Of course." For a few seconds he'd forgotten that there was no way she could read the note.

After he had translated the letter for her, she exclaimed, "How terrible for your brother. Locked up for three weeks in some dreadful hole. If he's as sick as Ivan says, you'd think they might put him in the Brett Hospital here in town—but they must have their own infirmary."

"I must do something." In a way, the news about Marco made him feel as if he'd been burned all over again. Fresh wounds.

"Tomorrow's Friday," Aunt Mattie said, more to herself than Alex and Otto. "Somehow we're going to have to watch that work party to see if Marco manages to join them Friday or Saturday. Of course, if he's well enough to work, they might send him off on one of the other crews—unless Ivan can do some manoeuvring."

On Friday some children were building a snowman in the park by the Cave Road and they allowed Alex to join in. When the work gang trooped by, Alex looked over and saw Ivan shake his head "no." Alex held a crooked branch up high for a second in response before attaching it to the torso of the snowman as an arm.

Aunt Mattie decided to come with him again on Saturday. She wore a different coat—this one was fur—and a hat with a veil that she used to cover most of her face. They walked as far as the Cave and Basin and mixed with a cluster of sight-seers at the pavilion as the work gangs made their way to the prisoners' compound. Several parties had gone by when Alex spotted the one with Ivan.

He was, Alex could see, keeping his spot toward the end of the line, and beside him was . . . Alex couldn't be sure until they were almost beside them, but yes, it was Marco.

"Marco!" The name escaped from Alex's lips. He wanted to run to the line of prisoners and grab hold of him, but Aunt Mattie suddenly linked her arm with his. Marco must have heard him. As he paused, one of the rear guards looked over at the group of them, and Aunt Mattie steered Alex toward the other visitors and began talking animatedly to a lady in a fur hat who was showing her sister-in-law the sights of the town.

"I'm an artist," Aunt Mattie told the woman. "The winter landscape here is quite spectacular and I'm determined to capture some scenes in oil. This is my nephew, Alex."

Alex nodded to the lady before turning his head to watch the prisoners disappearing around the corner of the pavilion.

The lady in the fur hat shook her head. "I find it very disturbing that they have these convicts going back and forth right in front of decent people. If they must have them here, there should be a back route for them to take to their camp."

"Come, Alex, we'd best be going."

She clung to his arm as they made their way down the steps and back onto the road.

"Marco," Alex whispered. "To see him . . ."

"I know." Aunt Mattie held his arm a bit tighter for a minute. "You've travelled such a long way to find him."

"But he is so thin!"

"Now that he is out of the camp jail and they've treated him in the infirmary, he'll get stronger with each day," Aunt Mattie reassured him.

"Ivan has the fear that he might not live," Alex reminded her.

They walked in silence across the bridge.

"Ivan, I think, will do all he can to look after him," Aunt Mattie said as they turned onto their street. "And you can write to him again, now, and know he'll be allowed to write to you in return. It should only take a day for the post office to process mail from right here in town."

As Otto served up reheated stew for supper, Alex tried to concentrate on a Tennyson poem Aunt Mattie suggested he memorize while she transferred a drawing from her sketchbook, outlining the details in blue paint on a newly primed canvas.

Alex turned Tennyson face down on an end table. "I will watch the camp tomorrow. From the back where the fence is.

Maybe Marco will be walking inside the yard. Maybe he will come close to the fence."

"I'm not sure that's wise, dear," Aunt Mattie said. "If you're spotted by a guard while trying to communicate . . . well, let's just say you risk being arrested. And they wouldn't keep you here. You're much younger than any of the other prisoners. But remember there are other camps all across Canada and, in some of them, there are children."

"I will hide. I will only come close if there is no guards by the fence."

"I won't forbid you," she added as Otto called them for supper. "But, as I said, I think it very unwise. I suppose it's difficult to be wise when you're this close."

The next morning Alex set off at about ten o'clock. Otto helped him make some sandwiches and packed them along with a small bottle of milk in a knapsack. Alex made a wide circle around the Cave and Basin, scrambling along the hillside, his boots plunging through the snow, finally finding more level ground close to the river west of the pavilion.

It seemed like an endless wait until the prisoners were allowed to exercise. From his hiding spot in a stand of pine trees, Alex could see they were heavily guarded. In fact, it looked like some official was reviewing the camp. Guards stood at attention and saluted him as he went by. For an instant, Alex thought he spotted Marco, at least someone a bit taller than most of the prisoners, his hat off, blonde hair catching sunlight. But only for an instant. The guards weren't allowing anyone near the fence. All too soon everyone was being herded back into the barracks.

Weary and disappointed, Alex trudged back to The Aerie. Aunt Mattie caught his eye as he came in but didn't say anything. She was rolling pastry on a piece of oilcloth on the kitchen table. The smudge of flour on her nose made Alex smile.

"You have a white end on your nose," he said.

"Oh, most likely." Aunt Mattie laughed. "I never could bake anything without getting well dusted with flour. How'd you make out?"

Alex recounted his hours of waiting.

"I'm not surprised the place was swarming with guards." Aunt Mattie trimmed the dough she'd pressed in to line a baking dish. "Anthea Billingsgate came by for tea this afternoon and said there was a brigadier general touring the camp today. Seems a guard died from flu a couple of weeks ago after he'd been left ailing in a bunkhouse for a week and then taken to the Brett Hospital in an open cart when it was extremely cold and snowy. There's a full-scale investigation. She thinks the brigadier general's there, too, because there was an escape by one of the prisoners last Monday while he was out doing park work."

"They escape?"

"Well, one escaped. In the fall, before Major Spence took

over, she said they were disappearing right and left whenever a guard so much as blinked."

What Aunt Mattie had said about the escaped prisoner stuck in Alex's mind as he penned a letter to Marco after supper. Reviewing all that had happened since he last wrote, but keeping in mind that a warden might be reading his every word, he made no mention of their staying in Banff. He ended by describing The Aerie as if it were a house on the edge of Calgary, using the Ukrainian words for "rock" and "logs."

> It is nice where I am staying and working. The house has kameinya around the bottom and kolody for walls. It is the last house on the street with trees and countryside beyond. Do you remember the colour of Mama's scarf she wore to church? The door and window trim is just that colour. I think of her every time I go out or come in.

He mailed the letter the next morning and every day he made certain he was somewhere along the Cave Road or the pavilion when the work party went by. Always, he stole a glance to see if Marco and Ivan were still in the line. On Wednesday, it looked as though they were there and Marco was pantomiming reading a letter. On Friday, when Alex returned to The Aerie, there was a letter forwarded from their Calgary address. Marco didn't say anything about being in the camp jail but wrote that he was happy to be out of the hospital and working on the rock-crushing crew with Ivan.

It is good to know where you are, Alex. It sounds like such a nice house and good people you live with. I am hoping we see you soon. Ivan too.

Alex showed the letter to Aunt Mattie.

"First chance," he said, "I think they will escape."

"And you've pretty well drawn them a map to The Aerie. Let's hope the guards don't keep track of such bits of information from letters." Aunt Mattie sounded a bit cross. But when she saw the stricken look on Alex's face, she patted his arm and said, "They've got over three hundred prisoners there. I'm sure they're not combing every letter for innuendo. But you have to realize, Alex, that prisoners have been shot and killed attempting to escape. Moreover, some who get away are caught immediately. And," she sighed, "there might be very serious consequences for anyone harbouring an escapee."

Chapter 16

ᴏɴ ꜱᴜɴᴅᴀʏ, Alex walked down to the Cave and Basin pavilion. From a vantage point at the edge of the structure, he could see the soldiers on parade. There were several other boys there, intrigued with the display, and Alex stayed with the group as they scrambled around later to look at the prisoners in the compound during their recreational period. The guards were more relaxed than they had been on the Sunday before, Alex noticed, and one of them chatted for a couple of minutes by the fence with the oldest boy in the group.

He looked like he was a couple of years older than Alex—someone called him Booth—and he lit a cigarette and held the pack out to the guard who said, "Thanks, mate," setting down his rifle long enough to get one lit for himself.

"How'd you get stuck with this job?" Booth asked him.

"Don't ask me," the guard complained. "Might as well be guarding cattle. Most of us have been begging to be relieved, get over to where the action is, where you can actually shoot the buggers."

"Yeah." Booth blew an elaborate smoke ring. "This must bore you out of your skull."

"I guess someone's gotta do it." The soldier sighed and then chuckled. "Every once in a while we get to do a little bayonet practice. Remind them who's running things." Then he saw that another guard was watching them.

"You better push off, kids," he said. He flicked his cigarette butt into the snow and held his rifle in parade position again.

As they turned to go, Alex saw Marco and Ivan just a few paces away from the guards. It was hard not to go running back to the fence, but Alex remained standing where he was and half raised his hand in a mittened wave.

The two grinned back at him. Ivan looked as sturdy as he had when they'd scrambled into a car in Vermilion. But Marco was gaunt, even thinner than he'd been when they were in Hamburg, when he was eighteen, before he'd gained a man's body working in the fields with Uncle Andrew. His cheeks were hollow and his hair was matted, raggedly cut. As he smiled, Alex could see he'd lost one of his front teeth.

When he realized the other kids were watching him, Alex turned and joined them as they straggled up the slope back of the compound.

"Who're you?" a freckle-faced boy asked him.

"Alex." He picked up a dead branch as if he might join a couple of the other boys who'd become engaged in a mock sword duel with branches they'd found.

"Alex Stephanson."

"What happened to your face?"

"Don't ask so many questions." Another boy gave the freckle-faced boy a shove. "You can see he was burned."

Alex ran on ahead and was relieved when he was past the pavilion entrance and the other boys were out of sight.

Later, as he went over the events of the day with her, Aunt Mattie added finishing touches to her painting while there was still some afternoon light coming in through the west windows.

"I think you're right." She set her brush down and stood back to look at the picture. "The more I think about it, I believe they are going to try to make a break for it. Imagine using bayonets on those men. Someone should talk to the brigadier general about that."

"I think they will try to come here." Alex knew, from what she'd said the day before, that Aunt Mattie was thinking the same thing. "What will we do?"

"If they make it?" Aunt Mattie put her brushes tip-end into a small jar of turpentine. "Put these out on the porch, will you, Alex."

She was taking off her painting smock when he returned.

"I don't think we can plan too much ahead on anything," she said. "What are their chances of evading the guards? If they do get away into the bush, there will be search parties looking for them. Imagine trying to make your way back into town and then finding The Aerie, a house they've never seen, without being noticed."

Alex helped move the easel to the corner of the room.

"Mind you, according to Anthea Billingsgate, there have been quite a few who did get away and have never been caught. We have to wonder where they found sanctuary."

There were groups of prisoners working on the recreation grounds by the Cave Road on Monday and Tuesday, so Alex waited up by the pavilion entrance again, tagging on to clusters of sightseers when possible. On Tuesday, as Ivan and Marco's party went by, Ivan made a quick thumbs up gesture when he spotted Alex.

When he got home, Alex found Aunt Mattie by the fire in the living room. "I think maybe soon, maybe tomorrow."

"We've been getting things ready." Aunt Mattie put down the newspaper she had been reading. "Take your coat off, Alex, and come in here and warm up."

"I am scared." Alex sank into a chair. "Maybe best they don't try. Maybe war will be ended soon and everyone goes home. But Marco, he is so thin. And sick. I think he has a bad sickness."

"It is a great concern," said Aunt Mattie. "And who knows how long this terrible war will continue. Only Marco himself can decide if it is worth the risk. But there is nothing we can do now except wait—and be ready."

Wait, Alex wondered, how would it be possible to get

through the coming hours—maybe days until the right time came?

Otto, seeing how anxious Alex was becoming, said, "We will now have supper—I have made a special dish, *Jäger Ein-topf*, so we should eat." He tamped down the tobacco in his pipe.

"It's a sort of shepherd's pie and quite delicious," said Aunt Mattie.

"And then you and I will play cribbage," said Otto. "It will make the time go faster."

Otto had been teaching him the game since they came to Banff. Alex tried hard to concentrate on the counting involved once supper was done and Otto brought the cribbage board and cards out. Was there anyone more patient than the German handyman? Aunt Mattie kept glancing up from the book she was reading, smiling as Otto patiently helped him figure out the scores of each hand.

On Wednesday, Alex couldn't wait and went early to the Cave Road end of the bridge. Snow had begun to fall, a soft, gentle snow. So beautiful, Alex thought, as it built up on the benches and tree branches. He scuffed through the fresh downfall along the walkway. How long would he have to wait for the work party to return? Perhaps a half hour? But he had only been there for about ten minutes when he saw a crew being hurried back ahead of time by the guards.

Ivan and Marco were not with them.

In a few minutes, soldiers on horseback galloped out of the compound, heading down the road from which the work party had returned.

Once they were out of sight, Alex raced back to The Aerie.

A large grey-haired woman with a couple of extra chins—Mrs. Billingsgate, Alex guessed—was having coffee with Aunt Mattie.

"Oh, there you are, dear." Aunt Mattie could see he was trembling with excitement and gave him a look that, Alex could tell, meant settle down. "Anthea, this is my godson I was telling you about. Alex, Mrs. Billingsgate."

He bowed to her.

"Pleased to meet you, Alex. I've heard from your godmother about your terrible accident. Isn't it wonderful you can be here for a winter holiday?"

"Wonderful," Alex echoed.

"Would you give Otto a hand with the wood, dear, while you have your coat on? His rheumatism is acting up today." Aunt Mattie smiled at him and he heard her saying to Mrs. Billingsgate as he headed out, "I'm hoping his brother can join us for a few days before we go back."

By the time Alex had filled the woodbox next to the cook stove and the bin by the fireplace, Mrs. Billingsgate had relinquished her coffee cup and was poised to leave. She seemed to initiate a conversation at each point of her departure, though, telling Aunt Mattie in great detail about a pattern for a tea cozy as she got on her wraps.

With her gloved hand on the doorknob, she remembered she hadn't told her about the gallstone operation Mrs. Wilberforce, who summered in Banff and once had tea at The Aerie, had at the end of August just after Aunt Mattie had returned to Calgary. Halfway out the door, she launched into an account of the complaint a neighbour woman had made to Major Spence over one of the workers leering at her as she passed a work crew on her way downtown.

Finally closing the door, Aunt Mattie looked like she'd beaten back a battalion.

"That woman would try the patience of a saint," she said, checking a side window to make certain Mrs. Billingsgate was indeed on her way and hadn't thought of some excuse to return. "Now tell me what happened that's making you as jumpy as a young mountain goat."

"They've run off. I'm sure." Alex quit pacing and told Aunt Mattie what he had witnessed along the Cave Road.

"Let's close our eyes and say a prayer for them," Aunt Mattie said. As she whispered some English words, Alex remembered the *Otche Nash*, the Lord's Prayer his mother had taught him. He was saying it over for a second time when he realized Aunt Mattie was now sitting quietly, listening to him.

"Your prayer—it has a beautiful, ancient sound to it." She took off her glasses and brushed at her eyes with a lace-edged handkerchief. "Now, what we need to do is make ourselves as busy as beavers or this evening is going to drag something awful. You can work ahead in your arithmetic book and I'm going to make jelly out of that cranberry juice I boiled up last summer. Maybe I'll make a couple of apple pies too. Somewhere in the middle of all this, we'll have supper. Otto bought a whitefish from a peddler a little earlier today. It would be nice baked . . ."

A little later, while he was working on a page of problems involving measurements and fractions to be solved, Alex noticed that Aunt Mattie was talking with Otto in the kitchen. Otto nodded his head seriously several times, and as soon as it became dark, he turned on the porch light. It was still snowing with flakes dancing in the soft light. Aunt Mattie tore into her pie-making project before supper and they had apple pie for dessert following the baked fish.

Alex could hardly eat. In his mind, he could envision Ivan and Marco struggling through the deep snow in the woods at the base of the mountains. Would they hear the patrols out looking for them? Were they in danger from mountain lions? Perhaps they'd been caught already, prodded with bayonets, hurled into that place of punishment, the hoosegow.

After he'd done the supper dishes, he decided he couldn't face another page of arithmetic and set about memorizing a poem Aunt Mattie wanted him to learn. Then, as she boiled up her cranberry jelly and got a bunch of pint sealers ready, Alex got his coat and boots on.

"I will just be close by," he said.

"Yes." Aunt Mattie looked at him with concern in her eyes. "Don't go far."

Even with the snow, the evening was mild and Alex loosened his scarf. The mildness of the night and the snow cover would be a bonus for Marco and Ivan if they were hiding out in the woods, he thought. There were few street lamps in this part of town and only a couple of the houses on the block where The Aerie sat on a corner had lights in their windows. The Aerie's porch light, Alex noted with satisfaction, caught the wine-red colour of Aunt Mattie's door, Mama's scarf colour, and there were lights shining from the windows in several rooms. Otto must have turned them on.

Behind the houses, the landscape quickly thickened into forest and Alex walked a ways into the woods, his boots at times breaking through the crust of snow beneath what had fallen over the past few hours. When he'd walked for about ten minutes, he stopped and turned. The lights of Banff twinkled dimly in the distance as he made his way back.

It was still only nine o'clock when he returned to The Aerie.

"Come," Aunt Mattie said, watching him pace the living room. "Let's see if we can put together a jigsaw puzzle."

"Jigsaw?"

"Martin and I used to do these on summer evenings when he was a boy. There are still a couple of boxes around." Aunt Mattie dug into a chest by the fireplace, pulling out books, decks of cards, a stereoscope like the one that Eric had, and finally held up a wooden box. "Here's one." She cleared everything off the dinner table and spilled the pieces out of the box.

"Pull up a chair, Alex. For the life of me, I can't remember what the picture is."

"Oh, this game I have seen in the home of a friend. In Lviv."

They began turning over the wooden pieces so they were all image-side up. It took them an hour to fit it all together, creating a picture of little girl trying to teach her pet dog to read.

Aunt Mattie chuckled. "I remember it now. I think it's called 'Compulsory Education.' Let's leave it there so we can have another look at it in the morning. I'm off to bed now." She gave Alex a kiss on his forehead. "I suppose there's no use in telling you to try and get some sleep. Otto will be ready if anyone shows up."

From an armchair in the corner where he was flipping through the pages of a seed catalogue, Otto gave him a reassuring nod. Alex opened his history text but gave up any pretense of reading it. Instead he watched the logs in the fireplace settle into embers.

The clock on the mantel chimed midnight.

"Go to bed, Alex," Otto said, before banking the fire in the cook stove and heading off into the little room by the kitchen where he'd made up a bed on an old iron cot. "I'm close enough to the door that if anyone comes, I'll hear."

Alex went to his bedroom but he didn't undress. Leaving his bedside lamp on, he lay on top of his bedcovers with a quilt pulled over him as the night grew colder. Sometime later—an hour? Two hours?—he must have drifted off but he woke with a start when he heard a light knocking sound against his window. There was someone there tapping fingers on the pane and Alex knew, he just knew it had to be . . .

He threw back the quilt, hurried to the front door, and rushed outside. There, beneath his bedroom window, Marco had sunk to the ground. He was moaning softly but when Alex knelt beside him and held him, he whispered, "Lexie, Lexie, I am here. I think I will never be here but I am here."

And he closed his eyes.

Chapter 17

❧

ALEX KNELT DOWN on the porch and put his arms around Marco. He could feel a stubble of whiskers as he kissed his cheek, and he could see that, despite the night cold, Marco's face was slick with sweat. Alex brushed a strand of hair from his forehead. It was wet too. Marco's eyes fluttered open and he returned Alex's hug, holding him with a brief, fierce energy.

"Lexie," he whispered, and then closed his eyes again. There were bits of pine brush caught in his coat and Alex could see a tear in his pants that exposed part of his leg and a deep scratch that had bled.

Otto was suddenly there at the door and he quickly switched off the porch light.

"Help me get him inside," he said to Alex. "Put him on my cot. It's the closest."

Aunt Mattie was there too, clutching the wrapper she'd put on over her nightdress. Before they eased Marco onto the bed, she unbuttoned his coat and took it off him.

"Otto," she said, "help me get him undressed, and, Alex, fill that basin from your bedroom with warm water. Bring a wash cloth and towels."

Returning with these, Alex held the basin as Aunt Mattie gently sponged Marco's face, then his chest and arms. Alex gasped at the way Marco's collar bones and his ribs were so apparent beneath his pale skin. When he became gripped by a fit of shivering, Aunt Mattie abandoned the washcloth and towels to pull a quilt up to his chin.

His eyes were open again. "Thank you," he murmured, the words catching on a coughing fit that seemed hard to stop. Aunt Mattie grabbed a towel and held it to his mouth.

"He's got a terrible fever." She spoke softly. "Empty this basin, Alex, and refill it with cold water. You can keep a cold cloth against his forehead."

Otto had turned the porch light on again in case Ivan was still looking for a building fitting the details in Alex's letter. Then he went through the house and turned off all the lights except for a small lamp in the kitchen that provided enough illumination for him to build up the cook stove fire and make a pot of coffee.

For about an hour, Alex stayed, replacing the cloth on

Marco's forehead with one freshly rinsed in the cold water every few minutes.

Then Otto came in. "I'll do that for a while." He felt Marco's forehead. "I think the fever's coming down a bit already. You go and have a cup of coffee. Miss Mattie's got it all ready for you."

"I wonder if Ivan got away," Alex said as Aunt Mattie cut him a piece of pie to have with his coffee.

"We'll know tomorrow. Right now Marco needs to sleep." She reached over and put her hand gently on top of Alex's. "His getting here is a gift. It's almost more than we could have hoped for. I'm something of a skeptic but maybe those small prayers we uttered earlier made some kind of difference. In any event, fate has managed to bring your brother back to your embrace. And into our hands. But we need to be careful, oh so careful now . . ."

Alex thought that probably no one except Marco slept much over the next few hours, and Marco continued sleeping through most of the following day. In the afternoon, Aunt Mattie took a jar of jelly over to Mrs. Billingsgate. She looked downcast as she returned from her visit.

"Ivan was caught," she said. "Mrs. Billingsgate's son is a friend of one of the officers and he told her they found him once they got the mounted patrol out. He said they're still looking for the other one today, maybe checking to see if he tried to connect up with some of the Ukrainian miners at the Georgetown Colleries."

"Poor Ivan." Alex closed the door to the little room off the kitchen where Marco was still sleeping. "He has no luck running away from police."

"How's our patient?"

"He was awake coughing for a little while but then went right back to sleep."

"What we need to do is get him away from Banff as soon as we can," Aunt Mattie sighed. "But right now I think I'll get busy and make some chicken soup so he'll have something he can tolerate when he wakes up."

Alex and Otto took turns checking on Marco and helping Aunt Mattie cut up vegetables to add to the broth she had simmering on the stove.

Alex was taking his turn sitting by the bed when Marco finally surfaced from his sleep. He was still perspiring a great deal and Alex was patting his face and neck with a towel when he realized Marco was watching him.

"You're awake," Alex said in Ukrainian.

"Or else it's a dream," Marco answered, also in Ukrainian. He reached out and grasped Alex's arm. "Let me look at you. Sometimes I thought I would never see you again, locked in that hole, eating slop, barely able to move. Now let me look at you closely. So you have a mark on your face now—so what's that! Your eyes are still the colour of the sky over Lviv on a day that's just a little cloudy. And, hey, that burn has not affected your ability to smile. If your hair caught fire, it comes back darker and curlier. Oh, Lexie!" He hugged him again.

Aunt Mattie had come to the door.

"Our helping angel," Marco said, switching back to English.

"An angel bearing chicken soup," Aunt Mattie laughed. She handed a bowl and a spoon to Alex. "See if you can get him to eat some of this. There's a cauldron out there if he wants more. We'll talk later."

Slowly, spoonful by spoonful, Alex fed the soup to Marco.

"I am a big baby." Marco shook his head sadly. "Remember I fed you like this in Hamburg when you were so sick. But you were a baby then."

"I don't think so. Eleven is not a baby."

"You've grown so big these last few months. Fourteen now? I would not know you."

"And you have been disappearing," Alex said. "I think I must weigh more than you. But you will put it back on now. Aunt Mattie and Otto are wonderful cooks and Alma, in Calgary, is even better. She makes a strudel . . ."

"You think they will have us live with them? Why?" Marco sank back into his pillow and closed his eyes.

"I ask that myself too." Alex fixed the quilt to keep Marco warm. "I have no answer. Why some people are good, like Mr. Bayles, Karl and Mr. Dallaine and his aunt—and other people would like to beat you down. Like Liz Eddy and Mr. Richards and Granger."

"That pig!" Marco muttered.

Alex suddenly remembered the things for Marco he had in

his bag. "Stella gave me your things, what you had left . . ."

But Marco had fallen back asleep.

When he woke up again, it was evening.

"I think I can get up," Marco said.

"Try it and see," Aunt Mattie suggested.

When he managed to walk into the kitchen, wearing Otto's housecoat, Aunt Mattie took over, sending Alex to run a bath, asking Otto to check through the closets for any clothing Marco might put on for the time being while she set the table for supper.

Alex shampooed Marco's hair as he soaked in the tub.

"You don't know how good this feels," Marco sighed. "Quite the haircut, eh? Ivan cut it with some dull scissors. Then I cut his and he looks even worse than me. I could weep for Ivan. He'll be thrown into that hellhole now, probably a month or longer."

As Alex helped Marco out of the tub, he was shocked again at how thin he had become. He was taller than Otto so his bony ankles stuck out beneath the trousers Otto had found, and his wrists, equally bony, showed beneath the cuffs of a checkered shirt.

Aunt Mattie had to laugh when she saw him.

"A scarecrow," she said. "But, at least, a clean scarecrow."

He was a scarecrow with an appetite and was able to get through stew and biscuits with only one coughing fit.

After he'd finished eating and was settled in a living room armchair by the fireplace, with a blanket around him, Alex handed him the package entrusted to him by Stella and the letter forwarded from Bayles' Corner. Marco tore the envelope open, reading the letter through twice before letting it drop into his lap as if the news it bore was too heavy to bear.

"Granger—he is beating her. Because of me..." Marco looked up at them, blushed, and refolded the letter.

He unwrapped the parcel Alex had carried with him since Stella had put it into his hands in the attic in the Granger farmhouse. "My vest, and some of my drawings." As he sorted through the sketchbook, a photograph dropped out. "Also a picture of Stella." Alex thought Marco blushed again as he examined the photo. He handed it over to him. "She is a pretty girl, yes? We are good friends . . . doing much talking and laughing together, which Granger does not like."

Alex remembered her from that farmhouse breakfast at Granger's, which seemed now like a lifetime ago. She was wearing a braid like a crown on her head, the way she had that morning at the farmhouse. The tiniest of smiles played on her lips.

Alex passed the photograph over to Aunt Mattie.

"She is a beautiful girl." Aunt Mattie held the picture up to the lamplight. "Look, Otto. What lovely eyes, and such light hair, it seems almost white."

"But she is not happy with Granger," Marco sighed. "She is of an age that could be his child not a wife."

"Was it his jealousy . . . ?" Aunt Mattie returned the photo to Marco.

"That makes him mad at me and keep much of the money I should be getting? Yes, I think that is so."

Alex thought of Maria's suspicion that Stella might be pregnant, but this was something he had never mentioned to Aunt Mattie. And the time wasn't right to bring it up now.

They were all exhausted, and Alex couldn't remember anything after crawling into bed and his head hitting the pillow, but Marco's coughing woke him a couple of hours after midnight. Once again he was bathed in sweat, and Alex brought him cool water in a basin and a couple of facecloths.

"I've been spitting blood," Marco said between coughs. "In the camp, they say a red flower on your handkerchief is the first flower in your funeral bouquet."

"You're not in the camp. Do not think such things." Once the racking coughs had subsided, Alex fixed the blankets around him. Otto had wakened too and looked in quickly, but seeing Alex there, went back to bed. One of Marco's thin hands lay outside the covers and Alex stroked it, just barely touching the skin. Butterfly fingers was the term Mama had used. "You want me to tickle you with butterfly fingers?" she would say when he'd ask her to stroke his back or arms to help him go to sleep. There was a song she would sing too. Softly, Alex hummed the tune and began fitting the words in.

A dream walks by your window here
And settles by the gate,
Asks Slumber where shall we fall asleep
Now that it's dark and growing late?

Why, there in the house so warm and snug,
That wakeful child will company keep
Touch his eyelids, tuck him in
And gently rock him back to sleep.

"Mama's song." Marco smiled. "Don't stop."

The next morning, Aunt Mattie watched Marco with concern as they ate breakfast. Alex had told her about the coughing spell and what Marco had said. But he was looking better and Otto watched with satisfaction as he ate a second helping of scrambled eggs and potatoes.

"Tell us about the camp," Aunt Mattie said, nursing her coffee.

"The camp!" Marco leaned back in his chair and Otto gave him one of his cigarettes. "Are there words to tell?" He lit the cigarette and inhaled with a satisfied sigh. "Ivan and me—we are put to working on the road gang when we come. Eight hours a day and our boots are cracked open and no warm clothes. If you think you can't work no more without making a rest, guards chain you to a tree. One guard, Cooper, right away does not like Ivan who laughs at him and—how do you say it—sometimes talks like he talks . . . ?"

"Mimics him?" offered Aunt Mattie.

"Yes. And I am with Ivan much of the time, so he does not like me too. One time at night I am drawing a funny picture of Cooper. He has ears that stick out and a little black Charlie Chaplin mustache, and he sees it and gets most angry. He grabs it and says, 'You think that's funny?' and Ivan says, 'I think it is funny.' He rips the picture up but many are laughing and I think he would like to kill all of us."

Alex remembered the cartoon of Granger in the pigpen. He had no doubt the farmer would have been ready to commit murder too if he had seen it.

"We are in Banff a few days and I get the flu, always running to the toilet, and tell the medic I cannot go out and work. Cooper is getting us ready to march. He says to the medic, 'This one is a lazy son of a bitch,' and I say back, 'You are the son of a bitch,' and he hits me with his rifle.

"I should think but I don't and I punch him in the face. Then I am grabbed by other guards. They put chains on me and I am locked in the hoosegow. Three weeks. Dark and stinky and only bread and water and sometimes a bit of slop to eat and I am coughing sometimes so I feel like my chest will break.

"When I get out, I cannot walk and I am put in the hospital. That is when Ivan tells me he has been seeing you when he comes back from working. 'If we run, he is there to help. But first you must be strong and get back out on the road.' I try walking in the hospital a little bit, and then more, and I tell the doctor I am being better and do not cough when he is checking me.

"The first day back on the gang, I think I will die. A guard ties me to a tree and lets me rest a couple of times."

As he finished his cigarette, Marco began coughing again,

a fit that sent him walking around the kitchen, holding a handkerchief to his mouth. Sinking back into his chair, he nodded to Aunt Mattie's offer of more coffee.

"Sorry—it is a cough that cannot stop sometimes."

"You got our letter?" Alex asked.

"Yes, and I know you are telling me where you are in Banff. We go out each day and I am a little stronger. Ivan and me, we wait for our chance. It is snowing and we are working on rock crushing and, when it is time for dynamite to make an explosion, everyone has to hide from flying rock. Where we hide, a guard cannot see us and, when the explosion comes, we crawl to where the trees are. Then we run but Ivan says run different ways and meet later at the house you tell us about in the letter.

"I am surprised I can run so fast. I hear guards crashing after me but I can hide and when I don't hear them I run some more. I am lucky that it is still snowing to cover tracks. It takes many hours, through the trees, never close to the road or the railway to get back to town and it is dark. I know your house is on the edge but not which edge. I wait until no one is on a street to look for the door that has the colour of Mama's scarf. I am hoping too that I see Ivan.

"Finally there is the street with a log house and stone bottom and it is the only house with the light on outside."

"It was such a relief when you found us." Aunt Mattie reached over and held Marco's hand. "Your brother would have walked every step of the way from that little town where the two of you lived with your uncle, if it took him a year, I think, to find you, to be close to you during this terrible time. When I think that you came to this country—a kind of golden dream before you—and this is what the dream turned into, it makes me ashamed. But it's one thing to hang your head and do nothing, and another to act. My husband, my dear Emile, always said we thrive on acts of kindness."

Marco reached his other hand over and placed it on top of Aunt Mattie's.

"Lord help us, there's Anthea Billingsgate coming down the street!" Aunt Mattie quickly wiped a tear from her eye. "Alex, get Marco into your room and close the door. Otto, clear these dishes into the sink or sure as shooting she'll be counting coffee cups."

Chapter 18

✑

MARCO LAY DOWN on Alex's bed, and Alex knelt by the door so he could listen to the conversation.

"That one alien is still at large." Alex thought Mrs. Billingsgate sounded more excited by the thought than alarmed. "John says there's Ruthenians and Jews all through the mountain passes who are just too willing to help an escaped prisoner. Storekeepers and mine workers and railway section crew. You have to wonder what the world's coming to. It makes my blood boil to think of the soldiers we have to keep here to keep those men . . . and chase them all over the place."

"There, there," Aunt Mattie crooned. "I've just made a fresh pot of coffee. That always makes me feel better."

"I know when they first came here everyone was saying how they'd help fix up the park and all. But Mathilde, I wish that camp'd never been set up. It was a mistake from the start, John says."

Alex could see that Marco was trying to hold back a coughing spell, but with little success. He held a pillow to his mouth to muffle the sound.

"My," Mrs. Billingsgate said, "someone's got a bad cold."

"Alex. I told him to be sure and keep his cap on yesterday, but you know boys. Played too hard, became too warm. Today he's in his room with a compress on his chest, but I think I'll try and get him back to Calgary today if we can get our act together, otherwise tomorrow."

"He and John must be cut from the same cloth," Mrs. Billingsgate said through a mouthful of something, likely an oatmeal cookie from a batch Aunt Mattie had baked a few days back. "I'd catch him running around midwinter, his coat flung open, no scarf . . ."

At the end of a second cup of coffee, Anthea Billingsgate declared she wished more than anything in the world that the return to Calgary might be postponed.

"I was thinking I would have a little social evening this coming Sunday and invite the minister."

"It's tempting," Aunt Mathilde said, "but Alex has a little bit of a history with chest problems and that's why I think we'd best get back to the city. The doctor there has looked after him before. The burns, you know . . ."

"Of course, but you must come back soon. And maybe your other godson—what was his name?—perhaps he can come and ski. Wouldn't that be nice, and John enjoys skiing too."

It sounded like Aunt Mattie was getting Mrs. Billingsgate her wraps. Alex gritted his teeth and rolled his eyes, making Marco stifle a laugh as the visitor took her usual time departing.

When they felt it was safe to emerge from the bedroom, Aunt Mattie was making a list of items for Otto to purchase on Banff Avenue.

"I think we need to catch a train today," she said. "What size boots do you wear, Marco? A long overcoat would be good if they have one and maybe some kind of boyish-looking cap. Wait, we might have something Martin's left here—I'll look in the storeroom closet."

"I am sorry—the trouble..." Was it embarrassment or the fever returning that brought a reddish flush to Marco's cheeks?

"And Otto, check the train schedule while you're downtown."

Alex helped to pack a food hamper while Aunt Mattie got a comb and scissors and did what she could to repair Marco's haircut.

It was a rush to get everything done but Otto had them down to the depot just before the train was due. He would close up the house and take a train back the next day.

"You look fine," Aunt Mattie whispered to Marco, taking his arm. She had on her fur coat and the hat with a veil that she'd worn when she and Alex had waited at the Cave and Basin pavilion. "We need to look touristy," she declared.

Otto had found an overcoat with a fur collar that was only a little too large for Marco. With leather gloves, new boots, and a hat that Martin had long ago decided was a little too jaunty for his taste, Marco did look fine, Alex thought.

Marco pulled the brim of the hat low over his eyes when a couple of soldiers entered the depot.

"Guards?" Alex whispered.

"I don't think so. They are not faces I remember."

Nonetheless, they were relieved to find seats in a different coach from them. Alex could tell Marco had been holding back a coughing spell at the station, which overtook him once they were seated.

Aunt Mattie smiled apologetically at a man in the seat across the aisle. "These winter colds . . ."

When the coughing persisted, the man got up, scowling, and headed to a seat at the other end of the coach.

As the train chugged its way through the darkening winter landscape to Calgary, Aunt Mattie retrieved a jar from the hamper. "This should help; it's a mixture of honey and lemon and ginger tea." She poured a cup for Marco.

He slumped back in his seat. "Sorry," he muttered.

"Tush." Aunt Mattie poured drinks for herself and Alex. "Don't fret. It's not a long trip to Calgary. We'll be home in just a little while."

Home. It had become home, Alex thought. Like the wandering brothers in one of the stories Mama would tell, they had made their way past monsters to find that place. Wasn't it always the youngest brother who found the way? And the helpers . . . not a feather from the firebird, it was true but . . .

"A penny for your thoughts." Aunt Mattie patted Alex's hand.

"Helpers," Alex said. "I think about people who help me find Marco. People helping us still."

"'Help' is a two-sided word. Those who give also receive." Aunt Mattie took a sip of her lemon tea. "Emile and I would have loved children. That didn't happen in the natural course of things, but we were blessed when Martin became our child. Oh, true, he had a father until a few years ago, but we were the family of Martin's heart. And since he's left the nest, I have been a very complacent old bird."

Both Alex and Marco laughed.

"It's true. Comfortable, just existing, painting mountain scenes when the mood took me. Drifting. I think the two of you were sent to me. You were meant to land on my doorstep."

At the Calgary station, Aunt Mattie had a porter find a taxi and Alma was waiting at the door when they got home.

"I got the bedsitting room at the top of the stairs, the one I've been using as a sewing room, all ready for the young man." Alma was already fussing over Marco. "And supper's all ready when you are. I've made a nice Welsh rarebit. Does the young man . . . ?"

"Marco." Aunt Mattie laughed. "Alma, this is Marco."

"Marco. And Alex." Alma gave Alex a hug. "Alex, you hang up coats and I'll put supper on the table."

Marco was close to falling asleep by the time Alma whisked away the rarebit and served dessert.

"Off to bed for you." Aunt Mattie nodded at Marco. "Alex, you take him up."

"A beautiful house," Marco said, "and paintings!" as Alex toured him through the schoolroom. He picked up one of Aunt Mattie's brushes and held it for a minute and touched, with a kind of reverence, the edge of the canvas on the easel.

"You'll be able to paint too," Alex said. "Aunt Mattie said as soon as you're feeling well enough."

"I feel better already." He smiled.

But as Alex helped him into bed, Marco began weeping, great racking sobs that seemed to tear from his entire body.

"What?" Alex gave him one of the handkerchiefs Alma had piled on the bureau. "What is it, Marco? You're home . . ."

He buried his face in a pillow to stifle the sound, but Alex could see his shoulders heaving with the sobs.

"Marco . . ."

Alex sat by his bed until he fell asleep and then he slipped back downstairs.

Aunt Mattie looked up from her newspaper. "You mustn't worry too much, Alex. These days have been, as you know, a trial that's difficult for us to imagine. With time . . ."

"Yes. Time."

"I phoned Dr. Abraham and he'll stop by tomorrow morning."

When the doctor examined Marco in his bedroom, Marco had a coughing fit that Alex and Aunt Mattie could hear from the living room downstairs. Alex could see Alma hovering in the hall. She'd been up early making a batch of cough syrup from a recipe she'd brought with her from the old country and was obviously distraught that Marco was still coughing.

"Will you take coffee, Sir?" Alma asked when the doctor came down, as if that had been the reason she was waiting there.

"Your coffee, and if it comes with strudel, I'll not pass it up." Dr. Abraham found a chair next to Aunt Mattie. He looked at her and shook his head.

"It's what you feared, Aaron?" Aunt Mattie took a deep breath.

"I'm afraid so. I'll have some tests done, of course. My guess is that it's moved rapidly to an advanced stage—little wonder with the kind of treatment he had in that camp. I understand that he was chained and locked up for the better part of a month in solitary?"

"Yes," Alex said. "When he got out he couldn't walk."

"You'd think we'd progressed some from the Middle Ages." Aunt Mattie got up and looked out the window for a couple of minutes. Alex thought she didn't want anyone to see her face.

"My sister Daphne, Martin's mother, died from tuberculosis. I was just remembering," she said, facing the doctor again. "What do you recommend we do?"

"You might consider a sanatorium." Dr. Abraham helped her back to her chair. "But I think, with everyone's help, you could look after him here. Your place is quiet and you can keep him fairly isolated. He'd have to be on complete bed rest, at least to begin with, and you could make use of that south balcony on warm days. Fresh air . . ."

"Daphne had a special diet too, I remember," Aunt Mattie said.

"Yes, I'll have one written up."

"Marco—he will be all right?" Alex searched the doctor's face. "He will be better?"

"We can hope." Dr. Abraham placed a hand on his shoulder. "Lots of rest, proper food. No gloomy faces. From what you've told me about him, I suspect he has a great will to live and it helps if he senses that desire for life all around him. Now, all of you in the household will need to take some special precautions . . ."

The doctor's voice became lost, though, as Alex thought about what the doctor had first said. There hadn't been much hope in his voice then.

"Excuse me, please," Alex said and, hiding his face, hurried upstairs.

Marco was still in bed, but he wasn't asleep. He was looking at the photograph of Stella. "I hope she writes again to Bayles' Corner. I hope she gets a place to live away from Granger." He propped the photo against a vase on his bedstand. "*Te hovoryv z likarem*?" Marco slipped into Ukrainian, asking him if he'd talked with the doctor.

"*Ne bahato.* A little . . ." Alex tried to keep his voice steady. "Aunt Mattie is talking with him."

"You didn't want to hear what he had to say?" Marco smiled wryly. "Tuberculosis. I asked him to tell me what is true."

Alex nodded but he couldn't think of anything to say. He directed his gaze back to Stella's photo. "I have written to Mr. Bayles so he knows where to forward mail."

"She is having a baby." Marco sighed. "I believe I am the father. In her letter she says Granger found out about the baby and that's when he beat her so bad. With her wrist broken she walked into town to the hospital."

"He knew, didn't he, about you and Stella? When you had the fight?"

"He guessed. That last day . . . we were thinking he had gone to Vegreville but he came back into the house when I was drawing a picture of Stella. She was wearing a shawl I gave her—one with flowers on it. It was a good picture. Granger flew into a rage and stuck his hook through it and said, 'Here is your money, get out.' I was only a little way into town when I looked inside the envelope and saw it was only half the money he owed me. I came back and told him to give me the rest. He hit me and we began to fight.

It was a bad fight. Things crashing in the house. I knocked him out and, while he was lying unconscious on the floor, I looked in his wallet and took the money he owed me. Stella was crying. Everything was so bad. I hurried away and while I was waiting—it was a few hours—for a train to come ..." Marco struggled for a moment to catch his breath, began to cough but was able to suppress it. "When Granger regained consciousness, he hurried into Vegreville before the train came and convinced the police to arrest me. I tried to run but they caught me."

"Oh, Marco ..." Alex felt that he could feel those policemen's hands on his own arms.

Marco lay back and closed his eyes. "I love Stella." His voice was a whisper. "But I think I have made things worse for her. I have a feeling she will have to go back to Granger. It will be too difficult for her to live on her own ... not just on her own, soon with a baby."

The next day's mail brought another letter from Stella, forwarded from Bayles' Corner. Marco shared a page of the letter with Alex.

Your brother has written to me at the hospital that you have been put in a camp in the mountains. I so long for a letter from you, though, and now Alex can give you an address. I stay with a friend of the doctor who looks after me. She is old and very crippled with arthritis and I help her around the house as much as I can. It is my left wrist that is in a cast and I can do quite a lot with my other hand. The baby will not be coming for four months and I hope my wrist will be all healed by then.

Edward has been trying to get me to come back to the farm and be his wife again but I have told him no. The doctor reported his beating of me to the police so he is being careful. I will never go back. Some days I visit Father Manihszyn at the church — Edward would never let me go there after we were married. The Father was your friend and now he is my friend too. He shows me the beautiful painting you did of St. Andrew blessing the hills of Kiev.

"You have a letter pad, Alex?" Marco asked. "The doctor says I should not get out of bed."

In the schoolroom, Alex hunted through his desk for writing paper. He sat down for a minute. He knew Marco must feel burdened with the weight of his actions, his responsibility to Stella. How that must be adding to his pain. Alex could feel it himself but he wished there were some way he could take on more of it to give Marco ease. He drew a long breath and then picked up the ceramic pot on his desk filled with sharpened pencils and crayons, balancing that with the writing pad as he returned to Marco's bedroom.

"Draw a picture for Stella at the end of your letter," Alex said. "She'd like that."

Chapter 19

OVER THE NEXT MONTH, Aunt Mattie and Alma took charge of Marco's sick room and the treatment Dr. Abraham outlined. The doctor himself stopped by weekly. Alex's studies, Aunt Mattie pointed out, were to be kept up.

"I want you to be able to go into grade eight next fall," she told him as she worked out a schedule of assignments. "There's no reason you can't. Then we'll look at possibilities for high school. Have you given any thought of what you'd like to do when you're through school?"

"I was so far behind . . . I didn't think . . ." Alex remembered how much bigger he'd been than the other students in Mr. Dallaine's class. "Maybe, when Marco is all better, we can go back to the farm. We have some pigs and a horse and a cow . . ."

"Would farming be your dream—if you could do anything you most wanted in the world? You think about it, dear."

Part of each day, Alex spent with Marco, reading to him, or playing the card games he'd learned at the Arnesons'. Aunt Mattie made certain he had a sketchpad and drawing implements at hand, and sometimes Alex would just sit and watch him draw. He sketched the geranium plants Otto kept on a windowsill to brighten the room. He sketched the elm tree whose branches scraped against the window glass on gusty days. He sketched characters from the stories Mama had told them, and fanciful creatures that came from nowhere except Marco's imagination. He sketched Stella from the photo he kept on the bureau by his bed. And sometimes he sketched Alex himself.

But often, whatever he was doing was interrupted by a coughing fit. Cards would scatter; pencil and pad would fall; a glass of milk would tip. Marco would punctuate the coughing spells with a string of Ukrainian oaths.

"What is he saying?" Aunt Mattie asked one day, walking into the bedroom after a sudden attack had caused a dark pencil to scoot across a *pysanka* pattern he'd been designing for an Easter egg.

"I don't think you want to know." Alex looked at her with a grin.

"Oh." Aunt Mattie raised her eyebrows and left the new *Saturday Evening Post* for Marco to read.

Mr. Dallaine came down to Calgary the second weekend after they'd returned from Banff. He brought Marco his breakfast tray on Sunday morning and stayed and visited with him for what seemed to Alex like a very long time. He thought about going up to find out what they were talking about but Aunt Mattie seemed to read his mind and said, "Let Martin get to know him a bit. We need to remember that Marco's been very much the focus of Martin's thoughts and energy since that day chance brought you to his classroom. There must be a great deal to talk about."

"He showed me his drawings," Mr. Dallaine said to them when he came back downstairs. "You're right, Alex, he has a great deal of talent. Don't you think so, Auntie?"

"Yes, and I'm going to have Otto make him a drawing board that he can use for watercolour paper or even tack canvas to." Aunt Mattie poured her nephew a fresh cup of coffee. "Something with a bit of a ledge for brushes and paint tubes that he can prop on his knees."

"When does Dr. Abraham think he might be getting out of bed . . . you know, for some exercise?"

Alex saw Aunt Mattie dart Mr. Dallaine a look, a look that seemed to say, "Don't ask." A swallow of orange juice stopped midway down Alex's throat and he ended up coughing it out into his napkin. Quickly, he excused himself and ran upstairs.

Later, in the schoolroom, Alex reviewed for Mr. Dallaine what he was studying. He showed him a composition he'd written about living on Uncle Andrew's farm that Aunt Mattie had praised. Mr. Dallaine nodded his head with approval as he read it over.

> *I remember the first summer. When Marco, my brother, and Uncle Andrew had planted the crops, there was some free time. Not a whole bunch. A little. Marco would walk with me and we would go past the fields to where the prairie was and it was yellow as far as the eye could see. A flower was in bloom called the golden bean. "Maybe magic beans," my brother said. "Like in a fairy tale." He laughed and made a silly look with his eyes but I think he liked seeing them because later he made a picture of them.*

"It is good, Alex. Aunt Mattie, you know, is a fine teacher. I think I learned more from her than I did from my schoolteachers when I was in grade school, and, when my mother died, she taught me some things about life . . ."

"Your mother . . ." Alex busied himself returning the composition to his writing folder. "She died from tuberculosis?"

"Yes." Alex felt Mr. Dallaine's hand on his shoulder. "I was seven when she became ill, and she passed away when I was nine. It's a terrible disease—I won't keep that from you. That last year, my father had her committed to a sanatorium so I didn't see a great deal of her. It seemed like she was slipping away from me more and more every time I visited. I think Aunt Mattie practically lived there, though, those months at the sanatorium. My mother was Mattie's younger sister, the only sibling she had.

"I remember my father saying, when she died, it was a relief. I think he meant for her to be free of pain, but I suppose he meant it was a relief for him in some ways too. But it was no relief to me. The only relief came with time and the love and kind attentions of my aunt and uncle."

"Do you . . . ?" The words stuck in Alex's throat. "Do you think Marco is going to die?"

Alex felt the grip on his shoulder tighten.

"There are always miracles," he said. "But I've talked to Aunt Mattie and we're sending some money to Stella and urging her to come down here. If she agrees, I'll meet her in Edmonton and then I'll put her on the train to Calgary. I won't be able to come myself. I've been telling Mr. Edgerton that I've needed days off for medical reasons but he cautioned me about taking any more. I think he's suspicious about the appointments always being on days connected with weekends—so I'd better not at the moment. You and Mattie can meet her at the station."

It took two weeks for the arrangements to meet Stella to be made. The Calgary streets were cleared enough of snow that Otto was able to take the car to the station.

"We can wait in the café," Aunt Mattie said, "until the arrival of the train is announced."

The cavernous, white-tiled restaurant bustled with activity, people finding tables, waiters taking orders or carrying trays crowded with pots of tea and coffee, sandwiches and hot meals under domed lids. If the train was on time, they had a half hour to wait.

All Alex could think about was Marco getting ready throughout the afternoon and becoming more and more exhausted as he bathed and shaved and got dressed, wearing the embroidered vest Alex had retrieved in Vegreville along with some dress pants, a white shirt and a striped tie from Mr. Dallaine's closet.

"I am well enough to come to the station," he had said to Aunt Mattie, making his way downstairs, where he lowered himself shakily into a parlour armchair. "Once I get my breathing..."

"You should stay here," Aunt Mattie said, gently but with the kind of firmness that didn't broach argument. "Dr. Abraham thinks you shouldn't even be out of bed these days. You want to greet Stella as rested as possible—not tire yourself out before she arrives."

Marco had watched from the parlour window as they got into the car. In the window he was a silhouette, a kind of shadow of himself, Alex thought. Every day, more of a shadow. What would Stella think, seeing him so thin?

In the café, Alex was just finishing his cup of hot chocolate when the train from Edmonton was announced. Aunt Mattie quickly settled the bill and they hurried through the walkway to the waiting room. Otto, Alex remembered, had met him and Mr. Dallaine those many weeks back out on the platform.

"I can go where the train is stopped?" Alex looked questioningly at Otto and Aunt Mattie. "Stella, she may be thinking about which way to go."

"Go ahead, Alex," Aunt Mattie said. "We'll just stay right here close to the doors."

The platform was busy with station staff moving wagons into place for unloading cargo and luggage, and a steady stream of people disembarking. Men in greatcoats and suits, others in winter work clothes, farmers, soldiers, women with children. One young woman wearing a large-brimmed hat, who seemed to be travelling alone, smiled at him as she went by. She was very pretty. Alex turned for a minute and followed her progress to the station doors.

When he turned back, he saw Stella at the far end of the platform. She wore a long black coat and a kerchief over her hair. She had set down a bag and was looking around her. One of the station lights shone on her face and Alex was struck by how it seemed to make her skin glow.

"Stella!" He called and raised his hand.

It took a second for her to spot him but when she did, she broke into a smile, waved back and, collecting her bag, hurried down the platform as he ran to meet her.

"Alex!"

They stood awkwardly for a couple of seconds. Stella set her bag down and then she hugged him. Carefully, Alex thought. Was her left wrist still hurting? Then she held him at arms' length for a good look at his face. "Your burns healed good—and you are bigger, more tall."

Alex picked up her bag. "Come and meet Aunt Mattie and Otto. They are happy to be knowing you. Happy for it to be something good for Marco. He needs . . . something good."

Stella clutched his coat sleeve and he saw the smile disappear from her face. "How is he, Alex? How is he really? Why isn't he with you?"

Alex drew breath. What could he say? "He is still very tired and the doctor is saying for him to be in bed. But today he is out of bed and waiting downstairs for you."

"Yes, let's hurry." Stella gave him a quick smile as they headed to the station doors.

There was no holding Aunt Mattie back. Before anyone could say anything, she had wrapped Stella in a hug that seemed to bring her fur wrap to life, the fox's sharp nose nuzzling the young woman's coat.

"Welcome, my dear!" Aunt Mattie stood back for a second and then hugged her again.

Otto nodded and tipped his cap.

As they made their way through the station to the parking area, Aunt Mattie plied Stella with questions. Did she have any trouble getting to Edmonton? Had she spent some time with Martin there? And the trip from Edmonton to Calgary, how was that? Stella's answers were shy and whispery.

Once the women were in the back seat of the car, Alex climbed into the front to sit by Otto. Aunt Mattie kept up the conversation but, in a pause, Stella said, "Thank you. It is so kind for you to let me visit, to see Marco. I thought I would never . . ."

"You must stay as long as you want. Alex and Marco are family now, and you shall be too."

Marco was waiting at the door when they got there.

"Stella!" Marco's voice cracked, and he stood back and sighed. It was a happy sigh. Alex recognized the smile on Marco's face, one he'd not seen since those summer days before he'd gone to Vegreville to find work. His hair, that deep gold of ripened barley, had grown since Aunt Mattie cut it, a curl falling over his forehead. His cheeks were flushed with colour.

At first, Stella was unable to hide her shock. Tears welled. Alex remembered how he had felt when he first saw Marco in Banff. Quickly, though, she brushed at her eyes and moved to embrace him.

"Just a kiss on the cheek." Marco laughed. "Dr. Abraham says we need to have . . . ?" He looked questioningly at Aunt Mattie.

"Precautions," she said.

"Precautions."

But Stella wrapped her arms around Marco and was crying and laughing at the same time and she wasn't just kissing him on his cheeks.

"Marco, why don't you take Stella upstairs and show her the room we've fixed up for her," Aunt Mattie suggested. "Dinner won't be ready for a little while yet."

An hour later Marco came down by himself.

"Stella—she is very tired and has gone asleep. I did not want to wake her." Marco looked like it had been an effort for him to return downstairs.

"Have something to eat and then you'd best go to bed yourself," Aunt Mattie said. "Alma's got everything ready and Stella can have some supper later if she feels like it."

"Thank you. Thank you for being so good to us."

Aunt Mattie put a finger to her lips to shush him and gestured to his place at the table.

Alex could see it was a struggle for Marco to work his way through the three-course dinner Alma had prepared. He excused himself before dessert was served.

"Alex, you go up with him," Aunt Mattie said.

"I am fine," Marco protested but Alex was already by his side, helping him up from his chair. It did look as if he could collapse at any minute. Alex could sense that he was holding back a cough, and, when they got to his room, he gave into it, grabbing a handkerchief from the pile by his bed. There was enough blood that Alex could see it seeping through the cloth.

The coughing wakened Stella in her room down the hall and she was there with them when his shuddering and hacking finally subsided. Alex noticed the terror in her eyes. She hurried to the bedside and helped Marco get out of his vest and undo his tie. When he leaned over to undo his boot laces, he began to fall forward. They both caught him and eased him up onto the bed.

He lay back and closed his eyes. A sound of disgust came from his throat. "I am weak and wobbly as old man Stremelsky." The words came out in Ukrainian.

"An old drunk guy we often see on the street where we live in the old country." Alex forced a small laugh. "Marco is saying he is like that. Falling over . . ."

Stella nodded and he remembered she was likely as fluent in Ukrainian as they were.

Once they helped him into bed, Alex urged Stella to go downstairs and have some supper.

"Shall I . . . I can stay here if you want me to?" Stella drew the comforter on the bed up and smoothed it across Marco's chest.

"No. Go. I am ready to sleep." He smiled wanly at her and Stella leaned over and kissed him on the forehead.

"Come with me, Alex." Stella's hand brushed his arm. "I will fix myself up a bit before we go down. I am all rumpled from falling asleep."

It took a while. When she emerged from her room, Alex could see that she had fixed the coil of hair and changed into another dress, a soft loose-fitting grey dress with a lace collar. The grey of the fabric was only a bit darker than the grey of her eyes. When she took hold of his arm as they descended the stairs, Alex inhaled a wafting of talcum and a scent that made him think of summer flowers. He felt something flutter through him and he had to catch his breath. More and more he could understand why Marco had fallen for this girl . . . this woman.

They found Aunt Mattie having her coffee in the parlour. Instantly she was up, though, directing them to the kitchen where Alma retrieved a plate of food from the warming oven.

"We'll join you at the kitchen table, Stella." Aunt Mattie bustled around, getting them all settled. "I've been waiting to have dessert with the two of you. Marco has gone to bed? Poor lad, I think he rather overextended himself today. Your nap did you good, though, Stella. Brought some colour to your cheeks. How are you feeling?"

Aunt Mattie kept a conversation afloat as Stella finished her plate of chicken and they all dug into a peach cobbler, Alma and Otto joining them. The kitchen was cozy and warm. A hanging lamp turned Stella's pale hair to gold. With his dessert finished, Alex began nodding off over the cup of cocoa Alma had fixed for him, topping it with some of the whipped cream she had prepared for the cobbler.

He felt Aunt Mattie's hand on his shoulder. "It's been a long day for you too, my dear. Off to slumbers for you."

Chapter 20

∽

"SOME OF THE POST is for you," Aunt Mattie said, popping into the study the next day where Alex was working on his assignments while both Marco and Stella were in their rooms, napping. "Two letters."

The hours had been dragging for Alex—he really wanted to be with Marco and Stella—but now he felt a pleasant rush as he accepted the envelopes. He studied the return addresses.

"One is from Mr. Bayles and the other is from Karl."

"Karl?"

"Arneson—where I was staying at his place in Edmonton."

"Take your time and enjoy reading them. I'm afraid my

letters are mostly business," Aunt Mattie sighed. "I'll tackle those downstairs by the fire."

He opened Mr. Bayles' letter first.

Dear Alex,

I hope this note finds you in good health and with your burns healed well. How are things in the big city of Calgary? Here at Bayles' Corner everything goes on quietly as usual. Miss Anderson, when she comes for mail or groceries, always asks about you. She was very happy when I told her that you have finally found your brother—although sad that he is in a work camp. Everyone hopes that the war will end soon and people in the camps can return home. She is also glad that a good family has taken you in and asks me to send along her best wishes. She misses you at school.

Last week I made a trip to Mrs. Eddy's. A parcel came from the war department and I knew it must be Robin's effects so I wanted to bring it to her myself. There were medals for his bravery, along with a photograph he must have had taken just shortly before he lost his life and a New Testament Bible with his name inside the front cover. Mrs. Eddy had a cry as she handled the items. Myrt was intrigued with the medals and wanted to wear them but Mrs. Eddy told her she could only touch them gently. Of course Myrt had a hundred questions. They both asked about you and I was able to fill them in with your news before Liz came in from the barnyard. Liz looked at the *objects in the parcel but couldn't bring herself to say anything, except to swear a bit. Then she just got her coat back on and went outside and disappeared. I think she still feels his loss more than anyone.*

As you know I am busy during the day running the post office and the store. But in the evenings I miss having you here for company. It is hard to tell what the future will bring but I hope you will return for a visit sometime. You are always most welcome and I send you my best wishes.

Yours,

Jack Bayles

Alex read the letter over twice. Mr. Bayles wrote in a spidery script that Alex had come to know, watching him maintaining ledgers, writing receipts and itemizing bills. He could almost smell the store with its paper and tin and rubber wares, the oil on the wood floor, the sharp odour if you got close to the big wheel of cheddar cheese. And the pervasive, sweetish aroma from Mr. Bayles' pipe smoke. He closed his eyes for a minute and was back in that upstairs apartment, light flickering from the stove grate and the kerosene lamp, the gramophone playing.

He thought of Miss Anderson and the Eddys too as he tucked the letter back into its envelope.

Karl's handwriting on the other envelope was very different from Mr. Bayles'. The words looked like they were crafted by someone who took as much care shaping letters as he did carving the design on a cabinet molding. When he unfolded the enclosed pages, he saw the letter from Karl was short but there were notes from Maria and Einar and Gunnar as well.

Dear Alex,

How is my coal-ghost from the wood scrap pile doing? I am glad you are in a good place in Calgary. Mr. Dallaine is very nice. He comes by to visit sometimes. He tells us you have found Marco and he is with you now, but sick. That part I am sorry to hear. It has been very busy at the shop but that is good because Jesse gives me a raise in pay. A small raise but that will help with the baby coming soon. Our Astrid has been asking about you. I think she really misses you. We all miss you and hope there will be a time when you can come back to see us. Maria will add something here.

Maria, Alex remembered, was left-handed and her writing, tiny and carefully formed, had an odd backwards slant to it.

Are you well, Alex? We think about you lots and sometimes it feels like you are maybe in the next room playing cards with the boys or helping get dinner ready in the kitchen. I know you will be helping where you are now. That is how you are. You are good and we been lucky to have you stay with us. I say prayers for your brother.

Your friend always, Maria Arneson

The boys each added their own page. Einar had drawn fine pencil lines to keep his writing straight.

Dear Alix,

I am writing with a pen and ink now. We are practising in school. Teacher tells me I am pretty good. Are you wining rummy games? Oops. Sumtimes ink runs off my pen when the nib gets stuck and it makes a spot. This one looks like a star don't you think? I bet you never thot you would get a star in a letter. I hope you are having fun and I hope your bruther is getting better.

Yours truly,

Einar Arneson

Gunnar's page was mainly a crayon picture with some printing below it.

ALEX this is for you. And for Marco. Tell him I am a drawer like him. It is a troll under a brij. Don't be to scared.

From GUNNAR

At the bottom of the page there was a dog's paw print. And beside it:

QUEENIE says hello and a lik with her tung

Alex spread the pages out on his desk. Gunnar's drawing made him smile. The troll had enormous eyes, a mouthful of pointed teeth and claws instead of fingers. He could picture

Gunnar labouring over it. And Einar proudly flourishing a straight pen.

Maria would likely be watching the ink bottle closely so it didn't spill. Maybe scolding Gunnar for sticking one of Queenie's dirty paws onto the bottom of his page. Did Karl pick up his violin after finishing his short note, playing "Danny Boy" or a jig tune while the others finished their letters? For a couple of minutes, Alex found it difficult to swallow. Was it possible to be homesick for a family he had been with for such a short time?

From her reflection in the window just beyond his desk, Alex saw Stella at the schoolroom doorway. A flash of red flowers on her shawl, the grey of her dress, the white gold of her hair.

"You are busy?" Whenever she spoke, Alex was struck by how quiet, how soft her voice was.

"No, just reading letters. Aunt Mattie said she has tea waiting for us when you wake up."

"I had a long sleep. Marco—he is still sleeping."

Downstairs, they found Alma setting out biscuits and raspberry jam to go with their tea.

"Let's hole up in the parlour by the fireplace. The dining room's always been a bit drafty in this old house." Once she was certain Stella was comfortable on the settee, Aunt Mattie had Alex read aloud his letters.

"I feel that I practically know Mr. Bayles and the Arnesons," she said. "Alex, you've talked so much about them and

Martin has been telling me as well about the Norwegian family."

"I got to meet them." Stella wiped a bit of jam caught on her lip. "Mr. Dallaine—Martin—took me over to meet the Arnesons the second night I was in Edmonton. They are . . ." She struggled to find the right words. "They are what I wish every family could be, people caring about each other, loving and laughing . . ." Stella's voice faded and she pulled her shawl around her.

"You came from a large family, didn't you?" Aunt Mattie poured herself a second cup of tea.

"Eleven children. But we were not much happy. Such hard work, not enough food. My mother in the field with my father. At first they don't even have a horse to pull the plough. They pull it themselves. They harvest by hand. Two older sisters trying to look after us little ones. Neighbours help some but they do not have much either.

"When we are in town one day, Edward sees me. I am thirteen, almost fourteen and he tells my father he will give him a good plough horse and some calves and pigs if I will marry him. Some money too. My father says wait until she is fifteen. My mother cried and I did too but I was made to go, to become Edward Granger's wife."

It was more than Stella had said at one time since she had come and the rush of words seemed to exhaust her.

"You can imagine . . ." A sob caught in Stella's throat. Aunt Mattie reached over and held her hand.

"I am forced to do housework just the way Edward wants. If he finds it is not right, he sometimes hits me. I ran away and went home one time but my father makes me go back." She was crying now.

"There, there. No need to tell us more, Stella."

Alex couldn't bear to watch her crying. He stared at the logs crackling in the fireplace.

But Stella must have felt a compulsion to keep talking. "Then Marco came. We had hired men before but no one like Marco. He worked so hard and he had ... joy. I think that is the right word. He brought joy with him. I think Edward does not like him but he was getting so much done. Marco was better than any hired hand we had before—as if he was working his own land, his own farm.

"You know how much Marco loves to tell stories and jokes, but Edward didn't like it when we laughed or talked Ukrainian so we tried not to laugh and only talk English when he was around. Marco would draw in his sketchbook in the evenings. I don't think Edward liked that either. And then we ..." Stella drew a deep breath. "We fell in love. If I knew it would lead to Marco going to a jail camp, would cause him to get so sick ..."

Alex looked away from the fire and noticed Aunt Mattie giving Stella's hand a little squeeze.

"There now. You mustn't blame yourself. Where the human heart is involved ..."

They were all startled to see Marco coming down the

stairs. He was dressed as he had been the day before, even wearing Mr. Dallaine's striped tie.

"Marco!" Stella and Aunt Mattie said his name at the same time.

"You shouldn't be out of bed," Aunt Mattie chided.

Stella started to rise from the settee but Marco moved across the room quickly to sit beside her.

"I'm feeling better," he laughed. "Maybe Stella and I should go dancing tonight, or roller-skating."

Alex noted there were beads of perspiration across his forehead.

"Oh yes, roller-skating for sure!" Stella laughed softly in turn. "You're looking good." She pushed back a curl that had fallen forward and then pulled a handkerchief from her sleeve to blot the moisture along his hairline.

He *was* looking good, Alex thought. His face actually seemed to shine like a candle whose wick has burrowed into the middle, the flame there but seen only as a glow through wax. And there was a brightness to his cheeks. Today, too, there was a sparkle to his eyes. A glimmer of the old Marco.

"I was thinking about Uncle Andrew," Marco said, looking at Alex. "Actually I had a dream about him. He and old man Potchak putting up fists to fight at a wedding and I was trying to stop them, but I don't get past the people crowded around them. You know how in a dream everything gets in your way? Remember how mad Potchak would get when Uncle Andrew would be teasing him at the hall? 'Pigs keeping you warm these days, Gregori?' he would say. When the Potchaks first settled on their homestead, people said they had their farm animals inside their house. I think many people did, but, Potchak, to him, it is what you call—"

"An insult?" Aunt Mattie offered.

"Yes, to make him mad on purpose. And then Potchak would yell back, 'You are the pig, Kaminsky.' And Uncle Andrew would go *oink oink* and laugh like crazy. Of course he would have been drinking. And I would dance sometimes with Olga Potchak, and her papa would have steam coming out of the ears like in the funny papers."

"She was your girlfriend?" Stella gave Marco a little poke with her elbow.

"One of hundreds," Marco laughed.

Aunt Mattie asked Marco to tell her more about their days homesteading with Uncle Andrew and what it was like living in a Ukrainian settlement. Marco talked about Uncle Andrew's socialist views that would certainly be getting him into trouble as the war went on, had he lived, and he talked about the exchanges of food and labour among neighbours.

Uncle Andrew's ability to distill a potent homebrew brought them a good deal of bartered goods, mainly for the pantry. Alex joined in to tell about their animals—he thought often about Popo his pig and Cossack, the big, gentle plough horse that he sometimes rode and their milk cow, Tsarina.

When the talk turned to Christmas dishes, Marco described his feeble efforts to recreate what Mama and Papa would lay out back in the old country. Stella even joined in, remembering her mother showing her how to make *kolach*, a braided sweet bread.

As it grew dark outside and the fire burned down, Alma came in to discuss dinner with Aunt Mattie.

"Where has the afternoon gone! This has been lovely." Aunt Mattie began gathering up the tea dishes. "I'm going to give Alma a hand and we'll have dinner before long."

"I will help too." Stella struggled a bit to get up from the settee. "I should not sit too long."

"No need—"

"Please. I would like to."

With the women gone, Marco leaned back and closed his eyes for a minute.

"You are tired?" Alex moved to a chair closer to the settee.

Marco opened his eyes again, shrugged his shoulders and reached over and clasped Alex's hand. "I want to not think about being tired and sick." He slipped into speaking Ukrainian and Alex felt comfort in the familiarity of the words. "But we need to think about the future. It may be a future without me."

"Marco!"

"I know—" he smiled wanly. "I want to be here to build a life with Stella. She has had such a bad life up until now. If by just wanting hard enough we could make wishes come true, wouldn't that be nice? Like in the fairy tales Mama would read to you when you were little. Yes, I would listen in—and remember them—because she told them to me too when I was small and the world was filled with wonder. Do you remember the story of Boris, Son of Three, with the firebird's magic feather?"

"Yes, that was my favourite." Alex sighed. "I think I liked it because it took so long to tell. Ivan forever getting a new quest from the Tsar."

"Maybe you have become the Son of Three—like Boris. Three fathers—Papa and Karl Arneson and Mr. Dallaine. Or maybe three fathers and one godmother."

"Aunt Mattie?"

"Yes. Her kindness to us and to Stella." With a cough coming on, Marco withdrew his hand from Alex to find a handkerchief. "Alex, if ... you must promise me to ..." But the cough took hold of Marco. "I've got to go up, lie down." Alex assisted him up the stairs.

He helped him get undressed and into bed.

"Promise me ..."

"Anything ..."

"Be always a friend to Stella. For the baby, be the best uncle."

Alex felt too choked to say anything but he nodded his head.

It was enough.

Chapter 21

STELLA, ALEX THOUGHT, was embarrassed by all of the attention Aunt Mattie and Alma lavished on her in the coming weeks. While they had settled her in a small bedroom down the second-floor corridor from Marco, they had also set up a daybed for her in the sunroom at the west side of the house on the main floor. Otto tended the plants there, coaxing blooms from leafy stalks in a variety of pots.

On a break from algebra, Alex found her there knitting something in a butter-yellow colour like the blossoms on a plant Otto had told him the name of, but Alex hadn't been able to figure out what he was saying.

"Stella." He was glad he'd found her alone. It was something that didn't happen often these days with Alma and

Aunt Mattie hovering around her making sure she was eating well and getting enough rest. Then there were the hours she spent with Marco in his bedsitting room which he rarely left.

"A hat for the baby?"

"Bonnet." Stella set the nest of wool and her needles aside. "Something I never learned. Alma's teaching me."

"A good colour." Alex let his fingers rest on the small half-finished garment before finding himself a wicker chair and pulling it over close to the daybed.

"Good for either a boy or a girl, they say." Stella smiled.

"What is the kind—?" Alex found himself trying not to look at the mound of Stella's belly, barely concealed by her smock. "What type do you wish?"

"Oh," Stella laughed. "I am not being fussy. Healthy. That's what I wish."

Wish. The word hung in the air, suspended somehow in the soft afternoon sunlight.

"I wish—" Alex paused. He saw Alma hurrying through the hallway, her arms loaded with fresh bed linens. Heading up to Marco's room no doubt. "I wish for Marco . . ." It seemed beyond sense to say it, but he finished. "To get better."

"Yes," Stella sighed. "We all wish that." She gasped suddenly, and then laughed. "It kicked. The baby kicked."

"A dancer?"

"I hope it doesn't try doing a polka." Stella placed her hand against her stomach.

Is she waiting to feel it move again? Alex wondered. "Marco says—a boy, he will be called Stephan, the name of our father."

"Yes. But Marco will be part of his name, too. Marco," Stella said decidedly. "And, if it is a little girl, Irene—after your mother. Sofia Irene—for my mother too."

Irene. He'd almost forgotten it. In the presence of his sons, their father had always called her Mama. When she became so ill, though, in Hamburg, he remembered the name on his father's lips. Irene. And how strange it was to hear him say it, almost as if it were a lover's term of endearment. *Irene, this tea is for you.* Mama, so still, her skin like the colour of thin tea itself. *Irene, just a few sips.*

"Marco says you have been teaching him, helping him improve his English. A born teacher, he says." Stella shifted her position, trying to get comfortable.

"Mama was a teacher. She told me that although she loved teaching the little ones, she could be firm with them—so that they learned.

"Not me. I never went past grade six." Stella picked up her knitting again. "My father said it was a waste. He wanted us to work at home. I think I cried for a week, and Pa practically wore out his razor strap on me. I was thirteen."

"And then you got married."

"In time. But I was at home for a couple of years, helping with the smaller children, cooking, cleaning the house, working in the garden and the field. My older sisters and one of my brothers move away to find work. My father—he was not a good farmer, or maybe it was just the land was no good. I think when Edward Granger tells him he wants to marry me, he thinks that is the best luck he ever had. It gets him a good plough horse, two calves, a brood sow and three small pigs."

Alex stood up and stretched. From the glassed walls of the sunroom he could see out to the neighbour's side yard where a couple of boys were playing catch, even though there was still some snow on the ground. They both had baseball gloves. As they ran and reached and the tan-coloured gloves sought the ball, Alex felt something tugging at his memory.

Baseball wasn't a game that was played back in Lviv. Two or three of the boys at Bayles' Corner had old gloves they brought out in the spring. No, it was something else. And then it came to him. Robin's glove on the shelf in his bedroom at Mrs. Eddy's. Dead Robin. The glove that would never fit to his hand again.

The immensity of it hit him—all the things that the hands of the living touch and hold continuing to be there after life has passed. A baseball glove, a harmonica, an embroidered vest, paint brushes, a sketchbook.

Marco lived to see the birth of his child. A boy. Aunt Mattie and Alex followed as Dr. Abraham brought the newborn in to Marco's bedroom.

"A strong, healthy child," Dr. Abraham said. "And the mother is doing well. She is ready to sleep now."

Marco was lying on top of his bed covers, fully dressed, and he sat up, reaching for the baby.

"*Ahh . . .*" was all he could say at first. His fingers traced the golden wisps of hair, touched each of his tiny fingers. "He's sleeping. What colour are his eyes?"

"Blue," Aunt Mattie said, "but most babies' eyes are blue when they're born."

"Little Stephan. He is perfect." Marco cuddled him for a minute. Then he caught Dr. Abraham's eye. "I should not be holding him."

Alma had come into the bedroom. "Yes, perfect," she said. "Give the little one to me and I'll put him in his crib."

"And I'll spend a bit of time checking on the father here." Dr. Abraham nodded toward the door, and Alex followed Aunt Mattie down the hall to the schoolroom.

"Finally, a baby in this house. It was something I always hoped for." Yawning, Aunt Mattie found a couple of cushions and curled into the window seat. She'd been up quite a bit of the night in Stella's room. "Stephan Marco—a good name. I think he looks like his father. I know that Stella worries about Granger tracking her down, maybe insisting the child is his. But we can hope not."

"He could find her?" Alex picked up one of the books on his desk, then put it down.

"We'll do everything we can to make her feel secure here. After all, this is the twentieth century. Slaves were freed in the last century; we're working on freeing women now." Aunt Mattie laughed. "I think we'll even get the right to vote this year. Stella can be strong—she will need to be strong . . ."

Alex opened his history text. He couldn't bear to pursue Aunt Mattie's conversation and where it was leading.

Marco died three weeks after Stephan Marco's birth. Crocuses at the base of the mountain ash tree in Aunt Mattie's back yard were in bloom, and daffodils that Otto tended in the beds against the wall ran splashes of gold against the grey stones. Alex had been sitting out on the porch swing reading and it was only Stella who was with Marco when it happened.

Alex wondered if she had screamed and he just hadn't heard her, but by the time Otto called him in Dr. Abraham was already there, and Aunt Mattie had taken Stella back to her room.

From the bedroom doorway, Alex could see Marco sprawled across his bed, his position written against the bedding by the spasm that killed him. Alex thought of the red blossom Marco had told him about. It had become a funeral bouquet, scarlet flowers strewn across Alma's snow-white sheets.

"A pulmonary hemorrhage," Dr. Abraham said, more to himself than to Alma who was standing by with a basin and a cloth, or to Alex, although when he did notice him in the doorway, he added, "I'm so sorry, Alex. I was thinking of taking him to the hospital and collapsing one of his lungs, but I'm afraid it was too advanced. Such a pity. You'd best let Alma clean him up and look after the room."

Aunt Mattie was out in the hall now. "Aaron," she called softly, "I think you might want to look in on Stella again before you leave."

Then she came over and put her arms around Alex and held him close to her.

"They killed him," Alex sobbed. "Granger and the police and that guard."

"There, there ..." Aunt Mattie stroked his hair. "We can blame a whole government. Whoever decided these poor souls should be treated less than human, whoever signed the papers. People can be so blind and stupid and uncaring during a war." She was crying now too. "Oh, Alex, if wishing and prayers could have kept him alive, he would have lived to be a hundred."

Later that evening Stella joined Alex and Mattie in the parlour. Her eyes were red, her face little different in colour from the white smock she wore. She smiled wanly at them.

"I was talking to Dr. Abraham." Aunt Mattie went over and put her arm around Stella on the settee. "We need to think about the funeral. Aaron thinks we shouldn't try to bury Marco with any indication of his real name or with the services of an orthodox priest. What do you think of us having a private ceremony, and we'll bury him in the Lafontaine family plot? For the record, we'll call him what we've been calling Alex. Stephanson. Marco Stephanson."

"Yes," Stella agreed. "Maybe we can leave the grave marker blank for the time being. There will be ... information to add."

"We'll know," Alex said. "We're all that need to know. For now."

Marco would have liked the warmth and sunshine of the day of his funeral, Alex thought. With schools on Easter break,

Mr. Dallaine was able to come down for the service, presided over by the minister from Aunt Mattie's church. For one of the readings, Mr. Dallaine recited the poem he'd had Alex write that first week of school in Edmonton. Aunt Mattie, who was sitting next to Alex, squeezed his hand ever so gently as Martin read the last stanza.

> It matters not how straight the gate,
> How charged with punishments the scroll,
> I am the master of my fate;
> I am the captain of my soul.

Alex knew his teacher had chosen this particular poem to remind him of what the poem could say to him, even though he couldn't elaborate it here in the presence of the minister and the few people gathered at the church. Marco had faced the locked gate, the punishments. Had he been master of his fate—or had forces beyond his control taken over? The captain of his soul? Yes, always the captain of his soul.

Aunt Mattie squeezing his hand ever so slightly was her little reminder, Alex guessed, of what she'd said when she found "Invictus" in his writing scribbler. Something about a good laugh now and then. That was the Marco to remember, Marco laughing, his head tossed back, teasing Uncle Andrew, flirting with the Potchak girl and even Miss Anderson, and always drawing funny cartoons.

Stella sat quietly on the other side of Alex. What were her thoughts, he wondered. She must have known the laughing

Marco too, but also Marco the lover. The first love she'd ever had?

In the graveyard, the Lafontaines had their own area marked off with an elaborate iron fence. Marco's coffin was lowered into place in one corner and when the minister said something about earth to earth and dust to dust, Alex had the job of scattering a small handful of soil over the casket and the spray of yellow roses Aunt Mattie placed on top of it.

Before they left, Alex noticed Aunt Mattie and her nephew stopped by a large gravestone with the words, on one half: *Emile Lafontaine, beloved husband* carved in relief. Aunt Mattie traced the carved letters with her gloved fingers and then brushed them along the other, smooth half. Mr. Dallaine placed some more roses in a granite urn beside an adjacent gravestone. The lettering on it stated: *Daphne Van Alston Dallaine and Victor Martinius Dallaine.* Below the names, in smaller lettering, were the words *Together in Eternity.*

Stella stopped and looked at the epitaph.

"My parents," Mr. Dallaine said, taking her arm.

"Together in eternity," Stella whispered and it was, Alex thought, almost a wish.

Alex was grateful to have Mr. Dallaine close by for the rest of the Easter holiday. He hadn't yet seen Stephan Marco and Alex had to smile at how awkward the teacher seemed holding the tiny baby.

"The Arnesons have an addition to the family too, Einar

tells me," Mr. Dallaine had told him when he first arrived. "Another boy. Norman." Alex could picture in his mind, Maria holding the baby. And Karl too, so gentle with little ones. The excitement of the other children: Einar and Gunnar and Astrid. He could almost hear their voices.

While he was there, Mr. Dallaine had the pianos tuned in the schoolroom and in the downstairs parlour. In the evening he played for them. Aunt Mattie, in her favourite wing-backed chair, watched and listened with evident pleasure. Was she remembering a time before Mr. Dallaine moved away, when this was a common occurrence?

His last evening before heading back, everyone gathered in the parlour while he played. Stella, with the baby in her arms, seemed to lose herself in the gentle music. Even Alma brought in her sewing and Otto pored over his gardening magazines within earshot.

"Chopin," Aunt Mattie said after Mr. Dallaine had finished a piece that made Alex think, for some reason, of Mama's butterfly fingers. "I think that's my favourite of the nocturnes."

Later, after the others had gone to bed, and Alex and Mr. Dallaine sat by themselves in the parlour listening to gramophone records, Mr. Dallaine picked up the sheet music of the piece he had been playing earlier.

"He died of tuberculosis, too," he said. "Chopin. And he wrote some of his most exquisite music when it must have been difficult for him to pick up a pen. Sometimes it's been called the artists' disease because so many artists died from it, musicians like Chopin, poets like Elizabeth Barrett Browning and John Keats."

"And the artist Marco Kaminsky," Alex added.

"And Marco."

Alex had Marco's sketchbook with him. He seldom let it leave his hands these days. Before he died, Marco had filled it almost to its last page.

"Here is a picture he did of Mama." Alex drew his chair closer to Mr. Dallaine's. "From remembrance . . ."

"Memory."

"From memory. The photographs burned in the house. But it is so real, I feel like I could reach out and touch her hair, and that is the kind of look she had. Like she knew a secret and it was funny to her. Just a little smile."

"It's a lovely portrait." Mr. Dallaine took the sketchbook in hand for a closer look beneath the lamp. "Did you give Aunt Mattie that little watercolour he did of her?"

"Yes, she will have it framed, she says. If you turn the next page you will see Ivan."

It was one of Alex's favourite pictures in the sketchbook. Marco had spent a good deal of time shading in the dark crosscurrents of Ivan's hair and the wide, black mustache. He was grinning, that same grin Alex remembered from the Vegreville kitchen where he joked with the priest's housekeeper while she served them tea. The collar from a shirt and the ribbed neck of a sweater surfaced from the bib of the overalls that prisoners had been given to wear.

"How is he doing?" Mr. Dallaine asked.

"He writes to us. In his last letter, he says rheumatism in his legs not so bad now with warm weather. Like Marco, he can hardly walk after getting out of the hoosegow, but he don't—doesn't—get sick in his chest. His work crew, they start to work on the golf course below the Banff Springs Hotel."

"Oh God, no! They've got the prisoners working on the golf links! I suppose the Vanderbilts and the Astors can sip tea on the terrace and watch the slaves below them extend their playground." Mr. Dallaine got up, limped over to the gramophone player and turned the record over.

"Aunt Mattie says she'd like you to go to school here in Calgary next fall. Take your grade eight. How do you feel about that?"

"I would like to. It feels like Marco is close to me here."

The music that spilled into the room was an air that shimmered with familiarity. Was it something Karl had played on the violin, or that Mr. Bayles had on one of his records?

"Maybe I will be a teacher," Alex said.

"A teacher . . ."

"A virtu—"

"A virtuoso? Why not." Mr. Dallaine smiled. "And we can pray the war will be over by then and the students can call you by your real name. Mr. Kaminsky."

Mr. Kaminsky. It sounded good. Alex returned Mr. Dallaine's smile. He closed Marco's sketchbook. Music surrounded them, the embers in the fireplace glowed, and Alex heard the soft rush of wings in the evening air.

AUTHOR'S NOTE

IT'S A SHAMEFUL CHAPTER in Canadian history less well known than the internment of Japanese Canadians during World War II, but during World War I, thousands of Eastern European immigrants were herded into makeshift camps across the country and put to work, virtually as slave labour.

Most of those interned were men of Ukrainian heritage who were no threat to Canadian security at all. In the hysteria that accompanied the outbreak of World War I, Ottawa issued an order-in-council calling for the registration and, in many cases, the imprisonment of aliens of "enemy nationality." In fact, these "enemy aliens" had come to Canada with a determination to escape the poverty and oppression experienced in Ukrainian provinces such as Galicia and Bukovyna, then part of the Austro-Hungarian empire.

In Western Canada before the war, Ukrainian immigrants homesteaded and established farms; others found work across the country as itinerant farmhands, factory and construction workers, lumbermen and miners. At the time, the British Foreign Office in Ottawa declared them to be "friendly aliens" and, in fact, many enlisted in the Expeditionary Forces.

By and large, however, the Canadian government during World

War I was hostile. Those whose papers were not in order, or who happened in some way to come adversely to the attention of the law, were ripe pickings for internment. Close to eight thousand were put behind barbed wire. More than one hundred died working as forced labour in the camps. Some managed to flee and go into hiding but six were shot and killed attempting to escape.

The Castle Mountain Camp consisted of tents within a dual barbed wire enclosure at the foot of Castle Mountain. As many as six hundred men were interned here. The tents, however, proved inadequate during the severe winter climate, forcing the camp to be relocated to military barracks built on the outskirts of the town of Banff, adjacent to the Cave and Basin, the site of the original Hot Springs. This camp was called the Cave and Basin but, causing confusion, it also sometimes went under the name of the Castle Mountain Camp.

Conditions in the camps were brutal. Often there were long marches to and from the work sites where rough terrain was being cleared and roads and bridges were being built. Clothing was inadequate for harsh winter weather.

Punishment sometimes involved being put into solitary confinement in a cramped "hoosegow" for weeks at a time—which could prove deadly. One internee wrote home: "The conditions here are very poor, so that we cannot go on much longer, we are not getting enough to eat—we are as hungry as dogs. They are sending us to work, as they don't believe us, and we are very weak." (Letter from Nick Olinyk, #98, Castle Mountain, Alberta, to his wife.)

The camps in Banff National Park were closed in July 1917. Forty-seven remaining prisoners were transferred to the camp in

Kapuskasing, Ontario. The last of the camps was closed in 1920.

The shame attached to these unjust internments did not disappear quickly. After being released, many internees found that their property and goods had been appropriated, and they needed to start over from scratch. It was not uncommon for those who had been in the camps to refuse to talk about the experience with their children and grandchildren.

In 2008, the Canadian government created a $10-million "First World War Internment Recognition Fund" to support commemoration projects. Among these projects are plaques in Banff acknowledging the injustice to those placed in the work camps along with praise for their accomplishments in building the park roads and bridges. There is now an interpretive centre open to visitors at the Cave and Basin Park.

FOR FURTHER READING

In recent decades, the Canadian internments of Ukrainians during World War I have been well researched. Along with the scholarly works listed here, I am indebted to the Alberta community histories of Vegreville and Vermilion and to other works offering Ukrainian folk literature.

In the Shadow of the Rockies: Diary of the Castle Mountain Internment Camp, 1915–1917. (Edited and introduced by Bohdan S. Kordan and Peter Melnycky.) Edmonton: Canadian Institute of Ukrainian Studies Press, 1991.

Kordan, Bohdan S. *Enemy Aliens, Prisoners of War: Internment in Canada during the Great War.* Montreal: McGill-Queen's University Press, 2002.

Livesay, Florence Randal. *Down Singing Centuries: Folk Literature of the Ukraine.* Westport: Hyperion, 1981.

Luciuk, Lubomyr Y. *In Fear of the Barbed Wire Fence: Canada's First National Internment Operations and the Ukrainian Canadians, 1914–1920.* Kingston: Kashtan Press, 2001.

Martynowych, Orest T. *The Ukrainian Bloc Settlement in East Central Alberta, 1890–1930.* Occasional Paper No. 10. Edmonton: Alberta Culture, 1985.

Sapergia, Barbara. *Blood and Salt*. Regina: Coteau Books, 2012.

Semchuk, Sandra. *The Stories Were Not Told: Canada's First World War Internment Camps*. Edmonton: University of Alberta Press, 2018.

Vegreville in Review: History of Vegreville and Surrounding Area, 1880–1980. Vegreville and District Historical Society, 1980.

Vermilion Memories: Compiled as a Centennial Project by the Vermilion Old Timers. Vermilion and District History, n.d.

Vovchok, Marko. *Ukrainian Folk Stories*. Kiev: Dnipro Publishers, 1974.

Waiser, Bill. *Park Prisoners: The Untold Story of Western Canada's National Parks, 1915–1946*. Markham: Fifth House, 1999.

ABOUT THE AUTHOR

 As a teacher and a learning resources consultant for Edmonton Public Schools, one of Glen Huser's special projects was his development of *Magpie*, a quarterly featuring writing and artwork by students in the Edmonton Public School Board system (published from 1978 to 2008). For several years he was a sessional lecturer in children's literature, information studies, and creative writing at the University of Alberta in Edmonton and at the University of British Columbia in Vancouver. His first novel *Grace Lake* was shortlisted for the 1992 W.H. Smith-Books in Canada First Novel Award. He has written several books for young adult readers including the Governor General's Award-winner *Stitches* and the GG finalist *Skinny-bones and the Wrinkle Queen*. More recently, he has crafted the texts for picture books such as *The Golden Touch* and *The Snuggly*. Glen's current home is Vancouver where he continues to write as well as pursue interests in art and film studies. Visit his website at www.glenhuser.com.

MARQUIS

Québec, Canada